THE SCREAM OF SINS

THE SCREAM OF SINS

Chris Nickson

SEVERN
HOUSE

First world edition published in Great Britain and the USA in 2024
by Severn House, an imprint of Canongate Books Ltd,
14 High Street, Edinburgh EH1 1TE.

severnhouse.com

British Library Cataloguing-in-Publication Data
A CIP catalogue record for this title is available from the British Library.

ISBN-13: 978-1-4483-1290-0 (cased)
ISBN-13: 978-1-4483-1337-2 (e-book)

All Severn House titles are printed on acid-free paper.

Typeset by Palimpsest Book Production Ltd., Falkirk,
Stirlingshire, Scotland.
Printed and bound in Great Britain by TJ Books,
Padstow, Cornwall.

Praise for the Simon Westow mysteries

"This gritty and surprise-filled mystery will enthrall both newcomers and series fans"
Publishers Weekly Starred Review of *The Dead Will Rise*

"Nickson's richly authentic descriptions of life in nineteenth-century Britain combine with a grisly plot and characters who jump off the page"
Booklist on *The Dead Will Rise*

"An action-packed mystery that provides interesting historical details about despicable crimes"
Kirkus Reviews on *The Dead Will Rise*

"Nickson does a superb job using the grim living and working conditions for the city's poor as a backdrop for a memorable and affecting plot. James Ellroy fans will be enthralled"
Publishers Weekly Starred Review of *The Blood Covenant*

"A gritty tale of perseverance, cruelty, rage, and redemption not for the faint of heart"
Kirkus Reviews on *The Blood Covenant*

"A fine choice for fans of British historical mysteries"
Booklist on *The Blood Covenant*

"Superior . . . The whodunit is enhanced by a grim portrait of life on the streets, embodied in a homeless child whom Jane befriends. Nickson again demonstrates mastery of the historical mystery"
Publishers Weekly Starred Review of *To The Dark*

About the author

Chris Nickson is the author of eleven Tom Harper mysteries, seven highly acclaimed novels in the Richard Nottingham series and six Simon Westow books. Born and raised in Leeds, he returned there to make his home a decade ago.

www.chrisnickson.co.uk

To all the lost children

ONE

E arly Sunday morning, and the silence in Leeds was eerie as Simon Westow walked along Swinegate. All the factories and mills were closed for the Sabbath, no machines or looms or pounding hammers ringing across the town.

A heavy mist deadened the sound of his footsteps on the pavement. Autumn, the season of fog. On the other side of the road he sensed someone passing, no more than the hint of an outline that appeared for a moment before being swallowed up again.

It was easy to believe the world had vanished. But he'd left his wife Rosie warm and asleep in bed, and glanced in on his twin boys, Amos and Richard, before he left. They were very much alive.

By the water, the air grew thicker. Simon moved without thinking, knowing every inch of this place. Where to turn, each little ginnel. He listened, straining in case there was the faint noise of anyone behind him. By habit, he checked to make sure he had all his weapons: the knife in his belt, the second tucked into his boot, and a third in a sheath up his sleeve.

The air turned colder; he felt the chill and the dampness on his skin as he pulled his greatcoat tight around his body.

Simon crossed Briggate. A few paces along he turned down Pitfall. It was a stub of a street no more than ten yards long, running down to the River Aire. A few yards away a barge rocked in the water, creaking and scraping against the pilings.

He was early. It gave him chance to check for anyone lying in wait. But he didn't notice a soul and leaned back against a wall that was layered with soot. Deep in the murk, he was well hidden. Whoever arrived would be blundering around.

His fingertips rubbed the note in his pocket. It had arrived the evening before, delivered by a boy who could only say a man had paid him to bring it. No name, no description.

Meet me at seven o'clock tomorrow morning on Pitfall.
Something important has been stolen from me and I need its
safe return as soon as possible. It's vital that no one else knows
about this. You will be well paid for your trouble.

No signature. That was mysterious in itself. Dangerous? God
knew, there were enough people around town who had no cause to
love him. Simon wasn't worried. He'd made his plan; everything
was in place. He was wary, but he'd discover the truth soon enough.
Simon Westow was a thief-taker, a man who recovered stolen items
and returned them for a fee.

TWO

The cobbles were damp and slick. The man limped cautiously down the street, all the way to the low wall above the water. Simon watched him turn, a blurred shape in the mist.

Half a minute and he was satisfied the man had come alone. He stepped forward, letting his hobnail boots scrape on the stone. Loud enough for the man's head to jerk around.

'Mr Westow?' An uncertain voice, filled with . . . what? Fear, perhaps? Worry?

'I'm Simon Westow.'

He heard the brief sigh of relief as the man approached, close enough now to pick out his face. A top hat, high collar, and a fashionable expensive woollen greatcoat with several short capes falling from the shoulders. An elaborate, wasteful fashion, he thought.

'Captain Holcomb.'

He recognized the man; they'd been introduced a few times. In his forties, short hair turning grey. Always a ready smile, Simon recalled, but just now his face was sharp and serious. He had shadowed circles under his eyes as if he hadn't enjoyed much sleep last night. No surprise, perhaps, if he needed a thief-taker.

'Thank you for coming out to meet me, Westow.' He raised his head. 'Dreadful weather. Can hardly see a yard ahead.'

Simon knew the man's story. Holcomb had been a cavalry officer, born and raised in Leeds and stationed in Norfolk. Home on leave, he'd met and quickly courted a local woman. A match of money and love, their wedding had been a big event in local society. Then, three years ago, Holcomb's horse had reared and thrown him while he was leading his troops on an exercise. His leg had been broken in two places, and even the surgeon's best efforts had left him with a cruel limp. Still able to ride, but not well enough for the cavalry. He'd resigned his commission and returned to Leeds to live a quiet, sedate life, the father of a young son.

'Your note said you need my services,' Simon said. 'What's been stolen?'

He wanted to come to the point quickly. Too often people would beat all around the bush rather than explain the problem.

The man stared down at the ground for a moment and took a breath. 'Someone took a bundle of letters and documents from my house and I need to have them back.'

'Are they valuable?'

Holcomb hesitated. 'No, not in terms of money. But they're extremely important to my family.'

Curious, but hardly the first time he'd come across something like that.

'How did you discover they were missing?'

'I went into the library yesterday morning and a drawer in the desk was slightly open. I'd been working down there the evening before and I must have forgotten to lock it. When I looked inside, the papers were gone.'

Simon nodded. 'Anything else?'

'A few bearer bonds, but they're not worth much. The upstairs maid had vanished, too.' Simon opened his mouth, but before he could speak, Holcomb continued, 'She can't read. She wouldn't know what was in those documents, and she certainly wouldn't have any idea what a bearer bond was.'

'Have you reported it to the constable?'

'No.' The captain lowered his voice, even though the fog gobbled up every sound. 'I don't want any official record. What's in those papers is very sensitive.' His eyes darted around, but there was nobody to see or hear; they were completely alone.

'What makes them so important?' He needed to know before he could begin to search. 'What's in them?'

'They involve my father.' He stayed silent for a minute, chewing on his lip as he decided how much to tell. 'Together, I suppose they make a confession of sorts. If they were to be made public, they'd bring disgrace on our name. Possibly more than that.'

'Confession of what?' It had to be something truly bad.

Another long moment of hesitation, then: 'I'd rather not give details.'

Simon frowned. Not a good beginning; he was going to need more than that to do his job. Maybe the man was simply cautious, but it seemed as if Holcomb was being deliberately spare with the truth. Just enough to try and lure him in. He decided to try changing tack. That might bring more.

'You said the upstairs maid had gone.'

'Yes. Her name's Sophie Jackson. She'd been with us for about half a year. Very biddable girl, always an eager worker. My wife liked her, she's still shocked Sophie has flown like that.' He reached into his coat and drew out a folded piece of paper. 'That's her family's address. We were pleased with her work.'

'I'll talk to her parents.'

'I spent much of yesterday trying to decide on the best way to recover the papers,' Holcomb told him. 'People assure me you're good. More important, that you're honest. I'll have to trust they're right.'

'This is my work.'

'I have money, Mr Westow, and the return of these papers matters a great deal to me. If you succeed, I can assure you that you'll be very well paid. Do we have an agreement?'

'I'll do what I can.' There was never a guarantee.

A brief handshake. 'That's enough for me. I don't want anyone else to know about this. That's why we're meeting here. Everything *must* be kept quiet. No visit to the house, no questions to the other servants, nothing like that.'

Simon considered the demand. Not a scrap of detail on what had been taken, and now this. The man seemed determined to make his job impossible. 'You'll be limiting me.'

'I'm aware of that. Please believe me, though, I have a good reason for it.'

Holcomb was paying the bills; it was his choice. It was up to Simon whether to agree to be hobbled or not. 'Has anything been stolen from your house before?'

'No, it's quite secure. I had no reason to believe anyone was likely to take anything.'

His footsteps, the slight drag of his limp, quickly faded, and Simon stood alone on Pitfall listening to the river lick against the wharves. Smelling it as much as hearing it, all its ugly perfumes, the sewage and the chemicals from the factories upstream.

A minute, then he felt her there.

'I didn't bother going after him,' Jane said. 'You know who he is.'

'Yes.'

She worked with him, a young woman who was the best he'd ever seen at following without being noticed. Dressed in her old green cloak, hood raised over her hair, she was almost invisible in the mist.

Back in the spring, Simon had stopped her taking revenge on a man who'd tried to kill her. He'd done it out of fear for her life, afraid the man would defeat her again. But Jane had felt betrayed; he'd ripped something away that was rightly hers.

Since that time they'd only done two brief jobs together where he needed her special skills. Easily done, soon finished, good money. But mending the ruptured relationship was like using string to knit together a broken bridge. Jane had huddled into a life with Mrs Shields, caring for the old woman in their small house behind a wall at the back of Green Dragon Yard. It was a serene place; she seemed content there, as if she'd found some peace after all the turbulence in her life. She'd learned to read and write and mastered her numbers.

Yet he knew she could still be deadly when she had to be.

Simon explained it all. Not that he'd managed to learn much.

'Finding the maid is the place to start.' He produced the paper and gave it to her. 'Sophie Jackson.'

A nod. She turned and disappeared.

THREE

J ane stood at the top of St Ann's Lane on Quarry Hill. The houses stretched out ahead of her looked exhausted, as if all the heart had been drawn out of them the day they rose from the ground. The bricks were grimy from the pall of soot and smoke that rarely vanished completely, not even in the stillness of Sunday.

Simon had come to see her the evening before, showing the note he'd received, asking if she'd be there, helping him once more. He want someone close, ready to follow whoever he was meeting.

She was reluctant; what he'd done in the spring had shattered all the trust between them. A man had tried to kill her. When she had her chance of vengeance, he tore it from her. For her own safety, he claimed. But who was Simon Westow to try to guide her life like God?

Jane had money, her half of all the fees they'd earned together; there was little need to go hunting. Instead, she was content to spend her days looking after Mrs Shields. The old woman was frail; she needed Jane more and more, the first person ever to rely on her.

It was Mrs Shields who'd taught her about the plants in their containers outside the house, how to water and care for them. So many other things she could never have imagined doing a few years before, back in the time she'd been built from anger, sharp edges and bitterness. But Catherine Shields had rubbed those away. Taught her to read, then to write. Books became one of her great pleasures. She joined a lending library, taking out a new novel every week. Jane had worn her good dress the first time she visited, still convinced they'd turn her away as undesirable. But she'd been made as welcome as everyone else, browsing the shelves and making her selections. Over the months she'd devoured everything from Miss Mitford's *Our Village* to the one she was reading now, *Ivanhoe*. No name for the author, but the story transported her to a time of rich imagination. Romance, knights and kings, chivalry, tournaments and love. It all came alive for her on the page. The perfect escape.

The work would be simple, Simon promised. Somewhere deep inside, she knew she owed him. She'd been living on the streets when they met. Working for him had brought her here, to this place she loved. To Catherine Shields. After a long hesitation, she'd nodded her agreement.

Now here she was going to talk to the maid's family. No danger in that; it shouldn't take her long.

The early fog had parted into shreds and tatters by the time she knocked on the door. All she heard was a mocking hollowness, and stood back on the pavement, eyes searching the windows for any sign of life.

Jane tried again, louder, and a neighbour came to stand on her step, arms folded as she watched.

'They've gone,' she said.

She felt a shiver run up her spine. 'Where? Do you know?'

'No idea, pet. They did a flit last night. Must have been not long after eleven. The church bells rang, then I fell off to sleep. Next thing I heard was some wheels on the cobbles and I saw him pushing the cart away. The father. His wife was beside him, along with their youngest girl. The only one still at home.'

'How many do they have?'

The woman laughed. 'Three, two of them off in service.'

'Sophie?'

A snort. 'Aye, she's one. A right little madam she is, too. Got herself a decent position and now she's too good for round here. Comes to see them once a month. Pops in for ten minutes then she's off again, like Lady Bountiful making a charity call.'

Now the family had vanished.

'Were the Jacksons behind on their rent?' Jane asked. Why had they run off? The timing was very suspicious.

The woman shook her head. 'They were behind on life, pet. You name a place, they owed money there. Harry Jackson couldn't hold on to a job if you nailed it to him, and the wife has a nasty side to her. We're better off without them on this street.'

'Did they have any friends? Someone who might know where they've gone?'

'Not that I ever saw.' She cocked her head. 'Why? Do they owe you, too?'

'Something like that.' Not the truth, but it would serve for now.

'Then I hope you have some luck.'

The door closed and Jane wandered off, down Coach Lane, across Jubilee Street, then over Harper Street, her feet edging slowly towards Simon's house. She passed a young couple. The man was bent from the weight of the pack on his back, the strain paining his face. He was probably carrying everything they owned. The woman shuffled beside him. A cotton dress with a pattern faded by years and a threadbare shawl that would do nothing to keep out the cold. She hugged a baby close to her body, her face empty of expression.

Leeds was an unforgiving town for the poor.

Simon wasn't at home; she told Rosie what she'd discovered.

'Not much to help us there.'

'No,' Jane agreed. A few short steps and she'd already reached a dead end.

'Never mind; you've done what you can. I know Simon's grateful. Now we can let him come up with the ideas.'

By the time she reached Boar Lane, Jane had already put it all from her mind. Off in the distance she heard the sound of a violin and followed her ears. Davy Cassidy, the blind fiddler who'd arrived in town at the height of summer and never left. His music had a soft, lilting tone; even the jigs and reels spun with an airy, pleasing grace. People would stop for a second and remain for several minutes, drawn in by the beauty, placing coins in the cup by his feet. Sometimes he'd sing in a keening voice that was filled with the ache of a man missing his home.

Jane took some money from her pocket and tossed it into his mug. Sunday was never a good day to try to make a musician's living.

'Thank you, miss,' he said without missing a beat. Somehow, he always knew it was a woman. From the swish of a skirt or the way she stepped, she supposed.

'Do you need anything?'

'Maybe another glass of cordial,' Catherine Shields answered with a kind smile. 'I've been very thirsty today.'

She watched as the woman took a sip from the cup, her movements always so small and birdlike. Tiny bites of food, little steps.

'Did things go well with Simon this morning?'

'There wasn't much for me to do. I went to find a family, but they'd moved.'

'What now?'

'That's all he asked me to do.' She glanced out of the window. 'The sun's out, it's warmed up a little. Would you like to take a walk in the garden?'

When Jane first moved here, Mrs Shields had looked after her. Now she was the one who took care of things. She shopped, she nursed, she was a companion. More than that; she felt like the woman's granddaughter.

Inside these walls was the first place she'd felt truly safe. Mrs Shields was the family she'd never known. Her father had raped her when she was eight. Her mother had thrown her out rather than risk losing a man's wage.

Jane had lived on the streets. She'd survived. She'd had to learn to be ruthless, to raise a shawl over her head so she became invisible to men, to kill when she needed, then walk away. Too many like her had gone under; she'd been lucky. Determined. Last year her father had returned to Leeds with news her mother had died and asked forgiveness for them both. A lie; all he wanted was someone to support him. He hadn't changed at all.

She'd paid back the debt that had been building for years.

'I'd better dress warmly,' the woman said.

'That's a good idea,' Jane agreed. 'Don't worry, I'll look after you.'

This was home. This was where she'd begun to understand happiness.

FOUR

'Do you think I'd be working on a Sunday if I was making money?' George Mudie asked. He tried to wipe the ink from his hands with an old rag; a losing battle in a print shop. He poured brandy into a glass, drank it down in a single swallow and smiled in satisfaction. 'Now, what do you want? I hope it's important.'

He didn't hide his frustration. It had been a poor year. Bills rising, not enough work. He was ground down, like so many others around town.

Simon chuckled. 'Would I be here on a Sunday if it weren't?'

Mudie sighed. 'Go on. What is it?'

'What do you know about Captain Holcomb and his family?'

'New clients?'

Simon shrugged and said nothing.

Mudie poured another drink as he gathered his thoughts. A stack of printed sheets sat by the press, a ballad called *The Sad Death of Christina Pearce*. He straightened the corners.

Outside, a coach broke the Sabbath silence. Hooves drummed over the cobbles and wheels rumbled. There and past in a moment.

Mudie had been a newspaper editor once, until an argument with the owner left him without a job. He'd tried writing and publishing his own sheet. A perfect way to lose money. Since then he'd struggled along as a printer. But curiosity about the town and its families still ran in his blood.

'They've had money for generations. That meant they married women who brought dowries so they became even richer.' He shook his head in disgust. 'The good captain, Thomas to his friends, managed to be appointed to Wellington's staff during the Peninsular campaign. Stayed in post until Waterloo and Napoleon was finished. Found himself with a few more medals and God knows how much in spoils. Cavalry posting, married, had his accident and retired. I'm surprised you don't know most of this, Simon.'

'I hardly move in the same circles as Holcomb.' He rubbed his chin, feeling the hard stubble. 'Do you think he's an honourable man? I only talked to him for two minutes.'

Mudie considered the idea. 'What an odd question. As far as I know, he is. But,' he added with care, 'he's a man of his class. Honour to those people is very different from the way you and I think about it.'

'Maybe so.' He understood what George meant, but hoped he was wrong.

'His father was a magistrate. You'd have been too young to have paid much attention, but he was the one who went after the machine breakers around here. The Luddites. That has to be over twenty years ago now.'

Possibly even closer to thirty, Simon decided. He'd barely been born, still part of a family, before his parents died and he ended up in the workhouse. He'd heard fragments of the stories here and there. Men wanting to destroy the new machines that would take away their livelihoods. Working men. Skilled men, many of them. There were several attempts around Leeds, more around the West Riding. A few were caught in the act, others betrayed. The ringleaders were hanged, the rest transported to the far side of the world.

'I don't think I ever knew his name.'

'Robert William Holcomb.' He raised the empty glass in a toast. 'May God rot his soul. As evil a bastard as ever walked in Yorkshire. He loathed ordinary people. Believed we ought to know our station. He'd send men and women and children to Van Diemen's Land for breathing the same air as him.'

'What about his son?'

He shrugged. 'I told you, he seems like a better man. But he's hardly had a difficult life. Everything handed to him on a plate. Never had to earn a damned thing.' His gaze moved across to the press and he snorted. 'Not like most of us. What does he want?'

'I didn't say he wanted anything.'

Mudie laughed. 'At least he probably pays his bills. More than his father did, according to the rumours. If someone came after him for what they were owed, he'd file suit against them. Keep them tied up in the courts for years.'

Simon cocked his head, suddenly thoughtful. He didn't want to have to fight for his money. 'You're sure you've heard nothing like that about the captain?'

'I've never even seen his name and lawyer in the same sentence.'

'Let's hope you're right.' He'd been lucky with his clients. They were always prompt with what they owed. But Simon was tall and broad, large enough to seem intimidating. His size served him well in his work. He nodded at the ballad. 'Is *Christina Pearce* going to be a best-seller?'

'God only knows. I don't care. I'm not the one taking a chance on this. Someone else placed the order. Whatever happens, I'll be paid. Speaking of . . .' He rubbed his hands together. 'I need to run off the rest of these.' Mudie snorted. 'Don't pay any attention to me. I'm a man coming to the end of his tether. Or maybe that's why you should pay attention. I don't care about gilding lilies any more. Just look out for yourself.'

'Would you be willing to help?' Simon asked.

He'd come to see Jane, the second time in two days. Finding the maid and the papers was going to be more than he could do alone.

'I already did what you asked,' she said.

'I know. You did it well. But this . . . I'd like someone with me. Half the fee.' He looked into her face. 'Please.'

The congregation was coming out of the Parish Church after evening service as Simon passed along Kirkgate and ducked into the Old Crown. Still early, only a few gathered around the hearth. One or two faces he recognized, men who walked with caution on the wrong side of the law. A couple of questions, no names mentioned, but none of them knew about any stolen papers.

It was the same everywhere he went, faces mystified when he asked. Not a whisper to be heard. That was strange. Usually someone would commit a crime, drink and begin to boast.

He moved through town, into the dram shops and the little parlours where an earnest landlady brewed and sold her beer. On to the bustling inns, doing a brisk trade as coaches came and left in a flurry of Sunday noise.

Nothing at all. At least he'd planted a few seeds, Simon thought as he ambled home. People would be wondering, maybe asking questions of their own. Things would rise to the surface.

Tomorrow he'd have to talk to Holcomb again. The man had set him on the hunt. Now he needed a better idea of what he was looking to find; it would help him understand where to search. At the moment there were too many pieces missing from the puzzle and that worried him.

It would all wait for morning.

FIVE

Mrs Shields thrashed and called out in her dreams. Plaintive little cries, names: Peter, Frederick, Henry.

Jane hurried into the bedroom and gently stroked the old woman's cheeks until she calmed and settled back into sleep. She hadn't woken, simply struggled under the surface. It was happening more often; this was the third time in as many weeks.

But whenever she mentioned it, Catherine Shields dismissed the idea there was any trouble.

'I'm perfectly well, child,' she said with her calm smile. 'You see me every day. Have you noticed a problem?'

She hadn't; certainly nothing obvious. That didn't stop the worry. The woman was older. Thinner, scarcely eating enough to keep a body going. She dozed several times a day as she sat in her chair. When Jane hugged her, her hand touched little more than bones covered in skin. No fat on her at all. Mrs Shields walked with a stick, and Jane had visions of the woman taking a fall and breaking something. If that happened, any recovery would be slow. At her age it might not happen at all.

How old was she? Each time Jane asked, she gently batted away the question.

'It's not something you should ask a lady. We like a little mystery about some things.'

Seventy? Eighty? She had no way of measuring. She wasn't even certain of her own age. Somewhere close to twenty, at a guess. When she had no home, she lost track of the days. The weeks, the years, slid together and became a blur.

Now she had chance to take pleasure in things she'd never been able to imagine before. That was why she wanted to care for Mrs Shields, to keep her here, safe, as long as possible.

As she settled back under the blanket in her own bed, Jane thought about this new job of Simon's. Nothing unusual in discovering a family had flitted. But the timing . . . was that more than coincidence? They could change their surname; it was easily done. They might be miles from Leeds by now.

Jane would see this through. She'd given Simon her promise on that. But she knew she wasn't the same person who'd started out in this trade. Back then it had seemed like her salvation. But all the desperation and fury that once drove her had paled. She'd banished the ghosts that tormented her thoughts. Even that bitterness at Simon had become empty. She'd complete this job; maybe it would be her last. Ample time to decide once it was over.

Monday morning and the coffee cart outside the Bull and Mouth was busy. People dashed aside as the early London coach rattled out of the yard, the driver cracking the whip to speed the horses down Briggate.

Simon had spent most of the last half-hour listening. A few juicy bits and pieces, but nobody had mentioned missing papers or Holcomb's name. Nothing had come out overnight.

Well before dawn, unseen, he'd slipped a letter under the captain's door. Soon enough, Simon made his way to the meeting place he'd suggested, the mill pond up in Sheepscar. Holcomb wanted everything to be secret. Out there they'd be safe from prying eyes.

He arrived early. Habit. A chance to refresh his memory of the landscape, to find somewhere hidden and make sure Holcomb arrived alone. No reason not to trust his client, but the man was concealing too much, and the years had made caution second nature.

The air was October crisp, a proper nip of autumn. It wouldn't be long before the first frost, Simon thought idly as he sat on a fallen log sheltered by a thicket of bushes. He pulled the watch from his waistcoat pocket and checked the time. Ten minutes yet.

Holcomb was prompt. He'd ridden over, guiding the horse across the uneven ground. Dressed for the morning in his caped greatcoat, low hat, and tall, polished boots. Simon met him by the water.

'Do you have any news for me?' the captain asked.

'At the moment, I barely know where to start looking.' A quick summary, but the only real thing it contained was the maid's family vanishing.

'Do you think they're involved?'

'I have no idea. That's why I need to talk to you again. You've told me next to nothing, Captain. Exactly what am I looking for? What's so important about these papers that someone would want to steal them?'

Holcomb kicked a stone into the water, watching as the ripples spread and faded before he answered.

'I told you.' A small, bitter laugh.

'You teased at it,' Simon answered. 'That's all. They're a confession, you said.'

'That's the truth.' The captain pursed his lips. 'I need to trust you.'

'There's no point in hiring me otherwise. Part of that is telling me what I need to know so I can do my job.'

Holcomb stared, considering how much to say.

'You'll have heard my father was a magistrate?'

'I have.'

'He was a hard man, Mr Westow. Not just with the people who appeared in front of him, but me and my sisters, too.' A half-frown of memories appeared, and just as suddenly he banished them. 'Have you met anyone like that?'

'Yes.' Men who were convinced their view of the world was always right. He'd seen too many who believed that.

'He saw himself as the defender of his class.' Holcomb cocked his head. 'Do you understand?'

'Not completely, no,' Simon admitted.

'Let me give you an example. When he received information about men intending to break machines in Leeds, he saw it as his duty to stop them. For the good of the country. The factory owners were businessmen who'd invested money in the machinery. Their own money, their faith in the future of the kingdom. In his eyes they were important men. The idea that a rabble might take the law into their own hands and try to destroy the ordained order of things outraged him. He saw it as the road to mobs and anarchy.'

'Go on.' Now he'd got Holcomb started, Simon wanted it all.

'He swore out warrants against the offenders and caught them before they could approach the factories. They were still out on the road, Mr Westow. But he claimed they'd been caught trying to break into the factories and handed down harsh sentences. Hanging for the ones who organized it, transportation for the rest. He refused to hear any arguments or protests they wanted to make.'

So far, none of it sounded worse than a hundred other magistrates. There had to be something else. 'What does this have to do with the stolen documents?'

'My father kept every little thing.' A rueful shake of the head.

'He believed it all had value. He had them all bound together with twine. After I inherited, I promised myself I'd go through his papers. But I never got around to it. There was always so much to do. Then last year my wife was ill, and I had a problem with my leg.' He shrugged. 'It never seemed important.'

'If you hadn't gone through the documents, how do you know they could damage your family?'

'Recently I skimmed them a little. There was plenty in there to hurt us. I'd considered putting everything on the fire, but I never did. After I've read it all, I told myself.' He gave a bitter smile. 'Now I'm going to pay the price.'

'Who knew about the papers?'

'Me, my wife. There used to be plenty of rumours. My father might even have encouraged them.' A long, difficult sigh.

Who could have seen them, though, if the maid couldn't read? How had anyone understood what was in them? Had she let someone in?

'How long ago did your father die?'

'A little over two years now. He was in his eighties and he'd been in decline. He only retired from the bench four years ago. His mind had begun to wander.' He gave a weary shrug. 'It might even have been God's blessing.'

The man's face didn't show any sorrow at the death. Simon tried to arrange his questions.

'How big a package did all these documents make?'

'Like this.' He held out his hands Perhaps fifteen inches by nine, Simon judged, and six inches thick. A fair size.

His thoughts moved along. 'You said Sophie had been with you for about six months?'

'Somewhere around there, yes.' Absently, he reached up and stroked the horse's nose. The animal laid its head along his shoulder.

'Nothing else disappeared in that time? No discipline problems? Entertaining young men in the house?'

'No, not that I'm aware.'

'Did she provide references?'

'I assume she did. My wife takes care of everything involving the servants. She feels betrayed. She'd been very pleased with Sophie.'

'Could you find the names of the people who recommended her?'

It seemed to take him by surprise. 'Of course, if you think it

will help.' He took a breath. When he spoke, his words were
measured and hesitant. 'I need these papers back, Mr Westow. As
well as his letters and legal documents, they include plenty of
personal papers and my father's notes. He could be inflammatory
in his opinions, especially in private. Does this give you enough
to help?'

'A little. It's a start.' A very thin one. He'd seemed to say a great
deal, but there was precious little substance. Still, one or two things
might prove helpful.

'I'll send you a note before noon with the names of Sophie's
references.'

'Thank you.'

Even with his bad leg, Holcomb mounted the horse in the single,
easy move of a born rider.

'I expect to hear from you soon, Mr Westow.'

Simon watched as the horse trotted away towards the turnpike.
The captain had painted a plausible and unflattering picture of his
father. He made everything so easy to believe. But Simon was certain
of one thing: it was very far from being the complete truth. Not
only about Robert William Holcomb, magistrate, but everything.
He'd been fed a few more scraps, but he sensed it was still a long
way short of a full meal. What was the captain holding back? What
was he hiding? Why?

Something about this was wrong. Exactly why or what, he didn't
know enough to say, and that was the problem. It niggled at him
and made him uneasy. Simon tried to puzzle it out as he walked
back to town, but the answers stayed out of reach.

'Holcomb.' Barnabas Wade rolled the name around his mouth. Simon
had found the man in the Talbot Inn, trying to peddle his worthless
stocks to travellers just arrived on the Carlisle coach. That was his
trade, a disbarred lawyer hawking paper with no value to people
eager for a quick fortune.

'How rich is the family?' Simon asked. Wealthy, he knew that
much, but it was a vague word. It would be useful to have a better
picture; the thief would likely try to sell the documents back to the
captain.

'Enough,' Wade answered after a little thought. 'They couldn't
buy the whole of Yorkshire, but they'll never have to stint
themselves.'

Able to afford a small fortune for whatever secrets were hidden in those papers. Much cheaper to pay a thief-taker to find and return them.

A little after noon he was home. The tutor was drilling the boys in their multiplication tables, making them recite in unison. More education than Simon had received. But he'd been a workhouse child, placed there when he became an orphan. His school had been a mill twelve hours a day from the time he turned six. The tutor was worth every penny; his sons would be able to make something of themselves.

'There's a note for you on the table,' Rosie said. She was kneading dough, grunting and sighing each time she slapped and pushed it down on the board. A pale mist of flour filled the kitchen. Better than all the soot outside.

It was a short list, only two names and addresses, the places Sophie Jackson claimed she'd worked before the Holcombs hired her. He didn't know either of them; neither did his wife.

She blinked quizzically. 'Where do they live?'

'One's on Leighton Lane, by Little Woodhouse,' he replied. 'The other's on Providence Row.'

Rosie pursed her lips. 'Reasonable addresses.'

'I'll ask Jane to talk to them.'

For the last six months she'd felt uncomfortable whenever Simon came to the small house, as if he was intruding on the careful peace she'd built around herself.

Mrs Shields made him welcome, filling the room with questions about Rosie and Richard and Amos as he sipped a glass of her cordial. All Jane wanted was to know the job he had for her, then close the door behind him. All too often when Simon was here she felt stifled, as if the walls were closing in and she couldn't breathe.

After he'd gone, she glanced at the piece of paper. Simple enough. But before she left she ran the whetstone over her knife blade. She hadn't used it in months, but she kept it sharp enough to kill. Habit, Jane thought as she slid it into the pocket of her dress. One day she might need it again.

She began on Providence Row. A street of identical, impressive villas that stood on a hill just to the north of Leeds. Jane turned, looking down on the town with its pall of smoke. Up here the air was cleaner, tasting almost sweet as she breathed deep.

The windows of the house gleamed, everything clean and polished, the paint on the doors shiny. Jane made her way to the back entrances, counting along until she came to the one she wanted.

A wait after she knocked, then a gaunt woman stood facing her. Pale skin, sunken cheeks, a plain black dress and hair gathered under a starched mop cap. So tall that she seemed to stretch almost to the lintel, with long, bony fingers.

'We're not taking anyone on.' A flat, final statement. She began to close the door again.

'I'm not looking and I'm not begging.'

That made the woman stop and give her a second look. 'What do you want, then?'

'To ask the housekeeper or the cook a question.'

Two years before she'd never have been able to do this. To stand her ground and talk. It still took an effort, but she'd mastered it. Things had shifted inside her.

'I'm the housekeeper. Miss Timms.' She gave Jane a searching, doubtful stare and clasped her hand together in front of her body. 'What are you after, girl?'

'I work with Simon Westow, the thief-taker.' Jane paused, letting the woman absorb the words. No need for any lie or subterfuge. A better chance of an honest answer here if she told the truth. 'We're looking for a young woman called Sophie Jackson. She was a servant.'

The woman shook her head. 'Not in this house, she wasn't.'

Jane widened her eyes. 'Never? She had a reference from here.'

'No.' Miss Timms didn't hesitate. 'I've run this place for eight years and I've never employed anyone with that name.' She pursed her lips. 'Definitely not. Do you know anything more about her?'

'I don't.' Had she made a mistake? 'Sophie Jackson,' she repeated and gave the address.

'You're at the right house,' Miss Timms said. Her voice was stern, unyielding. 'But if she claims she ever worked here, she's lying.'

'I'm sorry.'

The woman shrugged. 'It happens all the time. They hope someone will be lazy and not check. I've had them try it on with me before.'

It seemed a likely explanation, Jane decided as she stood on
Leighton Lane, wondering what she'd find. More grand houses. At
the back door, the answer was the same. No Sophie Jackson had
ever worked there; the cook had never heard of her.

Rosie turned to Simon after she'd listened to Jane. 'You're going
to need to talk to Holcomb again. Something's very strange.'

He nodded, questions flying around his mind. Did Sophie have
a young man who'd spotted a chance for some money? He sighed.
This was becoming a quagmire. 'I'll send him another note.'

'You could walk away,' Rosie told him.

'It's tempting,' he agreed. 'But not quite yet.' Simon turned to
Jane. 'Thank you.'

The fracture in their relationship would never completely mend,
but he valued her courage and abilities. He still trusted her; he had
no desire to lose all that. Stopping her, those months before . . .
perhaps some day she'd realize he was trying to save her life.

'What do you want me to do?'

There was no thread for them to tug. Nothing at all.

'See if anyone knows Sophie Jackson.'

It wasn't likely, but what else did they have? Desperate and they
both knew it.

'Do we know what she looks like?' Jane asked.

'I'll make sure Holcomb gives me a proper description.'

SIX

A new day, another meeting place. The Far Leylands this time, where Regent Street turned into a dusty, rutted track at the edge of fields. Nothing grew there, everything settling in for a long winter.

Holcomb eased off his horse and patted the animal affectionately on its neck.

'This is becoming tedious, Westow.' He sounded impatient. 'I hope it's as important as you said. I thought I'd given you everything you'd need. I hadn't expected you'd need a damned wet nurse.'

Both men were wrapped up warm against the crisp morning. The bitter cold was waiting around the corner. Simon pushed his hands deeper into the pocket of his greatcoat.

'Sophie Jackson.'

Holcomb's head jerked up. 'Didn't you receive my note with the names of her references?'

'Neither of them had heard of her.'

He studied the man's face, gauging his reaction. Astonishment and shock. 'But . . .' he began and ran out of words.

'No Sophie Jackson had ever worked in those places, Captain. Who checks the references in your house?'

'The cook,' he replied, as if he was struggling to make sense of it all. 'My wife supervises, but all the hirings and dismissals are the cook's responsibility.'

'Then she's let you down. What else haven't you told me, Captain?'

'I—' Holcomb stopped, took a breath and straightened his back. 'Everything I've told you I believed to be true, Mr Westow. I'll look into things.'

A very clever answer. The man should have been a politician. But they were weasel words, ones that hid so much in the corners. There was still a great deal the man hadn't said. Too much. At their first meeting, Holcomb had asked if he could trust Simon. Now it seemed the other way round: how far could he trust the captain? Something to consider.

'Can you describe Sophie?'

'According to him, she's middle height, somewhere around five feet four inches tall,' Simon said. 'Not slim, some meat on her bones. Light brown hair. Holcomb doesn't know how long it is, he only ever saw it under a cap. Oh, and he said she has a ready smile.'

Rosie snorted. 'Not a lot of use, is it?'

'Better than nothing. I suspect he hardly noticed her. He had to strain to come up with that much. There was nothing to make her stand out in his mind. But he did remember her saying that she had two sisters.' He turned to Jane and shrugged. 'Sorry, it's the best I could manage.'

'I'll go and ask.'

Back to St Ann's Lane and the woman who'd told her about the Jacksons flitting.

'They've not come back, if that's what you're hoping.' She folded her arms across a heavy chest and surveyed up and down the street before her gaze returned to Jane.

'You said the parents left with their youngest.'

'That's right, pet. Little Willette. She's seven, been working as a doffer girl at Souter's mill. What about her?'

'What does she look like?'

'Pretty little thing.' Ten more minutes and she had a full description of the girl, along with a wealth of other details about Sophie and the oldest sister, Elizabeth. Almost a family history. If she'd had her wits about her, she'd have asked on her first visit. But the Jacksons leaving so suddenly had taken her by surprise. Her mistake; she knew better than that. Stupid.

Simon chuckled. Jane had shamed him with everything she'd learned. But that was the difference between a woman's eye and a man's. No, not just that; between a neighbour and an employer.

He could almost picture Sophie in his mind now, he felt he'd know her if he saw her. Unlikely, of course. So many people in Leeds, and more arriving every single week, it was almost impossible to spot any face on the street. But there was one thing . . .

'I'll go to Souter's and see if the youngest daughter is still working there.' He gave Jane a quizzical look. 'Willette?'

She nodded. 'That's what she said.'

A curious name, but . . .

'The surname is Jackson?' the clerk asked. A few minutes before the end of his working day and the man was tired. The eagerness for home shone in his drawn face. He took a ledger from a cupboard, turned the pages and ran his finger down a row of names.

'She works here,' he said.

Simon slid a pair of shiny sixpences between his fingers and saw the clerk's eyes widen.

'Do you think you could write down the address for me? I know the family has moved.'

'I can,' the man agreed with a smile as he took the money. 'Just a moment.'

Jane was waiting outside, huddled in her cloak against the cold, a shawl underneath around her shoulders. It made sense for Simon to ask the questions; a man was more likely to get information from a factory office than a woman.

'Caroline Street,' he told her as he came out. She knew it. Just off Templar Street. Not far from where the Jacksons lived before their flit; just enough distance for them to arrive as strangers. She nodded and drifted away.

Plenty of hidden places around there; harder to discover somewhere out of the wind. Full dark, and she needed enough light to be able to pick out the small figure.

She didn't have long to wait. The shift must have ended on time. Jane heard a pair of high voices, then clogs running down the street.

With the hood of the cape raised over her hair, Jane knew that no one would notice her in the gloom. Still, she was careful, staying out of sight as the girl let herself into a house halfway along the terrace.

Once the door closed, Jane walked quietly up the road, paying attention to every detail so she'd know the house again.

She sensed them before she could see them. Her hand slipped into the pocket of her dress and gripped the knife, ready.

Her eyes flickered from side to side. The figures stood in the darkness, watching her. Jane twisted the gold ring Mrs Shields had given her long ago to keep her safe and kept walking at the same, steady pace. Wary, but not afraid. She wondered if they'd spotted her spying on the house, or were simply looking for any opportunity to rob.

'You.' Not a cry. More like a lulling invitation. She turned her head towards the voice. 'What do you think you're doing?'

No sound from the other one yet, but she knew he was keeping pace. Jane walked on.

A flurry of movement and they appeared in front of her, blocking her path. Very young, boys testing their mettle as men. Even in the cold, she could smell the stink of sweat and fear as they tried to look tough and cocksure. A rite of manhood.

'You're not from round here.' He sounded as if his voice had not long broken.

Their faces were hidden by the night, hats pulled low over their eyes. Bodies thin from a life of never having enough to eat.

'Well, are you?' The second one, trying to make his voice gruff and intimidating.

'We notice all the people who come through this way.' The first one again. She heard a faint tremor in his words, not sure how to act faced with someone who didn't show any fear.

Before he could say more, the tip of Jane's knife was pricking the skin under his chin.

'Be very careful.' Just enough pressure to pierce his flesh and let a drop of warm blood trickle down his neck. Suddenly he was silent and very, very still. 'Better tell your friend to run off or he'll be next.'

She never turned her head. No need; the second lad was already moving, a clatter of feet along the street. His courage had evaporated between heartbeats.

'What do you want?' He struggled to speak.

That bravado had withered to nothing, terror on his face. His eyes bulged; she could see he wanted to swallow but he was scared of moving his throat.

'Do you think you're a hard man?' Jane asked. 'Two of you against a woman on her own.' She moved forward, forcing him to shuffle back. Just for a second, all the months of anger and frustration threatened to rise inside her. It would be too easy to leave him on the ground.

No. She gave a sigh as weariness began to creep through her body. She'd done all this, done it far too often. He was hardly more than a child, with all the awkward, nervous movements of someone who hadn't grown into his body yet. One small push with the knife and he'd never have the chance to see what might be ahead. All because he believed he had to prove something.

Jane held the power over his life and realized that she didn't want it. Let him run and maybe he'd learn a lesson. Maybe. At least he'd still be alive in the morning.

'Go,' she told him. 'If I ever see you again, you'll be dead.'

Jane pulled the knife back, wiping it on her cloak. He was pelting hell for leather into the distance.

She needed to think, to try to make sense of all this. Her hand trembled as she slid the knife away.

Simon was waiting as the man left the house on Caroline Street. He appeared in the half-light of an early morning and took a furtive look around before he scurried down the road. As he turned the corner, Simon fell into step beside him.

'Mr Jackson, isn't it?'

The man blinked, helpless and fearful, a trapped animal. He had the bow-legged waddle of someone who'd grown up with bones shaped by disease. Gnarled knuckles, though he couldn't have been fifty yet. A muffler tied around a scrawny neck. A hawk nose and lines as deep as carved valleys across his face.

'Wrong man, mister. I don't know anyone called Jackson.'

Simon gave him an indulgent smile. 'You waited too long to say it.' His words turned into clouds in the air. 'I know which door is yours. Now, why don't we try that again? Good morning, Mr Jackson.'

The man hung his head, defeated. He'd probably had to do that often in his life.

'If you're looking for the back rent on the old house—'

'I'm not.'

Jackson turned his gaze sharply. 'Then what do you want?'

'You have a daughter.'

'I've got three of them, Mister . . .'

'Westow. I'm a thief-taker.'

Jackson stopped short, tensing to turn, thinking about running. 'I've not stolen anything.'

Around them, the morning was just beginning to come alive. A hint of brightness in the sky, a few people on the street, heads down as they made their way to work.

'I'm not accusing you.' Simon kept his voice low. 'I'm looking for Sophie.'

The man blinked again. 'She works for Captain Holcomb. You can find her there.'

'She's gone. Some things were stolen.'

'Sophie?' Jackson shook his head. He was confused, trying to make some sense of what he'd just heard. 'My Sophie? You've got the wrong girl. She'd never do something like that. She liked working there. Always her dream to be a maid in a good house.'

'Important enough to have someone forge references for her to get the job?'

The man coloured. 'That's why she'd never steal or run off.'

'She did. She vanished at the same time as some papers that were taken.'

'Papers?' the man asked. 'What, letters and things like that, you mean?'

'Yes.'

'Why? They'd be no good to her.' He frowned. 'Our Sophie doesn't know how to read. She's a maid, why would she need her letters and numbers?'

If she wasn't the thief . . . things began to click together in his brain.

'Is she courting?' Simon asked urgently. 'Stepping out with a young man?'

'Tommy Deacon.' The disapproval was right there in the way he spoke the name. 'I told her she could do better, but these lasses, they don't want to listen.'

'Where can I find him?'

'I don't know, mister, and that's the God's truth of it. She stopped bringing him round when she knew her mother and me weren't ever going to approve of him. We had rows over it. She used to give us a little of her wages, but a couple of months ago she stopped doing that.' He stared down at the ground again, then back at Simon. 'The money helped. Without it, we were always short on the rent. That's why we had to do the flit.'

'What does Deacon do?'

'Works for a wheelwright. That's what Sophie told us, anyway.

Not an apprentice, nowt so grand as that,' he added quickly. 'Just labour, and always full of ideas that could make him rich.'

'Which wheelwright?' There were plenty of them in Leeds.

He shook his head. 'She probably said, but . . . I think it began with an L, but I wouldn't swear to it.' A hesitation. 'Do you think our Sophie is all right, mister?'

'I'm sure she is,' Simon answered as he saw the plea in the man's eyes. He didn't know, but a little succour couldn't hurt. What else could he say? 'I'm sure she is.'

SEVEN

'You look like you lost sixpence and found a farthing,' Kate the pie-seller said. 'If that face of yours was any longer they'd have to pull your chin off the ground.'

Jane gave a tiny smile and bit into the pie Kate put in her hand.

'That's better. Come on now, what's the problem? It's nothing to do with Mrs Shields, is it?'

Not yet. But winter was galloping up rapidly and that was always hard on the old woman's chest.

'Nothing like that. It's . . .' She wasn't sure how to put it into words. All through the evening and long into the night, she'd turned it over and over. Backwards and forwards. In the past, she'd never have hesitated. She'd have given the boy a wound or a mark. A reminder to carry with him. But as she stood on that street, Jane felt she was watching herself and seeing someone she no longer wanted to be. A skin she needed to shed. Someone she'd once been, perhaps still was. Things were tangled, too hard to unravel.

She blurted it out. Kate listened as she took pies from her tray to sell to customers. They were standing in her usual spot on the corner of Boar Lane and Briggate, wind whipping about them.

Kate was a big woman with a forceful gaze. Married to a man much smaller than herself. She was big enough to crush him in her fist, but she still submitted to beatings from him if she didn't sell enough each day. It was something Jane could never understand; why would anyone stay for that?

'Do you still feel that way now? What would you do if it happened again?'

An age seemed to grind past before Jane answered. 'I don't know.'

'We all of us have our ups and downs, pet. Some more than others.' Kate frowned. 'You never knew that man Gregory Morgan, did you? The one who kept shouting then going quiet for a day or two. Before your time. His mood shifted quicker than the breeze. Believe me, you're not as bad as him.'

The woman was trying to make her feel better about things, but all Jane could do was nod her reply. What if this was something else, a deeper shift within her? Would she still be able to do this work? Did she care?

'Tell me this.' Kate interrupted her thoughts. 'If someone was coming for you, if he was going to harm you, could you hurt him? Kill him?'

Not a moment's hesitation. 'Yes. Of course.'

Kate smiled and placed a warm, fleshy hand on her arm. 'Then maybe you're just growing up and seeing there's more shades of colour to the world than you imagined.'

Wheelwrights. Simon could think of eight off the top of his head, and that was probably nowhere near the entire list. Mudie had a trade directory; he searched through it as the printer proofread a test sheet for an advertisement.

'Leatherbarrow.' Mudie raised his head. 'Doesn't he do some wheelwrighting?'

That was it. Paul Leatherbarrow. Simon could picture him now. Stringy hair, powerful arms. A paunch that arrived a full minute ahead of the rest of him.

He made a living of sorts, a workshop in Rockley Hall Yard, off the Head Row. Leatherbarrow was a Jack of all trades: some joinery, rough cabinets, doors. If it involved using his hands, he could do it. A little wheelwrighting if someone paid. Even bits of blacksmithing when there was a call for it; he had a small forge.

It wasn't in use today. Leatherbarrow was hunched over a lathe, turning it with a pedal as he moved his chisel across the revolving wood and muttered to himself. Simon waited until the man had finished the cut, straightened his back and taken a swig from a mug.

'Very demanding work.'

'Has to be exact or you ruin it.' He eyed Westow. 'You look familiar, but not like I'd enjoy your company.'

Simon smiled. 'Did you ever employ a lad named Tommy Deacon?'

'I might have,' Leatherbarrow answered cautiously. 'Who wants to know?'

'My name's Simon Westow.'

A nod. 'I've heard about you. What's he done?'

'I don't know.' He saw the astonishment on the man's face. 'It might be nothing. I'm trying to find him.'

Leatherbarrow snorted. 'He's quick to disappear when he wants, is young Tommy. Especially if there's any work around.'

'How long was he here?'

'Best part of a year. I turned him away a fortnight back.'

Something must have happened. 'Why?'

'He wouldn't show up. Even if he did, he wasn't paying attention. Not a scrap of use. I decided to save myself the wages.'

'Did he take anything?'

Leatherbarrow shook his head. 'Steal, you mean? Not from me. He wouldn't dare. If he tried, it would be a week before he'd be able to move again.'

'Where does he live?'

'His family's on Quarry Hill. Charles Street. I don't know how much time he spends there, mind. He's the type with just enough charm and education to worm his way into trouble.' The man rubbed his thumb against his fingertips. 'Wants money, but he thinks he deserves it without a lick of hard graft.'

Simon listened, forming a hazy image of Deacon.

'Charles Street?' Close enough where Sophie Jackson's family had lived.

'That's right.' The voice became suspicious. 'He's done something, hasn't he?'

'I'll have a better idea when I find him. How old is he?'

'I'm not right sure,' Leatherbarrow said, mulling the question. 'I never bothered to ask.' He pursed his lips. 'Twenty, I suppose. Could be a little older. Does it matter?'

Simon nodded. 'I'll find out.'

'I'll go.' Rosie offered to visit Deacon's parents.

She'd done more work with Simon over the summer, small jobs while the boys were learning under their tutor or playing with a neighbour's children. Picked up the slack, the jobs Jane didn't want. Before the twins, he and his wife had worked together every day; they'd always made a good team. Simon was happy to have her involved again.

'Do you think they'll talk to you?'

She nodded. 'We're both parents. That gives us something in common.'

She had the knack for drawing people out. 'Find out whatever you can,' he said. 'My guess is he's gone. But he might have left an address, some way to reach him.' A shrug. 'We can hope.'

'What do you want me to do?' Jane asked.

This morning she'd been even quieter than usual. Lost within herself, as if she was wrestling with a problem and not finding any answers. Her saw her fingertips absently stroke the old scars on her forearm where she'd cut herself. Years before. They were faded and pale now. No point in asking what was troubling her; Jane would never tell him. That had been her way as long as Simon had known her, even more since the splintering in the spring.

'Whatever you can discover about Thomas Deacon. The usual questions: does anyone know him, have they had any dealings with him. I've never come across the name, but maybe someone has.'

'All right.' She stood and made her way out. From the kitchen to the hall, and the quiet click of Simon's door closing behind her. Moving like a ghost.

'Leave her,' Rosie told him. 'She'll do the job.'

'I know. But—'

'Something's preying on her.' She gave him a soft smile. 'Let it lie.'

Yes. Better than losing her again.

Jane walked idly down Swinegate to stand by the bridge for a minute and watch the water flow past. She moved on, along the Calls, past the Parish Church and over towards Quarry Hill.

She felt as if she was full of holes, riddled with doubts. Unsure of herself, no longer certain who she was. It was nothing she could fight, not any kind of enemy she could see.

Her mood brightened a little as soon as she began to ask questions. Talking to boys and young men who lived on the streets. They spent all their days around the fringes of things, mostly just beyond the edge of the law. They heard names and gossip.

But none of them knew Tom Deacon. Even a few coins couldn't set their tongues chattering. The same with the girls. It was still far too early for most whores to be out and touting for business, but she was sure she'd simply hear the same from them. Deacon lived in a different world, one apart from most criminals.

During the afternoon she stopped in the small corner shops dotted around Quarry Hill. Only a tiny purchase in each: a little cheese, a twist of tea. Just enough to let her stand at the counter and talk for a moment or two.

'I heard that someone I know lived around here. A lad called Tommy Deacon.' Nothing more than that; let them make of it what they wanted.

One or two of the women running shops knew the family. Most hadn't heard the name. But one cocked her head.

'Funny you mention him, love. I saw him only last Sunday.' Her expression softened. 'I think he might have a room in Turkington's Yard. They were headed that way.'

Jane drew in a breath. She'd found him.

'They?' she asked slowly.

'Him and some lass.' The corners of her mouth turned down. 'I'm sorry if you're looking for him about anything like that.'

Jane laughed; the idea was ridiculous. 'No, I'm not.'

'My youngest knew him when they were little. That's why I recognized him. His face has hardly changed at all.'

But she knew people's memories all too often played them false. Maybe it really was him, maybe not.

'What was the woman like?'

A sly smile, as if her suspicion had been right all along. 'Bit more heft than you, I suppose. Not fat, mind, nothing like that. Just some weight.' She narrowed her eyes as she thought. 'Brown hair, a cape around her shoulders.' She stayed silent, trying to dredge up more, then shook her head. 'No, that's all. I hope he's worth it.'

'So do I,' she said as she hurried out.

Only a vague description, but it fitted what they knew about Sophie Jackson. She smiled. They were drawing close now.

Turkington's Yard. Jane stood, gazing at the place. Set back from Corn Hill, only one way in and out. Built cheaply, in a rush, and already starting to fall apart. She explored, seeking a hidden spot to watch any comings or goings, feeling her heart beating hard. Nobody gave her a second glance.

A nook close to the bottom of Cross Billet Street was perfect, sheltered from the wind, deeply shadowed but with a view across to the opening into the court. She spent a few minutes there before ambling back to Simon's house. The hunt had filled her mind for an hour or two. Now her thoughts returned to torment her as she tried to understand what had made her stay her hand the night before.

* * *

'They didn't come out and say it, but I think his parents were glad to see the back of him,' Rosie said. She sat at the table in her visiting gown of blood dark velvet, high-necked and modest. A matron's dress. A black hat with a tall feather lay in her lap.

She'd packed the boys out into the yard to play, deflecting their questions about why their ma was dressed in her good clothes. Rosie had listened as Jane told how she'd traced Deacon and the girl, then started with her own tale.

'How long ago did he leave?' Simon asked.

'About a month. No idea where he went, they haven't seen him since.'

'What about Sophie Jackson? Do they know her at all?'

'Thought she was quite common,' Rosie answered with an amused snort. 'Not that their son sounds much of a catch. He seems like he was a handful at home, had a habit of acquiring things that weren't his. He'd just shrug when his mother asked where they'd come from.'

Light fingers, Simon thought. Sly. Now that was interesting. But still, no reason for him to be taking papers and letters. Why would he want something like that?

'Could he read?'

She nodded. 'I asked. They had a neighbour, an old woman who taught the children when they were all young. The mother was very proud of that.'

That answered one question.

'When I told them that Sophie had vanished, too, they didn't seem surprised. My guess is they've washed their hands of him.' Rosie paused. He stared as a slow smile began to cross her face. 'Trying to, anyway. About the only thing that stirred them was when I said Sophie had worked for Captain Holcomb. The father came alive then. They hadn't known that. Ranted, began calling the Holcombs every name under the sun while his wife tried to calm him down.'

He cocked his head, puzzled. 'What brought that on?'

'Holcomb told you that his father was a magistrate and he went after the machine breakers,' she said.

'Was Tom Deacon's father involved in that?'

'Not him. His uncle. Arrested, tried, sentenced to transportation for fourteen years.' Her mouth turned down. 'He died on the voyage. You can see why the father is bitter.'

'Yes,' Simon replied, but his mind was already racing ahead. Tom Deacon's father had probably indoctrinated him with a hatred of the Holcombs. It would explain things. Maybe the young man saw a chance for some kind of revenge after he began courting Sophie Jackson. Maybe she sneaked him into the house, gave him a chance to search. He couldn't have known about the letters and diaries, but he must have been lucky, poking around here and there. Once he happened upon them, he'd realize they were perfect for blackmail, or to sell, the ideal scheme to make himself rich without working. He'd taken them, then he and Sophie had vanished. But few could ever completely disappear when someone was after them.

Tomorrow he'd go and see Tom Deacon.

EIGHT

Plenty of chatter around the coffee cart on Briggate by the time Simon arrived the next morning. He sipped from the tin mug, his body tensing as he heard the only topic of conversation: the body discovered in Turkington's Yard.

A man, that much was definite. Someone leaving early for work had stumbled over the corpse in the darkness and called for the watch.

He finished the drink and walked to the courthouse at the bottom of Park Row. It was home to the constable now, a grand sweep of a building, so much better than the ancient, crumbling stones of the Moot Hall.

Constable Porter was sitting at his desk, talking to the watch inspector. He raised his eyes as Simon entered.

'Might have guessed a dead body would bring you out of the woodwork, Westow.'

'Is it a young man?'

'Why do you want to know?'

'I'm searching for someone. For a client. I'd been told the man lived in the court.'

'What's his name?' The inspector's question was a snarl.

'Thomas Deacon. I was told he was around twenty.'

Porter shrugged. 'It's the same one. Somebody recognized him. Stabbed to death. But you wouldn't know anything about that, would you?'

'No.'

'Why were you after him, Westow?'

'He might have stolen something from a client of mine.'

'Is that right?' the constable asked, voice heavy with doubt. 'What's your client's name?'

Simon shook his head. 'Not without his permission.'

'Then you'd better get it from him before I pull you in as a suspect.'

It was the usual formal dance between them. Porter knew Simon had nothing to do with the killing, but he needed to establish his authority.

'I will. Have you searched his room?'

'Didn't know he had one. I was lucky enough just to find his name. What's he supposed to have taken?'

'I'll find out if I can tell you. But he was with a young woman.'

The constable raised his eyebrows and glanced at the inspector. 'Was he now? I don't suppose you know her name?'

Simon sifted through the possibilities. Could she have killed him? No, he couldn't see that; she'd run off with him willingly enough. If the body was Deacon, she was probably in danger. Telling the constable might save her, unless it was already too late. 'Sophie Jackson.'

Porter nodded to the inspector, who turned on his heel and left. In an hour or so the watch would be going through Turkington's Yard.

'Now it's just us, you can tell me the name of your client,' the constable said.

'Not until he allows me.'

His anger flickered like lightning. 'Then you'd better make sure he does, Westow. Get out of here.'

'We need to find her,' Simon said to Jane as they hurried through town. People filled the pavements on Briggate; they had to dodge and duck between carts and carriages to cross the street. A pig that had escaped from the Shambles slithered between people, drawing screams and shouts as it dashed towards freedom. 'We'd better hope the description we have is close.'

As soon as he'd arrived at Mrs Shields's house and explained the problem, she put on her cloak and laced up her heavy boots. No reticence, and he was grateful for that. After yesterday, he had no idea what was going through her mind.

'Where do we start? You said the watch is looking.'

'If we're quick we'll have a few minutes in the yard. You know what they're like. Always slow and lazy.'

'The body,' she began. 'Are they certain it was Tom Deacon?'

'So the constable says.'

Jane gave him a confused glance. 'Why, though? Who'd know what he had?'

That was the question he couldn't begin to answer.

When you paid pauper's wages, you didn't attract capable men. Some members of the watch were brave; he'd seen that for himself. But rarely clever. Many did no more than was needed.

It took less than five minutes for Simon to learn where Deacon and Sophie had their room. One or two people remembered seeing the young couple, but never any conversation beyond a good day or hello. They always appeared worried. Frightened, one neighbour said.

Now he stood at the door, Jane behind him. Knife in his right hand as his left came down lightly on the wood. No reply. He tried again, then reached for the knob. Locked, but the latch was flimsy, picked in ten seconds.

Empty.

Things were strewn across the floor. A comb, a cheap dress, a threadbare man's coat. Hurriedly, they began to search. Under the chest, tapping for loose floorboards.

No papers.

Sophie Jackson wasn't rich enough to leave clothes behind. Jane felt the cotton of the frock. Old but still wearable. Teeth were missing from the comb, strands of hair still tangled in it. She'd either run to save her life or she'd been taken.

'No blood,' he said. Deacon hadn't been killed here. That had to mean something. After five more minutes they were walking quickly down Corn Hill, past the Methodist chapel and on to Dyers Street where colours from all the works leached out on to the cobbles. Reds, deep blues, blacks; their boots scuffed over them.

'Why would anyone kill him?' Jane asked. 'We know he's light-fingered, but he doesn't have any kind of reputation as a thief.'

'The papers. It can't be anything else.'

'Sophie would never have left that dress or her comb if she'd had the choice.'

Simon nodded his agreement. 'Let's hope she *is* running, nothing more. And hope she still has the papers too.'

'There's no need for her to disappear otherwise.' They were the only things of value that Sophie possessed. 'Who would want them badly enough to kill for them?'

They'd barely started and already this was more tangled than a bramble bush. For a moment it all seemed too exhausting. She wished she could simply walk away and leave him to it. But she'd given Simon her word. For better or worse, she'd stay.

'Why don't you see if you can find anything more on Sophie?' he said after a moment's thought.

*   *   *

Who else would want those papers? Desire them badly enough to kill to possess them? That was the vital question, Simon thought as he strode up Briggate. What could anyone gain from them?

Deacon would have wanted . . . what? A payment to return them? He'd have sensed the opportunity of money. Yet Holcomb claimed he hadn't been approached. Might Tommy have wanted the truth of what happened to his uncle to come out? With the lad dead, he'd never have an answer to that. Sophie might know, but she was . . .

He drew in a breath. Where was she? They needed to pray she was still alive.

At Mudie's print shop he scribbled a note to Holcomb, giving a boy a ha'penny to deliver it.

'You look like a worried man, Simon. Something to do with that body they found?'

He exhaled. 'Everything to do with it.'

Mudie cocked his head. 'Let me guess, Simon. You've just sent Holcomb a letter.'

Simon shook his head. 'That would mean I'm working for him. I've never said that. Maybe you should be doing my job.'

'I could probably make more than I do from printing.'

'You wouldn't like the frustration of being a thief-taker. Or the hours.'

'Maybe not. But I'm sure I'd appreciate the money.'

Jane returned to St Ann's Lane. Sophie might have gone searching for the safety of her family. But half an hour of wandering and questions brought nothing.

She moved on to Caroline Street, keeping away from the house where the Jacksons lived. Whatever answers they gave her, she wouldn't know whether to believe them. No luck until she found a grubby boy, perhaps five years old, sitting by the corner pitching pebbles towards the wall, playing against himself to see which one could come closest.

He was absorbed in his game, not even hearing her until she squatted beside him. He turned his head, mouth wide.

'Do you live around here?'

He nodded, too shy to speak. Jane picked up a stone and rubbed it between her fingers. She'd done this when she lived on the streets, in the times when everything seemed too big and heavy for her. It had been an escape, a brief time when she didn't need to think about life.

'How long have you been sitting out here?' She tossed the stone. It hit the brick of a house and bounced back towards her. Too long out of practice. She picked it up and tried again. A little better. A third time, much the same.

'Since everyone else went to work,' he said finally.

She understood. Parents, brothers and sisters all gone to the mills or the factories and nobody to look after him, so the boy had to amuse himself all day.

'Do you know the house up the street?' She tilted her head to indicate. 'The one where the paint is peeling off the black door.'

He nodded again.

'Have you seen—' Jane tried to think how to describe Sophie Jackson in a way he'd understand '—a woman about my age go in there? Bigger than me. Have you seen anyone like that?'

He took a long time to answer.

'Yes.'

Jane took a breath, feeling her heart beating faster. 'Was she carrying anything?'

'It was all wrapped in a cloth. I thought it might have been a bairn.'

The papers. She still had them. Jane smiled with relief. 'How long ago was that? Is she still in there?'

A shake of the head. Patiently, she eased the answers from him. The woman had arrived with first light, just after he'd watched his family troop around the corner to work. She'd been looking around, as if she was scared someone would see her. A knock on the door and she hurried inside. Half an hour later she left, wearing a different cloak from the one she'd had before.

'You have very sharp eyes,' Jane said, watching him blush at the praise. 'Was she still carrying the package?' A nod. 'Do you remember the colour of the cloak?'

'Dark?' It was a question, not a statement. 'Black?' He'd told her everything he knew.

But there might be one more thing. 'Which way did she go?'

He pointed towards the centre of the town. The perfect place for Sophie Jackson to lose herself. Or for someone to find her.

She spilled out coins from her pocket. Pennies, threepence, a pair of sixpences and a shilling. His eyes widened at how much she had. She placed them in his small hand.

'Is there somewhere round here that sells used clothes?'

'Mrs Parker on the next street.'

Jane looked closely at him. As thin as a poor man's Sunday. Arms bare, covered in goose pimples. Holes in his clothes, shoes barely worthy of the name. Jane dug out another florin and placed it on top of the others.

'Go there and buy some things that will keep you warm.'

'But . . .' he began. He was too young to have the words he needed.

'When your mother asks, tell her the woman who works for the thief-taker gave you the money. You understand?'

'Yes,' he answered, but she wondered if he'd heard her. He was still staring at the coins, as if he couldn't believe they were real.

She tried the pebble again. It bounced away from the wall. Jane stood. He tore his eyes off the money to stare at her.

'Have some warm food, too,' she said and walked off. Money well spent, she decided. She knew Sophie Jackson was still alive and carrying the papers.

Where could she go?

Now it was time to see what the mother said.

NINE

'Not seen her in weeks.' The woman glared, daring Jane to call her a liar. 'Never been to this new place. There was a man, he talked to my husband.'

'Simon Westow.' She nodded. 'I work with him.'

'My Billy told him what I just said to you. We thought she was still up at the Holcombs.' A shift in the expression at the back of her eyes. 'I've been frantic with worry about her.'

'You haven't seen her?' A chance to see if the woman wanted to tell the truth.

'What did I just say?' Her temper flared for a hot moment. 'What's happened to her?'

'We're trying to find out. That young man of hers . . .'

'The Deacon lad? Never had much time for him. Decent family, but he's the black sheep.'

Time to say it and see how Mrs Jackson reacted. 'We know your daughter was with him. But he's dead. Someone murdered him in Turkington's Court.'

The woman's hands flew to her mouth, trying to stifle the moan. The shock was real. Sophie hadn't told her mother about that.

'Do you know where I can find her? She's in danger.'

A helpless shake of the head was Mrs Jackson's answer.

'We can keep her alive.'

A final look, all the hope draining from her, and she quietly closed the door.

They met on the road that rolled out along the valley to Meanwood village. Simon waited by a tree close to the beck. Most of the leaves had fallen, branches stark and bare and threatening.

Holcomb rode up at a canter, checking his horse to a smart halt, then dismounting.

'I trust it really is important. You're supposed to be working, not constantly running to me about this and that.' No small talk, nor greeting. The man was as immaculate as ever, coat freshly brushed, high boots gleaming with polish, his stock a fresh, clean white. 'What is it this damned time? It had best be good, Westow.'

'It is.' He explained about Deacon, watching the man's face darken.

'Tell me, why would anyone murder over these papers?' Simon asked when he'd finished. 'Who'd want to do something like that? What secrets are in there?'

Holcomb sighed. 'I don't know, Westow. I honestly don't. They're important to my family but—'

'Obviously to other people, too. What about the families of those your father ordered hanged or transported?'

A deep breath. 'Yes, of course. To them, too.'

'The young man who was killed, his uncle was one of those sent overseas.'

He gazed down at the ground as if it held an answer. 'I see.'

'He died on the voyage.'

'I'm truly sorry for the family,' Holcomb said. At least he sounded sincere. He gazed at the ground for a moment, scuffing his boot against the path. 'Was he carrying the papers?'

'They weren't found with his body, and they weren't in his room.'

A sharp look. 'Then where are they?'

'Possibly whoever killed him has them. Or Miss Jackson, if you're lucky. If she's even still alive. She's disappeared.'

'Disappeared?' Emptily, he repeated the word.

'We have no idea where she is. Someone's died for these papers, Captain. It might be more than one person. There has to be a very important reason. The constable wants to know more, too. He's been asking who's employed me.'

Holcomb led the horse by the reins, slowly pacing a circle, limping with each step. Simon watched him, hands deep in his pockets, feeling the sting of the cold air against his face.

'Whoever has them can blackmail me,' the captain said. 'They can threaten to publish the documents and ruin my family unless I pay them. Tell the constable your client refuses to let you say anything.'

Maybe this was just his way, a man too used to others obeying him without question. That his decision was the always the right one. Perhaps not as different from his father as he imagined, after all.

'You've definitely had no demands of any kind?'

A quick shake of the head. 'I'd have told you if I had. I suppose the other possibility is that whoever has the papers intends to publish them. A form of revenge for what my father did.'

'You told me about the machine breakers. That's common knowledge. I can't believe something like that is likely to hurt you. What else did he do? There has to be something.'

'All sorts. He believed in punishing people who opposed anything to do with the way he saw things.'

'You told me you didn't have much love for him.'

'No. He grovelled to people with power and titles, but he bullied everyone else, including his children. There was precious little to respect about him.'

'But you want to stop anyone publishing the papers that damn him.'

'Yes, I do.' He sounded adamant. 'I know full well what he was like. But he's dead now. What good would it do to bring everything out? It won't change a damned thing. All that will happen is his sins will fall on us. Me, my sisters, my wife, my son. I've done everything I can to make sure I'm not like my father. If this comes out, people will assume . . .' He took a breath. 'Do you see?'

'Yes,' Simon told him. It all sounded so plausible. As far as he knew, the captain had tried to live an upright life.

'There has to be something else in there.'

He snorted. 'Isn't that enough, Westow? It seems like it to me. He protected men sometimes, people of his class, even when he knew they'd committed crimes.'

He mounted and rode off. Simon watched him leave. What crimes had the magistrate covered up? There was still too much hidden. Rosie was right. He should walk away. But not quite yet.

Simon stood at the top of Briggate, wondering where to go next, when Jane appeared from nowhere.

'She was definitely still carrying the parcel when she left her parents' house?' he asked when she'd told him what she'd learned.

'That's what the boy said.'

At least Sophie Jackson was alive. But who was pursuing her? Who had killed Tom Deacon?

He gazed down the street, off towards she river. The town spread wide, the pall of smoke a low cloud over everything. She was somewhere in all that. Where could Sophie go?

'She's going to need somewhere to sleep. Can you go out tonight and try to spot her?' Jane could drift around the homeless groups without being noticed. If Sophie was with one of them, Jane would find her.

'What do you want me to do if I see her?'

'Stay close,' he told her after a little thought. 'Just watch and make sure she's safe for now. If someone tries to hurt her or take the papers . . .' Jane knew what to do. 'See where she goes in the morning.'

A nod and she vanished.

He'd just turned on to Commercial Street when Constable Porter fell in step beside him. His day for company.

'Found out anything more about the killing?' Simon asked.

The man shook his head. 'We discovered his room but there wasn't much to find.'

No, Simon thought, it was the things that weren't there that mattered.

'Have you talked to your client?'

'He still doesn't want me to say anything.'

Colour rose over the constable's cheeks. 'Then how the devil am I supposed to work? I've got a killer who's free—'

'There's a young woman, too.' Simon cut him off. 'Remember her? We need to find out what's happened to her.'

No need to tip his hand. The change in direction might distract Porter.

'Anything you *do* discover . . .'

TEN

The bell at the Parish Church had just rung five o'clock: full autumn dark. People moved through the streets, stooped and quiet. Already the ones with no home were gathering wood, whatever they could find, to build fires in the empty buildings.

Some warmth, a shelter to try and see them through the night. It would keep away the roaming packs of dogs that could drag off an unattended baby. Jane had seen that happen when she first lived on the streets. Back then she'd been too scared to try to stop the animals.

Sophie Jackson would be terrified out here. Her life might never have been rich, but it had been settled. She'd had a bed to sleep in. Now everything had fallen apart and she was scrambling to survive, with no idea which way to turn.

For three hours Jane drifted around the places she knew, others that people mentioned. Murmurs of conversation and lost faces in the firelight. A few had a little food; others watched them jealously. Sophie would be alone, not knowing a single soul out here, not daring to trust anyone.

The fleeting visit to her mother's house had been desperation. Sophie would only go back there again as a final resort; it looked as if she'd been trying to protect her family from her danger.

Here and there Jane saw faces she recognized. A hasty question or two, pressing a penny into someone's palm, then she'd move on.

By nine she'd seen nobody who resembled Sophie Jackson. Plenty who were frightened and huddled, curling over to make themselves small. Jane had given up, turning towards home and the comfort of Mrs Shields's house, when she heard the skitter of feet on the cobbles.

She turned, searching the darkness, one hand gripping the hilt of her knife.

'Did you find that woman, miss?'

A small, timid voice. A girl, young, with a wide, guileless face.

'Not yet. Have you seen her?'

There was just enough light from a window to see the nod of the head. A dirty face and hands and haunted eyes.

'Maybe. I don't know.'

'Where?' Jane asked.

'That warehouse by the river. The one that smells of fire.'

She knew it well. The place had burned up during the summer, blazing so bright in the night sky it was as if day had never ended. Only the husk remained, walls that might collapse at any moment, no roof. Filled with a dead, charred stink inside. She'd been there earlier and hadn't spotted anyone.

'When did you see her there?'

'A little while ago. She's on her own, I thought it might be her.'

Jane thought. Some way to identify Sophie. 'Was she carrying something?'

The girl thought. 'I'm not sure.'

The honest answer surprised her. This one hadn't been on the streets long enough to become sly. 'Show me. I'll pay you if it's her.'

She'd never seen Sophie Jackson, but as soon as she spotted the woman, she knew. It had to be her. Tucked into the shadows, keeping just close enough to the fire and the people in the building to feel the comfort, yet far enough away to hide. Looking very scared and clutching something close.

Jane gave money to the girl who'd brought her here, enough to make her gasp in surprise.

'Miss . . .' she began, and suddenly there was a little hope in her voice.

'What?'

'Do you look for people? Is that what you do?'

'Not really. This time I am.'

For a moment, the girl looked as though she wanted to say more. Then a man barged past, sending her tumbling out of the way. When Jane looked again, the girl had gone.

She settled where Sophie wouldn't notice her and drew the cloak close around her body, hand on the knife in her pocket.

She'd spent many nights in these places, back when anywhere out of the weather felt like salvation. Hoping she'd still be alive in the morning, yet knowing it would only bring more of the same. As her eyes slowly adjusted to the gloom, she could pick out the silhouettes, the empty faces that only wanted to last through to first light.

Eventually, Sophie lay down on the cold floor, clutching the bundle against her body and pulling up her legs. Hoping for some sleep. Jane sat, keeping watch over her. Eventually the noise fell away. No more talking. Coughing, snuffling. A few tears. The sharp cry of a baby. The moan of a nightmare.

She wasn't the only one with an eye on Sophie. She felt someone else out there. No hope of discovering who before dawn. The fire began to crackle and burn low as another hour passed. Jane flexed her fingers to bring some feeling to them.

Mrs Shields would be worried about her, but she'd understand; this wasn't the first time Jane had been out all night when she worked for Simon. The woman would still be able to sleep.

From the corner of her eye she caught a movement and tensed, gripping her knife tighter. Just a mother drawing her baby close enough to give it some heat.

Well before the earliest sign of day, people began to rise and leave. Some pissed in the far corners before they made their way outside. Others didn't bother going that far.

Jane eased the ache from her legs and pulled the cloak tighter. From too much bitter experience, she knew this was the coldest part of the night. Her gaze hadn't wandered far from Sophie Jackson.

The woman woke, cautiously raising her head. She stood, stretching, trying to ease the cold from her bones, keeping the package close. A defeated glance around and she began to shuffle towards the doorway and the Calls.

Further away, another figure rose and followed. A man. On his feet with surprising grace for someone who'd spent a night here. Keeping his distance, he stayed behind Sophie.

Jane pulled the hood of her cloak over her hair. She kept back, just another shape on the street, wondering who he was and what he wanted with the woman. He never glanced over his shoulder. Too confident by half.

Sophie kept turning her head, checking, nervous, but she never spotted him as she wandered around Leeds: from the centre of town, out past the Head Row and into the Leylands, where houses gave way to fields. Back, and down to Park Square.

Each step looked like an effort. The man remained, falling away as she slowed, never approaching her. Jane couldn't understand what he was he doing. He'd had plenty of chances to try and steal her bundle during the night, even kill her if he wanted. Was he hoping Sophie would lead him somewhere?

She stayed clear of Quarry Hill and Turkington's Yard, didn't venture anywhere near Holcomb's house, anywhere she might be recognized. Was she passing time or searching for somewhere safe? Or had she already realized safety and comfort were just dreams when you had no home?

ELEVEN

Sophie kept walking. She returned to Leeds Bridge and the river. The man stayed forty yards or more away, never needing to conceal himself. As the clock on the Parish Church struck seven, Sophie picked up her pace, crossing into Hunslet and following Meadow Lane until she reached South Market. It stretched out across the open ground, all the way to Hunslet Lane, a stone cross at its heart.

She made for the covered area where traders were setting out their wares. Some late apples and pears, their skins starting to wrinkle. Old clothes that had seen better days. Boots and shoes held together with hope and shoddy repairs.

Jane hung back. No need to go too close. She could see everything.

Sophie stopped at the used clothes stall, talking to a woman who was pulling goods from a sack. A handcart stood behind her. They knew each other; the smiles made that obvious. Two minutes of talk, then Sophie handed the woman the bundle she'd been carrying, straightening up as if she'd let go of a heavy weight.

With a swift glance around, the woman tucked it away in the sack, then placed it under the wheels of the cart, tying it to one of the spokes.

Hard to steal. But whatever was in there had already cost Tom Deacon his life.

Sophie was moving away. Her step was lighter, freer. The man seemed torn. Jane could imagine his quandary: stay and watch the package or follow Sophie? Almost half a minute passed before he ducked away after the young woman.

Jane turned and slowly walked back towards the river, her head full of possibilities.

'Once the boys are with the tutor, I'll go over and talk to the woman at this stall,' Rosie offered.

Simon nodded, eyes on Jane. 'You look like you need to go home and rest.'

'That man,' she said with a frown. 'I can't make head nor tail of what he wants. He had plenty of chances to take the papers, but all he did was follow her.'

'It sounds as if she's probably safe. For now, at least. That's something. We'll find her later.'

Jane woke and stretched in the bed, slipping out from the blanket and dressing quickly. From the light outside, the day was half gone.

Mrs Shields was in the kitchen, crumbling dried herbs to add to a soup.

'I suppose you're going out again,' she said with her gentle smile.

'I am.'

'Put something warm in yourself first. You know how cold it is out there.'

Jane nodded. Sensible advice.

By the time she reached Simon's house, her face was chapped by the wind and the cold rattled through her. She settled at the table, grateful for the soup and bread Mrs Shields had made her eat.

'I talked to that woman,' Rosie said. 'At first she claimed she didn't know anything about a bundle.'

'What did you tell her?' Simon asked.

'I didn't try to accuse her.' Rosie smiled. 'That wouldn't have helped. We talked. It turns out she's a friend of Sophie's older sister, Elizabeth. I think that's why Sophie went there. Someone she knew, that she felt she could trust. At first she didn't want to believe me about Tom Deacon. Sophie hadn't mentioned that.'

Keeping it from her mother and then this woman. What had been going through her mind, Jane wondered. Then she answered her own question: fear.

'As soon as she realized I was telling the truth, she was horrified. Even more when I said someone was following Sophie. After that she told me the girl had asked her to keep the package safe, that there was something important in it.'

'Did Sophie say when she'd come back?' Jane asked.

'As soon as she could.' Rosie drew in a breath. 'Nothing more than that. The woman asked where she'd be, but she didn't say.'

'She probably doesn't know,' Simon said. 'I don't suppose she let you look inside the bundle.'

'No. I didn't want to press her. But she told me she lives in Holbeck.' Her eyes moved to the clock. 'The market finishes in an hour. I thought one of you could follow her. Make sure she was telling the truth and that she's safe. She knows me, and the boys will be done with their lessons.'

'I'll go,' Jane said. 'I've seen her. After that I'll look for Sophie.'

'We need to find out who's watching her.' Simon pursed his lips and shook his head.

South Market was growing emptier by the minute. Half the stall-holders has left, the rest packing up their wares. The woman with the used clothes was loading everything into bags and placing them on the handcart.

Jane kept out of sight, turning her head, searching for anyone else who might be watching. Nobody. No sign of the man who'd seen Sophie hand over the bundle. Curious.

She had no time to think as the woman grasped the handles of her cart and began to walk. Out along Water Lane, jolting over the cobbles as Hunslet edged into Holbeck. Still the same cramped streets, though, with the air heavy from the foundries and the black bulk of Marshall's Mill that towered towards the sky.

The woman arrived at a yard, unlocked the gate and dragged the cart through. Two minutes and she was back, staring around as she turned the key and keeping the package tight against her body as she hurried to a small house a street away. Holbeck, just as she'd said.

Dark out. People passed, going home or on their way to the shops to buy a little food. A baby wailed and an infant joined in. Jane waited until she was certain that nobody would come.

The cold had numbed her; moving brought some warmth. But she had another long night ahead.

She started at the place she'd seen Sophie. Staring at the lost faces, but no trace of the woman or the man who'd been trailing her.

It was the same everywhere else. Maybe she'd decided to leave Leeds for a spell; it would be safer. Two hours and she was certain Sophie wasn't seeking shelter with any of the groups. The wind had shifted, bringing an angry, stinging rain. No one would stay outside in this if they could find somewhere dry.

Could she have gone back to her family? Jane stopped close to Caroline Street, thinking as she watched people dash past. No, she decided. Not yet. Sophie hadn't told them about Deacon; she'd try to keep them free of her troubles as long as she could.

At home, with her clothes hanging in front of the fire to dry, she settled under the blanket to read *Ivanhoe*. By the time sleep arrived, she was lost in the past.

Morning, and the rain had ended. The streets glistened, the air bitter enough for a thin rime of frost on the windows. Simon stood at the coffee cart, enjoying the heat from the drink as he listened.

It had been a quiet night, there was little gossip; the weather had kept people indoors. He returned the mug to the shaky trestle, starting to turn away as a man dashed up Briggate. Conversation fell away. Everyone watched as he stopped at the cart, gulping for breath.

'Bodies,' he gasped. 'In the beck by Water Lane.'

Talk exploded as voices climbed over each other.

'A man and a woman,' the man said above the clamour. 'That's all I know.'

Unnoticed, Simon eased away, striding over the bridge and along into Holbeck. It might be nothing, not connected to his case. But deep inside he didn't believe that. He *knew*.

It was easy enough to find the spot. A crowd had gathered, drawn by the ugliness of death, the way they always were.

Two men from the watch had dragged the corpses from the water and covered them with stained sacking. As Simon approached, one raised a hand to stop him until Constable Porter called out, 'Let him through.'

He'd never seen Sophie in the flesh, but the sodden corpse could have been her. Her skin was icy to the touch. Tenderly, Simon turned her head and saw the wound. A single blow, hard enough to shatter the back of the skull. He closed his eyes for a moment. No matter what she'd stolen, this was no way for her life to end.

The man had died the same way, but he looked as if his head taken a pounding before he died. Cheekbone snapped, an eye gone, nose squashed across his face. Someone had wanted him to suffer.

A little older than the woman, as far as he could judge. Curly fair hair, slim built. No rings on his fingers. The only remarkable thing about him was murder.

'Know them, Westow?' Porter asked.

'She might be Sophie Jackson. If it is, she was with the Deacon lad in Turkington's Yard. Her parents live on Caroline Street.'

'What about him?' He glanced at the man's corpse.

'I have no idea.' He wasn't going to tell Porter that Jane had

seen a man following Sophie. No need for her to be involved at all.
'Anything on him?'

The constable shook his head. 'Nothing to identify the body.' He
turned his head and spat. 'I need to know who's employing you.
It's urgent. That's three dead now.'

'I'll ask him again.'

'Don't ask this time, Westow. Tell him.'

Simon scuffled around, but there was nothing to spot. Any tracks
or footsteps had been obliterated by the throng. He edged his way
through, grabbing the wrist of a man who tried to pick his pocket
and pushing him down the ground, before wandering off, trying to
put all the pieces together.

TWELVE

'Go and see the woman with the clothes stall,' he told Jane. 'Didn't you say she lives in Holbeck?'

'Not far from Marshall's Mill.'

'The news is going be all over the area. See if she'll give you the bundle.'

'Do you think she will? Why should she trust us? We could be the ones who did the killing.'

He sighed. She was right. The woman had no reason to believe a word. 'Ask her anyway. Say Rosie sent you. That might work. If she still says no, we'll let it go for now.' In the hall the longclock struck quarter to the hour.

Over to Hunslet. The clothes seller hadn't arrived at the market. Jane moved around, listening to the chatter, reading the signs and the advertisements pasted to the walls and hoardings with her appetite for words.

Half an hour passed and the woman still hadn't come. Plenty of customers walking around. A few paused at the empty space, curious. When Jane asked, none of the other stallholders knew why the woman wasn't there.

'Maybe she's poorly, pet.' A shrug and the man blew some warmth on to his hands. 'This weather, wouldn't be much of a surprise.'

No answer at the house. Door locked. The cart was still in the yard. Something strange was going on.

Porter sat in his office at the courthouse, scratching a few notes in a ledger. He glanced up as Simon entered.

'That body was definitely the Jackson girl. I took her father to the infirmary. He identified her.'

How could anyone stand to see his own daughter, empty of life on a slab?

'What about the man?'

'He didn't recognize him at all. What does your employer have to say?'

'I haven't talked to him yet.'

'Make sure it's soon.' He had a solid note of anger in his voice. 'I don't care if he's the Lord Lieutenant of the bloody county, my patience is running thin on this.'

'I'll send you a message later today.'

The constable seemed to weigh the idea, then agreed with a nod.

Somewhere off in the distance, Jane could hear Davy Cassidy, the blind fiddler, playing. Sweet, plaintive music.

'Miss. Miss.' The voice dragged her away from the beauty.

Jane stopped in mid-stride on Boar Lane, glancing down to see the girl who'd led her to Sophie Jackson. Scrawny. Shivering and shaking from cold, but with eyes full of hope in the dirty face. The other night she'd had a question on the tip of her tongue. Maybe she felt ready to ask it now.

First, though, the girl looked as if she needed food. Nobody ever had a full belly on the streets.

'Are you hungry?' Jane asked and the girl gave a tentative nod. 'Come on, then.'

Side by side they walked down to the corner of Briggate and Boar Lane, where Kate the pie-seller raised her eyebrows as she saw them.

'Three, please,' Jane asked.

'Be careful, they're still hot,' Kate warned as she nodded at the girl. 'Who's your friend?'

'I'm don't know yet.' She balanced the pies and told the girl to take two.

'Can I, miss?' She seemed astonished by the offer. Polite, not grasping. She couldn't have been living like this for too long.

'Yes.'

Jane leaned against the stone of a building to eat. Her cloak would be smeared with soot, but everyone carried that mark somewhere; it came with living in Leeds.

She watched as the girl took small, dainty bites. Somewhere she'd been taught manners and they'd stuck, even out here, where she would always be famished and grasping at anything on offer. She'd been properly schooled. Delicate movements, although she'd learned enough to look around and guard her food. She studied the girl's clothes. Filthy now, torn. But the material had once been good wool.

'What's your name?'

The girl glanced up at her, then hurriedly back down at the ground as she licked the last crumbs from her grubby fingers.

'Emma, Miss.'

'I'm Jane. You have a lot on your mind, don't you?'

The girl was silent, trying to pull together scraps of bravery. 'You were looking for that woman the other night, miss.'

'I was.'

'Do you find many people?'

'Not really.' How could she explain it? 'It's usually things that have been stolen. I work with a man who does that.'

'Oh.' Her face flooded with disappointment.

'Sometimes we do have to look for people, though.'

Emma took a deep breath. 'How much do you charge, miss?'

'It depends how much the thing is worth.' Jane cocked her head. 'Why?'

'I only have a ha'penny left from what you gave me. That's not enough, is it?'

She'd finished eating, and stood shivering from fear and cold.

'You wanted to ask me something the other night, didn't you? What have you lost?'

'My sister.'

Warmer clothes. The girl desperately needed those. She looked so gaunt and cold that it was painful. A thick cloak to keep out the weather. Gloves. Stockings and boots that weren't falling apart. A heavy shawl. Jane found them all at the market on the corner of Kirkgate and Vicar Lane.

Emma looked scared.

'I can't ever pay you back for these, miss.'

'Don't worry about that. It's better than having you freeze to death.' Jane stood back and inspected the girl before nodding her head with satisfaction. 'Does that feel warmer?'

'Yes, miss.' She blushed. 'Thank you.'

'Good. We're going to see someone.'

'Simon's gone to talk to Holcomb,' Rosie said. She looked at the girl who sat timidly on the bench.

'He needs to hear this,' Jane said and turned to Emma, gently putting her arm around the girl's shoulders. 'This is Rosie. Why don't you tell her what you told me?

*   *   *

'I will not have the law involved,' Holcomb said.

'You're too late,' Simon told him. 'They already are. Three people have been murdered because of these papers of yours. Sophie Jackson is one of them. Your upstairs maid, the woman who used to work for you. The constable needs to talk to you and find out what's going on.'

'Then you'd better stop him.'

'No.'

The captain's face was rigid with fury. 'No?'

'You hired me to retrieve something stolen. It's what I do, even if I'm certain you haven't given me anywhere near the whole truth about it.' He stared at the captain. 'There's more to this than you've ever said.'

'I've told you the truth,' Holcomb replied slowly.

'Certainly not the whole of it,' he said. 'Just a drip, drip, drip that's meant to satisfy me. I'm not a fool, Captain.'

'It was all you needed to hear.'

His words confirmed what Simon suspected. There were currents moving under the surface of this. 'You don't believe what's happened changes any of that?'

'You know what you need to do the job.'

'Is that how you were with your soldiers?'

'I learned from my Lord Wellington.' He stood, proud and straight-backed. 'A infantryman charging the enemy doesn't need to know the whole battle plan.'

Simon exhaled, trying to keep his temper in check. He remembered what George Mudie had said: *Honour to these people is very different from the way you and I think about it.* 'This isn't war, Captain, and I'm not your soldier. I don't charge at guns and I will not defy the police for you.'

'What do you mean?'

'I'm withdrawing from this, and I shall give the constable your name. He and I sometimes have a fractious relationship, but this is *his* job.'

'Keep me out of it, Westow.'

Simon shook his head. 'It's much too late for that. Good day to you.'

As he walked away, he heard Holcomb's voice: 'Be sure you don't live to regret this.'

THIRTEEN

'Please listen to what she has to say.' Jane's voice carried a tone he'd never heard from her before. 'Please.'

Simon stayed quiet and glanced at his wife. She was sitting beside a child, a young girl, stroking her back and her hair. He'd come home breathing fire about Holcomb and found this. Rosie looked up at him and nodded.

'Her name is Emma,' Jane told him.

The girl was quivering, eyes darting around, holding her arms across her tiny chest. Amos and Richard were still with their tutor, a reassuring drone of voices coming from the front room.

'What's happened to you, Emma?' Simon asked. He squatted in front of the girl, so she wouldn't have to stare up at him.

Jane turned to her. 'You can tell him. This is the thief-taker I work with. He might be able to help.' Help? How?

'I . . .' Emma began. 'I was with my sister. Her name is Harriet and she's four years old.' Her voice wavered, gaining a little strength as she continued. 'Our governess took us to the park. Me and Harriet decided to play a trick on her, so we ran and hid. Two men found us. They took us away. When I tried to scream, they covered my mouth and hit me hard, again and again.' She stopped; her hand trembled as she reached for a mug and took a drink. The room was quiet. Waiting.

'They pushed us into a box. I tried to struggle but they just hit me again. Harriet was crying and holding on to me. We must have been in a carriage or a cart. I could hear the hooves and feel the wheels. The ground was very rough.'

'You must have been absolutely petrified,' Rosie said softly.

The girl nodded. A tear trickled down her cheek, then another.

'I didn't know what to do. I didn't know where they were taking us or what was going to happen. I tried calling out and screaming, but nobody came. I thought they were going to kill us. I think we must have been in there for a very long time. After they stopped, they dragged us out of the box. We were in a stable. I could smell the horses. A man was looking at us. He pointed at Harriet and

said, "I'll pay you good money for her. The other one's too old." I
started to scream and I tried to stop them, but one of the men hit
me again so I passed out. When I woke up I was next to a midden
in Leeds.'

Rosie pulled a handkerchief from her apron and handed it to
Emma. The girl dabbed at her eyes.

'I'm sorry,' she said.

'Don't apologize.' Simon's voice was soft. 'There's no need.
You're safe now.' It was hard to take in, men doing that to girls.
First things first. He had to find her family and see her home again.
'Where were you living when they snatched you?'

'Tadcaster, sir. Me, mama and papa and Harriet and the servants.
My dog, too.'

'How long ago did this happen?' Rosie asked.

Emma was hesitant. 'I'm not sure, miss. I *think* it was two weeks.
It's hard to keep count.'

'Have you had anywhere to sleep?'

She shook her head. 'No, sir. Just where I could.'

'What's your surname?'

'Caldwell, sir. I know my mama and papa must be frightened,
but I had no idea how to find them. I couldn't get anyone to listen
to me until Jane.'

'You don't need to worry now,' Simon assured her. 'We'll make
sure your parents know. They'll be thrilled to hear you're fine.
They'll come for you as soon as they can.'

'But what about Harriet?' Her gaze moved frantically from one
face to the next. 'They always said that I was older, so I had to
look after her. I've been searching everywhere and I can't find her.'

He felt Jane's eyes on him and saw the determination on her
face.

'We'll hunt for your sister,' he said. 'We'll do everything we can.
I promise.'

Emma blinked. 'But what if you can't find her?'

Nobody spoke for a few seconds. Then Rosie stirred.

'We have a room upstairs, in the attic.' She smiled, trying to offer
some comfort. 'Jane used to sleep there. Come with me.' She held
out her hand. 'I'll make the bed and bring you some hot water to
wash yourself and then you can have a proper rest.'

More talk as they climbed the steps, leaving Simon and Jane in
the kitchen.

'My God,' he said.

'I believe her.'

He pressed his lips together. 'So do I. She comes from money; you can hear it in the way she speaks.' He ran a hand through his hair and kneaded the back of his neck. 'You know what this means.'

She'd understood it as soon as Emma told her. Someone was seizing girls to order, taking them a distance from home where they were unlikely to be found. Very young girls. A little past that age and they were already too old. There was at least one man willing to buy them.

'I'm going to find Harriet,' she said.

'If she's still alive.'

'She is.' Jane spoke with such faith that he didn't question it. The girl was somewhere near Leeds, enduring her own hell, but her heart was still beating.

'We'll do it together.'

She looked at him, uncertain. 'Are you honestly willing?'

'Yes,' he told her. 'I am. I'll write to her parents. They . . . I can't start to imagine what they're feeling. Both their daughters taken. They must be off their heads with grief. You know we have to tell the constable.'

'Why?'

'Why?' He stared at her in utter disbelief. 'Two young girls have been snatched. One's still missing, very likely close to town, and we need to find her as soon as we can. If Emma is right, it's already been too long.'

'But—'

'Look, Porter has the watch working for him.' He drew in a breath. 'We need as many people as possible out there searching for her. Can't you see that? We have to *find* her, and I don't know if we can do that by ourselves.'

Jane opened her mouth, then closed it again before nodding agreement. Every pair of eyes would help. A fortnight . . . Christ Almighty, he thought, that was long enough for anything to happen.

'There's something I don't understand,' she said. 'There are plenty of children without any homes on the streets here. Why wouldn't he take one of them? It would be simple enough. Nobody would miss them. People wouldn't even realize they'd gone.'

'I don't know.' He sighed. 'Whoever ordered this, it sounds like he's wealthy. Maybe he has very particular tastes.' Whatever they were, the bastard was twisted. Not difficult to think of things he intended for the girl.

'I cleaned her up a little and put her to bed,' Rosie said after she returned. 'She's down to skin and bone. Poor little thing closed her eyes as soon as the blanket was on top of her. Probably the first time she's slept inside since . . .'

'Since she was stolen.' Jane finished the sentence.

'What are we going to do, Simon?' Rosie asked. 'That's girl's from a good family.'

'We make sure she goes home again.'

'What about her sister?'

'Harriet.' Jane spoke the name. She needed to hear it, to make it solid and real in her mind.

'I asked what she looks like,' Rosie said. 'Emma started to cry. She think her parents are going to hate her because she didn't stop the men. It was her idea to run and hide from the governess. She's blaming herself, poor little thing.'

'Did she manage to give you a description in the end?' Simon asked.

'After a fashion. Fair hair. Very pale, Emma said. Blue eyes. Thin. She tried to show me how tall, it's probably a little over three feet.' She shrugged. 'I know it's not much, but it's the best she can manage for now.'

'I'll go and talk to Porter.'

'He won't know where to begin.' Jane's fists were clenched on the table, the knuckles white.

'Do we?' he asked.

'We'll find her.' He could see her determination. She wasn't going to allow a shred of doubt into her voice. 'Before Emma found me, I went to look for the clothes seller at South Market first thing this morning. She never turned up. I tried her house, but there was no answer, doors locked, no sign of anyone inside. Her cart was still in the yard, though.'

'Maybe she'd heard about the bodies in the beck,' Simon said. As he explained, Rosie's face fell in sorrow. 'One of them is Sophie. Her father identified her. No idea on the man.' He turned the mug of ale, leaving damp rings on the table.

'They found her,' Jane said.

Simon felt their eyes on him. 'I told Holcomb we're not working for him any longer.'

'Well, I'm glad you did,' his wife said. 'What tipped the balance?'

'Even with all the bodies, Holcomb still refuses to talk to the law. The deaths don't seem to matter. He refused to let me give Porter his name. When I said it didn't sound as if he'd told me everything, he agreed. He'd only given me what he believed I needed to know.' He looked from his wife to Jane. 'That was the end of it. We're not going to work like that.'

'What now?' Rosie asked.

'I told the constable Holcomb had hired us. He can do whatever he wants with it.' Simon drank and sat back.

'It's over, then?' Jane asked. 'All of it?'

'No,' he replied carefully. 'Holcomb believes it is. That's what I want him to think. But Sophie Jackson deserves something better than that. Even Tommy Deacon and the other one who had his skull beaten in. Now that clothes seller has gone, too. Someone's done all that. We're going to find those papers and bring them all some justice. All very quietly, though.' His eyes moved from Jane to Rosie. 'If we don't, who will?'

'What about Harriet?' Jane asked.

'We look for her,' he said. 'That will be the most important thing.' Her eyes glistened. With a nod, she left.

'How did the captain react when you told him?' Rosie asked.

'Said I ought to be sure I don't regret my decision.'

She raised her eyebrows. 'That sounds like a threat.'

Simon smiled. 'We've had plenty of those before. We're still here.'

'Be careful.' Her voice was serious. 'Men like that aren't used to people refusing them.'

'It's too late now. I've done it. Like I said, we'll keep our investigation very quiet.'

'Holcomb would have paid well,' she said wistfully.

'His father had a history of taking people to court if he owed them money.' He shook his head. 'Someone else can wade through his muck. I gave him plenty of chances to tell me the truth. We'll do things our way.' He raised his head towards the ceiling and Emma up in the attic. 'Besides, we have something more on our plate.'

'Jane needs this, you know. To find the girl.'

'If she's still alive.'

'I asked Emma about her family when I was washing her. She told me her father owns a stone quarry.'

'Money.'

'That was obvious as soon as she mentioned a governess.'

He glanced towards the window. 'The miracle is that someone like Emma survived out there.'

'Don't underestimate her, Simon,' Rosie told him. 'She's stronger than she looks.'

'She must be.'

'Jane knows.' She reached out and squeezed his hand. 'Remember, she lived it for years. She understands more about that life than we ever can. We have no idea what she had to do.'

No, he thought, and they never would. She'd always kept it locked away, not spoken a word about it. Even Mrs Shields probably didn't know everything. But helping her with this . . . it might go some way towards healing the rift between them.

'There are things you can do that Jane can't,' Rosie reminded him. 'People you can talk to who'd never speak to her.'

He wrote to the Caldwells in Tadcaster and put the letter in his pocket, ready to take to the post office. First he strode down to Park Row to the courthouse. The constable was smoking a pipe and reading through documents.

'Can't keep you away, Westow. What is it this time? Looking for a job? Want to join the night watch?'

Simon grinned. 'I can't afford the drop in pay. Have you talked to Captain Holcomb?'

'I sent the inspector to see him, but the captain appears to have suddenly gone away for a few days with his wife and son.' He raised his eyebrows. 'None of the servants seem certain where.'

'Very convenient.' Interesting, too. If the man had really gone away, he wouldn't know Simon was still investigating. If.

'Isn't it?'

'This is about something else.'

By the time he'd finished, Porter was ashen.

'In Leeds?' He ran his hands down his cheeks and stumbled over the words. 'Jesus dear God. Are you certain this girl's telling the truth?'

'Positive,' Simon told him. 'We have a four-year-old girl who's been bought by someone. I don't want to think what he's done to her. But he has to be somewhere close to Leeds if they dumped the sister here.'

'I'll have every man on the watch looking.' The constable glanced up. 'What about you?'

'I'll be searching.'

'That lass. Jane.'

'She brought Emma to me. She's taking charge.'

'Her?' Porter asked in surprise. 'Why?'

'The sister came to her. She knows about life on the streets. If there's anything to hear, she'll make sure she knows it.'

'I don't think we'll find the answers there.'

'Probably not,' he agreed. 'But someone might have information we can use.'

'I want the man behind this, Westow.'

'So do I.' The pair of them needed to hope Jane didn't find him first. 'You know it's almost certainly someone powerful.'

'I don't care,' Porter said. 'That's not going to protect him. I know we butt heads sometimes, Westow, but can we work together on this?'

'Yes.'

He picked up a nib. 'I'll send a rider to Tadcaster and tell the family. They deserve to know as soon as possible, don't you think?'

Of course he did. Faster than the post. A nod of gratitude and he left. Where to begin?

Jane watched the children. They lived in the shadows, darting out to scavenge anything that fell, stealing if they could get away with it. Food from a barrow, quick fingers picking a pocket or a purse. After a few minutes she singled out the ringleader, a hard-faced girl who looked to be around eleven or twelve, wearing a tattered shawl around her shoulders and a cotton dress that might once have been a pale, pretty blue.

She directed the others, telling them where to go. The girl had sharp eyes, but she hadn't seen Jane come up behind them.

A cough. The younger ones turned their heads, then scattered like birds. The girl tensed, pausing as Jane let some coins jingle in her hand.

'What do you want?' Deep suspicion in her voice, fingers easing towards the knife in her belt.

'I'm not here to hurt you. Questions, that's all.'

'Is that right? What kind of questions?'

'Ones that can help me.'

'Why would I care about you?'

'Because I can give you a little money for answers.' A moment until the girl nodded. 'How long have you been out here?'

A hard, bitter smile and a shrug. 'Does it matter? A year? Forever? Same thing, isn't it?'

'Most of the time.'

She saw the girl staring into her face. 'You have the look.'

'I've done it.'

'How many did you have to kill?'

'Enough.' No need for details, although she remembered every one of them. The first had seemed impossible. After that it became easier, a matter of survival. If she hadn't done it, she'd be dead herself. 'What's your name?'

'Sally.' A surname was extra weight, part of a past that had been shed. 'You didn't come to ask about me.'

'Did you ever see someone called Emma?'

Another shrug. 'Emma, Elaine, Elizabeth. Seen them all.'

'Recently. Fair hair. She'd have looked lost—'

'They all do at first.'

'She was snatched, along with her sister.'

Sally cocked her head, narrowing her eyes, interested. 'Go on.'

'Emma's eight, her sister is four. The man who paid for them to be taken said Emma was too old. They dumped her out here.'

'And she lasted?'

'She's safe now.'

'Safe?' The girl snorted. 'What does that mean?'

'Have you heard of anyone snatching girls, using them?' She placed two pennies in Sally's palm and heard the girl rubbing them together, a glint in her eyes.

'I could take the rest of that money off you.'

Jane shook her head. 'It would be the last thing you tried.' The knife appeared in her hand. 'Better if we keep this friendly.'

'All right. Men come around all the time. You ought to know that.'

'I do. And people disappear.' Two more pennies, seeing the girl's eyes widen. 'Ask. There's more in it for honest answers.'

Sally weighed the idea. 'If I come across something, how do I find you?'

Jane thought. 'Do you know Kate the pie-seller?'

'On Briggate? Big woman?'

'She'll pass on a message. Say it's for Jane. Or look for Dodson, the old soldier with one leg who begs.'

'I've seen him.'

'Where do you sleep?'

'Depends.' She glanced at the money in her hand and smiled. 'Tonight it might be a lodging house and a real bed.' The girl studied her again. 'How did you manage to find a way out of all this?'

'Luck.'

Another hour of walking. Questions, whenever Jane found someone to ask. She'd have more chance after night fell and people gathered for shelter and warmth.

FOURTEEN

How could he begin to ask questions no one would dare answer? Simon walked up Briggate, watching the faces of the men he passed. He'd never heard any whisper of men paying to have girls taken.

George Mudie's face filled with outrage as Simon told him.

'That little girl . . .' Mudie said. 'What sort of bastard—?'

'One we're going to stop,' Simon told him.

'I hope you do and it's not too late.'

'It won't have been the first time for this man. I'm certain of that.'

'Christ.' Mudie closed his eyes for a moment and took a drink of brandy. 'There have always been rumours about things like this, but they were nothing more than words. Never any meat to them.'

'Who?' Simon pressed.

'I don't recall, I'll need to dig back. But Simon, I looked into them then and came up with nothing. People like to spread lies, you know that.'

'You're talking to the wrong people,' Rosie said as they sat down to eat. Amos and Richard stopped chewing to stare at her, suddenly curious. He knew they'd reached that age, asking more about his work, following conversations.

'You're right,' he answered, understanding her meaning.

His wife turned to the boys. 'We have a guest. Just for a little while. A girl. Her name's Emma.'

'Why?' Amos asked.

'She was lost,' Rosie answered with a smile. 'Jane found her and brought her here because we have room upstairs. Her mother and father will be coming to take her home soon. When you see her, be kind,' she warned. 'She's been very frightened.'

The boys gave solemn nods and returned to their food.

'I'll go and see if she's awake,' Simon said. Time to ask one or two more questions while he had the chance.

Climbing the stairs, he thought about his wife's remark. She was right. Where could he look? People at the top of society? No, they wouldn't tell him anything. They'd keep their secrets and dirt very close. Deal with everything themselves. The way in was from the underbelly. He'd begin once dark arrived.

Emma was awake, sitting on the bed, hunched over. Her head jerked up as he entered, eyes wide.

'No need to worry,' he told her. Washed, with her hair brushed, he could see how delicate she looked, skin pale and eyes so anxious. Thin, tiny fingers, the nails bitten all the way down. 'We've sent word to your parents.'

She hung her head. 'They'll hate me.'

'No they won't,' he said softly. 'They'll be overjoyed to have you home again. Did you manage to sleep?'

'Yes, sir.' The guilt licked at her face. She was here in comfort while her sister . . .

He asked a few things, hoping for some sort of clue that might identify the man who'd bought Harriet or where he lived. But Emma had been too terrified to notice much. They were in a barn or a stable. The air had felt wide and open, maybe a farm, not in a town. The man had worn good clothes. He seemed very old, but she couldn't guess at his age. What would be old to a girl of eight? A big man, she thought, but no idea how tall or broad.

Simon listened, never pushing, absorbing every scrap, trying to build a picture. But in the end, there was little.

'Come on down to the kitchen,' he said as he rose. 'You can meet my sons.' Simon saw her hesitation. 'It's fine; they're harmless, and Rosie's there. It'll be warmer.'

'Are my mama and papa really going to come?' she asked as she followed him down the stairs.

'They are. If they're not here later, they'll arrive first thing in the morning.'

She was wary around Amos and Richard, perched on the very edge of the bench trying to make herself small, invisible. The boys were quiet, not sure how to act. Simon waited until Rosie nodded at him; she had it all under control.

A little while yet. Ample time after the twins were asleep.

'You're on edge, child.' Mrs Shields looked up from her book. 'You can't sit still for five minutes.'

'I have to go out again later.'

She looked quizzical. 'I thought that business was done.'

'It is. This is different . . .' Jane began to talk, letting it all spill out, seeing the horror spread across the old woman's face.

'Are you going to find her? Can you?' The old woman looked stunned, but it was impossible not to be. This was beyond crime. This was evil.

'Yes.' She daren't allow any doubt. If that arrived, it could over-whelm everything else. She spent a quarter of an hour sitting with the whetstone, running the blade back and forth until it was sharp enough to cut the air. Mrs Shields kept glancing at her with a worried expression but kept her silence.

A little after seven, she rose, spread a shawl around her shoulders, the cloak on top. She kissed the old woman on her head.

'I pray you can do it, child.'

'So do I,' Jane replied, but prayer would have little to aid her success.

The pall of factory smoke lingered in the darkness. She heard people cough as they moved along the streets. Slivers of light shone between closed curtains.

When she first met Emma, the girl had taken her to the building where Sophie Jackson spent the night. It seemed a place to begin, to start asking her questions. Two women remembered Emma: the name, the fair hair. No more than that, though. Where she went, who she knew . . . they had no idea.

Another place, damper and more shadowed than the last. She found a boy who lifted his head when she spoke Emma's name. In the flickering light of the fire, he could have been about ten, with long, stringy hair and sad eyes. No chance of edging closer to the blaze; that was for the bigger boys and their favoured ones. But even this was better than outdoors.

'What's your name?' Jane asked, but he shook his head.

'I haven't seen Emma since yesterday. Has something happened to her?'

'She's safe.'

He smiled. 'I was worried. I usually see her somewhere during the day.'

'Do you look after her?'

He chewed on his bottom lip as he considered the question. 'I showed Emma what she needed to know.' He turned his head. 'Do you see?'

'Yes.'

'She kept talking about her sister.'

'Harriet,' Jane said and he gave her a sharp look.

'She told me they'd been snatched.'

'They were,' she said. 'I'm going to find Harriet.'

'You?' He couldn't hide his surprise.

'Me.'

'I wanted to believe her, but . . .'

'Stories.' She'd heard so many of them when she was out here. Lies, hopes, wishes, sometimes the truth, all tangled together until it became impossible to tell what was real. 'Have you heard of children being snatched like that?'

He stared at the boys and girls all around. 'Why bother? There are plenty here. One or two go missing every day. Then more come.'

The boy's voice was bitter, the anger simmering just below the surface.

'Was it a brother or a sister?' Jane asked.

Hesitation before he answered, long enough for the memories to pour in. 'Brother. His name was Robbie.'

She waited, watching his face.

'Last winter,' he said. 'It was very cold. At night. I looked after him. He was younger than me. We settled down together. When I woke up, he wasn't there. I searched everywhere for him. Asked all the people I knew. But I never saw him again. I still hope . . .'

A year. Nothing she could say would ever help him.

'I have to stay out here. He might come back, you see. He'll need me here if he does.'

The boy had to believe that, to keep grasping at the possibility. It was probably the only thing that kept him going through the days.

'Girls,' she prompted softly. He shook his head.

'I don't know anything.'

'If you hear, look for me.' She pressed two coins into his hand. 'There's more for information.'

'Can you find my brother, too?'

Jane tensed. The question she hadn't wanted him to ask.

'A year . . .'

A sorrowful nod. She rose and moved off into the night.

Three other places where the fires burned and people crowded together, young and old. Four who remembered Emma talking about her sister. But what could they do? They'd never seen the little girl.

Folk always talked of children vanishing, but who knew how true
it ever was?

Tales, Jane thought as she came out into the cold air. Probably
little different from the stories she read. Truth or made up; eventually it all became . . . she frowned as she searched for the word.
Bigger than life. A legend.

Time to go home and be grateful she had a bed and a warm place
to live. As she turned the corner, she sensed someone ahead. Her
hand slipped into the pocket of her dress and brought out the knife,
holding it down by her side.

Closer. Closer.

'I've been watching you.'

Sally. The girl she'd met earlier. But she hadn't been aware of
anyone as she'd gone around Leeds. That was worrying.

'I didn't have any luck.'

'That boy you were talking to, don't believe too much of what
he says. Maybe he has a brother, maybe not. Sometimes he claims
he ran off because the man he worked for beat him every day. He's
not right in his head.'

Stories and legends. Myths.

'Have you found out anything about the little girl?'

A small hesitation. Then, with slyness in her voice: 'Maybe. Can
you meet me later?'

'Where?'

'Outside the Parish Church. When it rings eleven. I might have
something for you then.'

'All right.' Perhaps she would or it might be a trap to try and
rob her. She understood Sally all too well; that was why she didn't
trust her.

She brought out two pennies and wrapped the girl's fingers around
them.

'I'll be there.'

Simon told the boys a story as they lay in their beds. Something
he half-remembered, half pulled from the air. Ten minutes and their
eyes had closed as the rhythm of their breathing shifted into sleep.
A final look and he left them, holding the lantern high. He heard
Rosie up in the attic, talking to Emma.

He'd go out soon enough. But the kind of men he needed to see
wouldn't be around yet; they haunted the late nights. He'd barely

had chance to sit when someone hammered at the door. Constable Porter, escorting a couple in their late thirties, well-dressed, their faces tight with terror. A carriage sat on Swinegate, spattered with mud, the horses lathered in sweat.

'Come in.' He showed them through to the kitchen, and heard feet on the stairs. Rosie first. Behind her, treading hesitantly, Emma. Simon watched the joy and relief spread across the mother's face as she saw the girl and opened her arms. A moment before Emma launched herself into the embrace, the pair of them in tears.

Mr Caldwell extended a hand. Simon shook it.

'Mr Westow, we came as soon as the constable's man told us. I don't know how to . . .'

'We just gave Emma somewhere to stay. It was my assistant who brought her here.'

A surprised nod. 'I'd like to thank him—'

'Her. Jane. She's out looking for Harriet.'

Caldwell blinked in astonishment. 'Her, then.' He picked Emma up as if she weighed nothing, pressing her close against his shoulder as his expression began to ease and his eyes glistened. A moment, then he let her down again, gave a small cough and a light touch on his wife's shoulder, the signal for her to ease their daughter out to the coach. The girl curtseyed to Simon, hugged Rosie, and she was gone.

'Sir, if you can imagine how we're feeling now . . .'

'We have two boys,' Rosie answered. 'We understand.'

'You've given Emma back to us. We've been praying every night for the return of our girls. My wife and I can never thank you enough for this.' He took a breath. 'The constable tells me you're a thief-taker. You find things that have been stolen.' Simon could see the pleading in the man's eyes. 'Can I employ you to find Harriet?'

Working for someone would make things simpler. A chance to earn for a job he'd do anyway.

'Yes,' he replied. 'Gladly.'

Porter lingered after Caldwell had gone.

'No sign of her yet,' he said as he sat at the table. 'I didn't want to say it while he was here.'

'We'll find her,' Rosie told him, and Simon hoped they could. The girl had been gone for far too long.

'The watch is doing everything they can. Plenty of them have children.'

'What about the murders? Sophie Jackson, Tommy Deacon, the other man.'

The constable shrugged. 'Nothing so far, and Holcomb hasn't returned, according to the servants.'

'There's someone else.' Rosie explained about the clothes seller at South Market and the bundle Sophie had passed to her.

'You should have said so earlier.' For a second anger rippled across Porter's eyes. 'We'll try to find her. *You've* heard nothing more from the captain, I take it?'

'Not a word. But I'm not likely to, since I don't work for him any longer.'

A nod as he stood and gathered up his hat. 'If you find any information on any of it . . .'

'We'll tell you,' Rosie assured him.

'I'll leave with you,' Simon said. 'I need to go hunting.'

'I don't believe there's much likelihood we'll find her alive,' Porter said as they moved along Swinegate.

The man was probably right, but saying the words didn't help. 'We need to try. We're her only chance.'

'These killings. Do you have any idea at all who's behind them?'

'None.' He'd keep looking, softly, quietly. But trying to find Harriet Caldwell was far more urgent for now.

Jane waited in the burial ground across from the Parish Church. A clear view of the entrance, hidden from sight in the cold darkness as she stood motionless among the gravestones. Five minutes to eleven, and a flicker of light from the lantern that hung in the church porch gave a little illumination.

Earlier she hadn't felt Sally watching her. She hadn't been aware that the girl was anywhere close. Were her senses deserting her? Was Sally better than her at this?

A small movement and she tensed, tightening her grip on the knife. Someone was over there. Two figures. All she could make out were faint outlines. Slowly, keeping away from any lights, Jane edged around, listening for voices, the shuffling of feet, anything at all.

No sense of a trap. Just the pair at the church porch, nobody lurking elsewhere. She hadn't lost all her abilities. A touch on the gold ring for luck.

Jane waited a final few moments to be certain of everything.

Before she could speak, a head turned and Sally said, 'You're here. Good. This is Anne.'

Jane inspected the girl. Thin as wire, brittle, with hollow cheeks. A face that had known anger and pain. Eyes that had learned to trust no one.

'My name's Jane. Do you know about girls being snatched?

She saw Sally nod and give a small touch on Anne's arm.

'I've heard about it.'

On its own, that meant nothing. 'What have you heard? When?'

'A while ago,' Anne said. 'I don't know how long.'

Out here, the only time that existed was now and tomorrow. The rest didn't matter.

'What happened?'

'Two men came around. I was still new then. Still learning to get by out here. I'd never seen the men before. But a lot of the lasses must have known them because they ran off. I turned around and they'd gone. There was just me and this other girl and a boy left. They looked us over and one said, "They're too old. He'll never pay for these. I told you we'd do better looking for the kind of girl he wants. Someone decent, not like this."'

'Decent?' Jane asked.

Anne nodded her head. 'That's what he said. I can still hear his voice. Remember every word.'

She sounded sure and firm, gaze steady, her right hand hidden in the fold of a tattered dress. She'd be holding a knife, always ready to use it. 'One of them was older. He said, "This is easier," and the other one said, "Not if we don't find no girl for him, it's not." They went away after that.'

'Where did this happen?'

'Dock Street. Where the boat yard used to be.'

Another place lost to fire and the choking smell of burning wood that lingered around Leeds for days. That had happened about nine months ago.

'Can you tell me anything else about them?'

Anne squinted, trying to see the men in her mind. 'One of them had a beard. Dark. There was something about him.'

'What do you mean, something?'

'Dangerous. You know, one of those men who starts shouting and hitting for no reason.'

Maybe the girl's father had been that way, Jane thought. Or someone else.

'What about the other one?' she asked, but the girl shook her head.

'I don't know. The one with the beard, though, he scared me.'

'Have they been back?'

'Twice. I ran off and hid so they wouldn't see me.'

Jane put coins in her hand, seeing Anne grasp them tight before hurrying away.

'How do you know her?'

Sally gave a shrug. 'Met her one night. She told me about it. When you came around I remembered, so I went looking for her.'

'Have you ever seen these men?'

'No. But I believe they exist.' Jane could feel the girl watching her. 'You do, too.'

'Yes.' Anne's words had the ring of truth. That note of pure fear. Find those men and they could lead her to Harriet and the one who'd handed over money for her.

More coins for Sally. 'You did a good job.'

'What are you going to do?'

'Hunt.'

'You need someone who's out here. Who can talk to them. Who knows what it's like.'

'I spent enough time—'

Sally shook her head. 'How long ago was that?'

'I—'

'You need to stand in front of the mirror and take a proper look at yourself. When was the last time you went hungry? Those clothes you're wearing, they're too good for out here. Your hands and your face, they're *clean*.'

The girl spat the word, a mix of envy and insult and pain.

'What do you suggest?'

'I could help you.'

'Why?'

Sally jingled the money she was holding. 'This. You can help me, too.'

'Help you? How?'

'I want to get away from this. You said you managed it.'

'I told you that was luck.'

'Maybe your luck can rub off on me.'

She was gone into the night, leaving Jane in the church porch with her thoughts. She began to walk, her steps leaden as she let the conversation ring through her head.

Sally was right. It was a hard truth, but years had passed since Jane had survived outside. However much she liked to believe she still fitted, she was a stranger now. She *was* fed, proper meals, not scavenging. She *was* clean. She'd never have been able to find someone like Anne.

For a while longer she moved through the buildings, asking a question or two, listening to the chatter, stopping to talk to half-remembered faces who were still awake. A few claimed they'd seen the men and run off at the first glimpse of them. Had anyone been taken? They didn't know.

After two hours, she stood by the river, trying to make sense of the last few days. First, pulling back from hurting someone, now those images of herself that the girl had held up in front of her face. For too long she'd believed herself to be one thing. Now she'd have to come to terms with a different truth.

Jane felt someone approaching. She knew who it was, but turned anyway, the knife in her hand.

'Made up your mind yet?'

'What do you want me to do?'

'I told you: I'll help you and you help me.'

'All right,' Jane agreed.

'Go home to your bed now. I'll find you in the morning.'

FIFTEEN

Cheap candles threw a pale light across the dram shop, small mountains of wax mounting on the rough tables. It was a tiny place, no more than the ground floor of a filthy terraced house off Hunslet Lane. Three people were finding oblivion in the gin, but no sign of the man Simon wanted.

'Michael Day?' the landlord said. He had a lively face, eyes amused by the world. 'Not been here in a week or more. Owes you money, does he?'

Simon shook his head. 'I'm looking to put a little in his pocket.'

'Tried the Masons Arms?'

A grand name for a place almost as dingy as this one. 'Not yet.'

'Worth a look. If he comes in, do you have a message?'

He wanted to take Day by surprise. 'No. I'll find him.'

Not at the Arms, but he'd been there the night before.

'Cock fight.' The owner paged through a copy of the *Leeds Mercury*. 'That's why it's so dead.'

'Where is it?'

'That open ground beyond the brass foundry in Holbeck.'

Bitter, biting cold in the night, but it was busy, knots of men talking, betting their wages. A couple of fires built from rubbish. Boards and posts and straw bales formed a crude ring, topped by lanterns that illuminated the fighting birds. Roars of encouragement and misery. The end of a bout, the smell of blood and victory. Money was changing hands as Simon pushed through the press, watching everyone until he spotted Day.

He was tall, with a face like stone and dark eyes that showed nothing at all. Two fingers missing from his left hand. He liked to flex it as he threatened people.

Simon waited until the man finished his conversation.

'Hello, Michael.'

Day turned slowly. 'You want something, Westow?'

'A few questions.' He nodded towards bird owners setting up for the next fight. 'A little money for you to lose here.'

'When I bet, I win.'

Everyone knew the lie of that. Day lost far more often than he walked off with money. Always scrambling for a few coins to see him through the day.

Simon gave him a smile. 'Then you'll be able to take home even more.'

'Go on.' Still no expression in his voice.

'Have you ever heard of young girls being snatched?'

The silence was uncomfortable. Day's left hand bunched into a fist and Simon started to reach into his sleeve for his knife.

'I might have.'

Simon had dreaded words like that. Useful, but still terrible. All too real.

'Facts or rumours?'

'Things,' Day said.

'What kind?' Simon asked.

'Some rich men involved.'

'Men?' he asked, feeling the bile rise and his heart begin to thump. 'More than one?

Day shrugged. 'I don't know. I keep my distance from anything like that.'

'Why?'

'Don't trust them. Once you start mixing with those kinds of people, it's easy to die.'

'Have they killed anyone?'

'Nobody's ever said so.'

'Some names.' Simon jingled the coins in his pocket.

'Even if I knew, I wouldn't tell you. Word gets out . . . they have a long reach.'

'Who might be willing to say?'

'Nobody, if they have an ounce of sense.' His voice was dark as the grave.

'And if they don't?'

Day shook his head and started to turn away.

'Don't you want some money?'

'Keep it. If you carry on asking questions, your widow's going to need it for your funeral.'

The men behind all this terrified Michael Day. Anyone who could do that was dangerous.

* * *

Sunday morning arrived grey and misty, spitting an icy rain. In the kitchen on Swinegate, Jane recounted what Anne had said the night before, and Simon repeated his conversation with Day.

Rosie stared down at the table, scratching at the wood with a fingernail. Sounds came from upstairs: the boys, working at the lessons the tutor had given them to complete.

'How do we stop it all?' she asked in a bleak voice.

'We find them,' Simon replied.

'Even if we can, what then? Powerful men, that's what he said to you.' She stared at her husband. 'Men. More than one. And he refused to give you any names.'

He put his hands on the table in front of him, spreading his fingers wide.

'It might not mean anything. I'll go and talk to Porter and George Mudie.' Simon turned to Jane. 'What about you?'

Before she could reply, a fist thudded on the front door and he vanished to answer it. When he returned, he was holding a piece of paper, shaking his head in amused disbelief as he read the words.

'What is it?' Rosie said.

'Holcomb's filing suit against me.' He exhaled slowly. This couldn't be real, could it? 'For slander. Delivered on a Sunday, too. He must have paid a lawyer well for that.'

'What slander?' Her voice came out as a furious screech. She snatched the document from his fingers. A quick read and she tossed it down on the table. 'There's nothing here. What does this mean? "To all and sundry."'

'It means he doesn't know anything. I never slandered him. The only person who knows that I worked for him is Porter.'

'He didn't want you revealing his name. This is his revenge.'

'Maybe it is,' he agreed, folding the letter and slipping it into his pocket, 'but I still need to see lawyer Pollard in the morning.' He tightened his mouth, feeling the fury grow. 'I think the captain is beginning to panic. All the more reason to keep digging, isn't it?'

Jane had tossed in her bed until the sky began to lighten. She fought it, tried to deny it to herself, but all the things Sally said were true: after years of scrabbling for every meal, her stomach always empty, she enjoyed having a full belly. That feeling of clean hair and looking down at a hand that wasn't always grimy. Her clothes were old, but still far better than any she'd worn when she survived on the streets.

Sturdy boots to keep her feet dry. She had a bed, somewhere warm and safe to consider these things.

The truth had come as a slap, but Jane realized she felt no regrets. She remembered the way things had once been; so much better now. She ran her fingers over the old scars on her forearm. She'd tried to lock the past away, but some things were too strong, and would always edge their way back.

The church bell rang nine, calling people to the service. Jane kept walking, along Briggate, down the Head Row, then Vicar Lane, turn on to Kirkgate, all the way to Timble Bridge. Back, then along the Calls, seeing barges at the wharves, but no activity on the Sabbath.

Up on Leeds Bridge, she gazed down at the water. A prickle ran up her spine and she turned around. Sally, limping and grimacing. A cut down her cheek and a bruise by her eye.

Jane put her arm around the girl and gently leaned her against the bridge. 'Who hurt you?'

Sally took time to catch her breath, pushing a hand against her side. She tried to hide the pain but it stood out stark on her face.

'I used some of that money. Went to a lodging house. A man there took a fancy to me and thought I was too small to refuse him.'

'Did he . . .?'

She shook her head. Sally tried to smile, but it turned into a grimace. 'Never gave him the chance. He made me pay for it, though.' A few shallow breaths. 'I hurt him. He won't bother anyone else for a long time.'

'It's nothing to do with the snatched girl?'

The girl was pale, arms and hands shaking. Jane took off her cloak and placed it around her; at least she'd be a little warmer.

'No. This was him and me.'

'You need some help.'

A snort. 'Where? Do you see anyone?'

A moment of hesitation before she made the decision. 'How well can you walk?'

Sally was curled up in Jane's bed. Asleep, all the hatred and suspicion left her face and she looked like the child she was. It had been a slow journey. The girl winced with every step, stopping often to rub her hip and press down on her side.

Mrs Shields had washed her and tended the wounds. Fed her

warm soup and bread, then made her drink a tincture to help her rest.

'He broke two of her ribs,' she told Jane. 'I've strapped them. I don't think there's any damage inside. That seems to be the worst of it. They'll mend in time. Her hip is badly bruised. He must have kicked her there.' She stood in the kitchen, her voice little more than a whisper filled with worry. 'Child, child, you know we don't have room for her here.'

Jane nodded. Sally needed care and she hadn't known where else to take her.

'I'll find her a room.'

The old woman studied her carefully. 'Why her?'

She'd expected the question, but she couldn't find an answer she could put into words. Nothing more than a feeling that she needed to do this, that it was right.

'I don't know.'

'Do you see your past in her, child? Is that it?'

Maybe, just in some small way. Jane had possessed nothing, no chance of escaping the streets until Simon employed her. All because she could follow people without being seen, become invisible in a crowd. But that had seemed like survival rather than skill.

'I don't know,' she repeated.

The woman laid her hand on Jane's arm, a touch so light she had to glance down to be certain it was there.

'There are hundreds like her. You can't look after them all.'

'I know. It's just until tomorrow. I promise.'

'The girl will probably sleep most of the day. Rest and warmth will help.'

'Thank you.' A kindly hug, a kiss on the old woman's dry cheek.

Harriet Caldwell was still missing. Jane moved around the autumn streets. Few people were out walking in the Sunday cold. Those without homes were huddled away from the weather. They barely seemed to listen as she asked her questions.

Two hours of nothing. Failure. Jane rubbed a fingertip over that line of scars she'd made on her arm, then walked on.

'I know Day,' Porter said. 'He'd sooner hurt someone than eat a hot meal. Do you believe him?'

'He turned down money. Too scared of these men to give me any names.'

'That's not like him,' the constable agreed. 'But all it means is we have shadows, Westow. Until we get a glimmer of who they are, if they actually exist, what can we do? At the moment it sounds like someone's dark dream.'

Simon had thought about it. The man was right. Still, the law knew now. More people to ask questions. Maybe they could shine some light on those shadows.

'By the way, Holcomb's suing me for slander.'

The constable snorted. 'Good luck to him on that. I thought you'd walked away from him.'

'I did. My guess is he's trying to keep me cowed, make sure I don't poke my nose into his business.'

'Will you?'

Simon smiled. 'Who knows?'

Mudie was busy but listened carefully as Simon went through his encounter with Day.

'I hope it's a lie. For the love of God, Simon . . .' For once he was lost for words.

'You said there were once rumours.'

'With no substance. I told you, I checked.'

'Go back. Please. Anything at all.'

A weary sigh. 'All right.'

He brooded through the evening. Tonight, telling the boys their bedtime story brought only a brittle joy. By the time the longclock gently struck ten he was on his feet and buttoning up his greatcoat.

'Simon . . .' Rosie began and he heard the warning in her tone. She knew his anger at Holcomb's letter was simmering below the surface. It would take very little for it to explode.

'I'll watch my temper.'

He went around the alehouses where the drink was cheap and tasted like piss. Men came all the same because they couldn't afford better. Walter Rainsford was in the third place he visited. Simon placed a full mug in front of him and waited until the man raised his head.

His eyes were clouded with cataracts that grew worse each year.

Food stains coloured the front of his clothes. He'd been a hard man once, with a successful trade in violence. Then his vision started to fail. Too fearful to risk the surgeon, he began to drink.

Now he lived on the shrinking charity of friends. His muscles had wasted, and each time Simon saw him, the man seemed more and more weary of living.

'Westow? It looks like you.'

Simon sat across the table as Rainsford struggled to focus. 'It is.'

'Don't often see you in such a grand establishment.' His laugh was a hoarse rasp. 'Moving up in the world, are you?'

He smiled. 'Maybe I'm looking for you.'

'You'll always find me where I can quaff the finest drink and mingle with the most gallant company.' He swept an arm around at the few scattered around the room. 'Invariably stimulating conversation here. What can I do for you, Westow?'

'Who do you know who'd be involved in something like that?' Simon asked after he'd told the little he knew about the sisters being snatched.

'I'd have done it myself if I'd still been able,' Rainsford said and gave a grim look. 'Shock you, does it?'

'Disgusts me.'

The man shrugged. 'I did worse than that in my time and never thought twice about it as long as the job paid. At least a child doesn't give too many problems. There are others who think the same.'

'Who?'

'Harpy Faulkner. Mind you, he's probably too feeble by now. John Bedford. Maybe what's-his-name, used to do work for Macallan.'

'Erskine.'

'That's the one. Ginger Liddell. They always used to work together.'

'Are they doing much these days?' Simon asked.

'How would I know?' An edge of friction in his tone. 'You wanted names. I'm giving them to you.'

It was more than he'd had when he walked in. He didn't really know Faulkner, but the others . . . he could readily believe any of them doing a job like that. Like Rainsford. Passing on the names for a mug of weak beer. Simon put three coins on the table.

'You can put in a word for me with St Peter.' Rainsford gave another raw, bitter laugh. 'Maybe it'll be enough to let me in.

SIXTEEN

A grey Monday morning, and Simon was pacing up and down outside the lawyer's office on Boar Lane, pulling out his watch every minute.

'You must be anxious about something,' Pollard said when he arrived, a clerk carrying a pair of thick ledgers hurrying along behind him.

Anxious didn't begin to cover his feelings. He knew Holcomb had nothing, but the letter had preyed on him all night. He'd read it over and over until he could recite it by heart.

'Come inside. Let's see the problem.'

Pollard read the letter with a bemused expression. When he finished, he removed his spectacles, took a handkerchief from his pocket and polished the lenses before sitting back in his chair,

'Well?' Simon asked.

'First of all, you can calm down. This has no merit at all. I'm going to be very clear on that. If it ever reaches court – and I don't for one second believe it will – it will be thrown out immediately.'

That was one weight lifted. He'd thought it, hoped for it, but he'd needed the legal confirmation.

'Tell me, what did you do to anger him, Simon?'

Two minutes to give a brief explanation as Pollard listened with his hands steepled under his chin.

'Holcomb wouldn't be panicking over that sort of information coming out. I doubt it would damage his family that much. His father must have done something much worse than he told you.'

Simon nodded. 'That's my guess, too. I was sure he wasn't telling me everything.'

'Did you give his name to the constable?'

'Yes, but *only* to him. I never talked about Holcomb to anyone else.'

'No conversations where you insulted him?'

Simon smiled. 'Nothing at all.'

'Then you don't need to worry.' He flicked his fingers at the letter. 'This is nothing more than an attempt to warn you off. To keep you away from his affairs. I'll send a reply today and that should be the end of it.'

He narrowed his eyes. 'Should?'

Pollard shrugged. 'If the man has any sense, that *will* be all. His attorney is bound to advise him to leave it. But—' he paused '—in the end it's Holcomb's decision. Don't worry, Simon. If he proceeds, he'll lose, and he'll do it in the public eye. Things would come out. If he's so eager to keep his father's life private, that's the very last thing he's likely to want.'

'But until he decides, this is hanging over me.'

'That's probably the aim of it. The uncertainty. To keep you guessing. Honestly, though, you can put it from your mind. He has absolutely no grounds for slander. However,' he added, 'make sure you don't talk about this, or him. Don't give him any ammunition.'

This was why he paid the man. Solid, reliable advice. Even with a wind whipping at him out of the west, he felt the relief as he stepped out on to the street.

'Westow!' The shout made him stop and turn. Porter with his inspector.

'Any more word?' Simon asked and the constable gave a shake of his head.

'No trace of a young girl.'

'She'll be hidden away in someone's house. Someone who has plenty of room. Emma said she thought they were on a farm.'

'The watch have been out to some farms around town.'

'As best they can,' the inspector said. He was a man with a sour face, mouth pursed and disapproving of life. 'There are too many, then there's the size of those damned places and all the buildings. All the woods and fields.' He shook his head.

At least they were doing something, Simon thought.

'We need to hope she's still alive.' Porter's voice was dull and empty.

'He's paid for her. He'll want his money's worth.' Christ, what a cold thing to have to say. To even think. He shuddered.

'All the watch want her found.'

'What about these rich men?'

A shake of the head was his reply.

'Nothing more on the other business?'

'The clothes seller hasn't been back to South Market,' the inspector told him. 'None of the others there have heard from her.' He shrugged. 'They didn't seem to know her well.'

'What about her handcart? The one locked in the yard.'

'I went and examined it myself. Just sacks of old clothes. An oilcloth over everything to keep off the weather.' Without thinking, he glanced up at the sky. At least the wind was forcing the smoke away. The air felt clearer and sharper. 'Her name's Janet Bristol. We'll keep our eyes open for her. We haven't had any female bodies turning up.'

'Have you been inside her house?'

'Let's simply say she's not there,' the inspector said.

A nod. He had men to find, the names Walter Rainsford had given him.

The room was shabby, with creaking floorboards and glass that rattled in the window frames, but Sally hobbled around, touching everything cautiously, as if she believed it might all be snatched away from her. A battered old metal brazier, a pallet with fresh straw for a mattress. A table and chair, ewer and basin.

It was dry. It was reasonably clean. More than anything, it was out of the weather.

The landlord had stayed close while Jane inspected the room. The thoughts were plain on his face: she'd try to steal something, then run off. But he changed as soon as she gave him the rent, insisting on a receipt. For a few extra pennies he was happy to bring up a bucket of charcoal and another of water.

'All of this is for me? Just me?'

Jane placed the key in her hand. 'Yours.'

The girl had still been stiff when she woke. Bruises clearer on her face, the cut beginning to scab over. Her ribs hurt when she breathed. Mrs Shields made her drink a tonic and put porridge in her belly.

'I never believed you'd help me.'

'We made a bargain.'

'People say things. They never mean them.' The girl rubbed her eyes and tried to smile.

Jane took out some coins. 'You'll need food and blankets. A proper knife.'

'I have—'

Jane showed her blade, oiled, shiny. Lovingly sharpened. A thief-taker's weapon.

'Are you sure you want to work with me?' she asked. 'You don't have to. That's not the price for this room.'

Only a moment's hesitation before Sally nodded. 'I'm sure.'

Jane waited as the girl locked the door, moving the key to and fro with pride.

'I've looked back and I can't find anything at all. Not a scrap,' Mudie said. 'If I made notes, they're long gone. But I know for damned sure there was nothing. It was smoke, Simon.'

'You're positive you don't remember any names?'

'I can't even be sure I ever heard any. That's how little there was to it. If I'd come across something, I'd have followed it.'

'What about the man who has Harriet? Someone with land, maybe a farm.' Simon thought of Emma being dumped on a midden in Leeds. 'Somewhere quite close to town.'

Mudie shook his head. 'Too many possibilities. Come on, there are dozens of places like that all around. Men make their money and set themselves up with a small country estate like lords of the manor.'

'What about the people who work for them? Someone has to know.'

'Listen to yourself: so far all you have is maybe this and possibly that. Show me one single fact in there. None of it is going to help you find this man. The question I'd be asking is why he's not grabbing girls living on the streets here. For the love of God, we have enough of them. What is it about taking girls from families?'

'He's looking for decent girls, whatever that means. Jane found out.' A pause. 'If it hadn't been for Emma, we'd never have heard about any of this.'

'Now you have, get Porter to write to other constables. Young girls from good homes who've gone missing.'

Christ, what kind of picture might that reveal? How long it had been going on, how many girls had been taken . . .

'Do we want to know that truth?' Simon asked in an empty voice.

'I'll set the clerk to work on it,' Porter said.

'We know he's going to have her somewhere away from people. Where they can't hear her scream and cry.'

'Space to bury a small body, too,' the inspector added.

*　　*　　*

Sally leaned against Jane's arm as she walked. It gave her a chance to study the girl's face. Each step was an effort, but she never gave up or complained as they moved from one group of children to another. They all appeared relieved to see her, worried that she'd abandoned them or died.

They started in one of the old yards off Briggate, close to the Talbot. Sally talked to the children, listened, praised and chided as if they were all her charges. Some orders before they crossed to a ginnel by the fish market. More children. One girl who hung back until the end, when she darted forward to speak quickly to Sally. A nod, an arm on the shoulder to guide her to Jane.

'She knew Emma. Her name is Hannah.'

The girl spoke in shy stubs of sentences that fitted together like pieces of a jigsaw. Emma cried often, she said, too nervous to trust a soul.

'You've got to be hard out here,' Hannah said. 'Everybody knows that. You're dead elsewise.' She halted and glanced at their faces. 'You look and listen and see who'll help you. She didn't have that. She was lost. When I didn't see her I thought she were dead.' She raised eyes that held no expression. 'Surprised she lasted that long.'

'Did she talk about her sister?'

The girl shrugged. 'They all talk about someone. I did it. You learn to shut up and try to live.'

Jane remembered. The tears, the sorrow that had turned to cold anger. The determination to survive.

'Anything else you can recall?'

'What's the point in listening? Someone's going to have another tale tomorrow.' That wasn't toughness; it was protection.

'Do you remember if Emma said she and her sister had been snatched?'

'Not really. She's not the first.'

Jane watched close for any hint of a lie. 'Who else?'

Hannah frowned and turned to Sally. 'That girl with the red hair. Months back. Remember her?'

A slow nod. 'She had those wild eyes. Kept shouting.'

'She always said she and her sister had been stolen.'

'I never talked to her,' Sally said. 'It was only a few days before she vanished.'

'Do you remember her name?'

Both girls shook their heads.

A few pennies for Hannah, noticing the girl eyeing her pocket to try and pick it in the future. On to two other places; no joy from either. All Jane had for her work was a teasing glimpse of someone long gone. Months, Anne had said. Now this. Two weeks for Emma. No pattern to it.

Somewhere close by, off around a corner, she heard a fiddle and followed the sound. Davy Cassidy, the blind fiddler, bow moving slowly over the strings and letting the melody sing for him.

Jane stood and listened, letting the music fill her. For a minute or two, all seemed well with the world. Then Sally began to shuffle her feet impatiently.

'Don't you like it?'

'It's just there, isn't it?

Jane put money in the cup, heard his thanks, and they walked on. Dodson, the beggar soldier with the wooden leg, was sitting on the pavement on Vicar Lane. He'd acquired an army greatcoat from somewhere and a second shirt. More warmth for the winter ahead.

'From an old comrade,' he explained when Jane admired it. 'A generous man.'

She rattled money into his cup and introduced Sally.

'I've seen you around.' He gave a welcoming smile; the man approved of her.

He wasn't likely to know about girls being snatched. But he heard things as people passed; who paid any mind to a beggar?

'There was one strange conversation.' Dodson frowned. 'I didn't know what it meant. I tried to puzzle it out, but I couldn't make sense of it.' He looked at Sally. 'I listen, and there's not much to do here but think.'

Jane cocked her head. 'What was it?'

He stared at the ground, trying to conjure up what he'd heard.

'It must have been on Saturday. Two men were arguing. They stopped about as close to me as you are now. One of them was trying to light his pipe. He was saying the money was too good to turn down. The other told him he'd had enough, people were starting to ask questions. He didn't like having to deal with girls.'

Jane felt her pulse race. Dodson was an honest man; he'd never say it if it hadn't happened.

'Anything more? What did they look like?' Her voice was low and urgent, hoping something had stuck in his mind.

'They moved on after that. I think one of them had dark hair and a beard, but I can't be sure.' A few more moments of thought. 'He made me think of a sergeant I had in the army, I don't know why. He liked to hurt people, have them flogged for no reason.'

That sounded like the man Anne had described.

'What about the other one?' she asked, but he shook his head. 'No.'

A little more money in his mug. She had her first hint. Faint, but real.

'You think it's them, don't you?' Sally asked as they walked away.

'I know it is.'

'What are you going to do?'

'Find them.'

Food from Kate the pie-seller, the meat still warm inside the crust. Sally was quiet as she ate.

'How long have you paid the rent for on that room?'

'A week.' That was an age when you lived on the street. Forever.

'What about after that?'

'We'll think about it closer to the time.' The clock at the Parish Church struck one. 'I need to go. Rest yourself.'

'I promised to help you.'

'Then find me later today.'

SEVENTEEN

Harpy Faulkner wasn't going to snatch any girls. Simon watched him from the other side of the Rose and Crown, dragging his left leg as he moved slowly towards the bar. His dangerous days were over. Now he struggled to put together the words to order another drink and his hands shook wildly as he fumbled money from his pocket. A bad palsy, someone said.

John Bedford was elusive. Someone claimed he'd left Leeds almost a year before, but the man sitting beside him in the beer shop claimed it wasn't two months since he'd seen him. One to pursue later.

Erskine and Ginger Liddell. He'd seen them here and there, always together. With wild ginger hair barely crammed under a hat, Liddell was impossible to miss.

'You wouldn't know him now, it started falling out, coming away in clumps,' a man told him when Simon began asking questions. He laughed. 'Some disease or other. No surprise, given the type of whores he buys.'

'Where will I find them?'

'Around and about.' The man shrugged. 'Saw them in here two nights back. Sat right over there.' He nodded towards a table against the wall.

'Any idea what they're doing these days?'

A snort. 'Won't be honest work, you can bet on that.'

But would they be willing to snatch girls? He'd try tonight when the dregs circulated.

'Dark hair and a beard?' Simon asked. He was watching as Richard completed his homework sums. Amos liked to work alone, upstairs, but his brother always preferred company.

'That's what Dodson told me,' Jane said.

'Now we have two girls who've talked about being snatched.' Rosie's voice was thoughtful. 'One of them mentioned a bearded man who seemed violent and then your soldier heard someone talk. It's a possibility.'

'But not enough to say more than that,' he pointed out.

'It's them,' Jane said.

Simon turned his head to look into her face. Not a glimmer of doubt in her eye. No use trying to dissuade her. He'd agreed to follow her lead in this. To believe in her.

'Then we'd better find them,' he said.

She rose. In the doorway she pulled her cloak tight around her body and then she was gone.

Jane sat at home until dark. Trying to read, talking to Mrs Shields, sharpening her knife over the whetstone. A little food, enough to take the edge off her appetite.

When night fell, she laced up her boots and kissed the old woman's cheek. Mrs Shields reached out and took hold of her hand.

'Please look after yourself out there, child.'

'I will.' She gave the fingers a gentle squeeze.

'Take special care.'

The way she said it was enough to make Jane pause. 'I promise.'

Coming out past the wall behind Green Dragon Yard, she twisted the gold ring on her finger. No sense of anybody following. Jane raised her hood and blended into the shadows.

No rain, but the air felt wet. Everything she touched was damp under her hand. November already. An hour passed before she spotted Sally in a half-demolished building on Call Lane. The girl glanced up as Jane entered, then turned back to her conversation. Five or six children were gathered around her, all competing for her attention.

'I need anything you can find about girls who say they've been snatched. Any man who looks like the one I told you about. Especially if he's with someone else. Where they are, too.'

Once they'd all flown off, Sally pushed herself to her feet, pained by the movement.

'They listen to you.'

The girl shrugged. 'I've helped them stay alive. I know how to do that.'

'What will they do when you go?'

'Someone else will come along.'

Would they? Jane had never seen anybody like that when she was out here. Or perhaps she'd never trusted anybody enough to find out.

'Can you read?'

The girl laughed. 'Me? What's the point? Can you?'

'I learned. I can write a little, too, and I know my numbers.'

'I don't see what good it does.' She began to hobble, pressing a hand against the broken ribs that Mrs Shields had strapped.

'How bad is it?'

'I'll mend.'

Another place, the warehouse down by the river where Jane had found Sophie Jackson. The fire was low, not so many around it tonight. She watched Sally pass the word, then they were moving again.

They finished far beyond Fearn's Island. She had no sense that anyone was watching. Plenty of people gathered inside the walls, a blaze of wood crackled and threw up sparks. Someone had dragged along a sack of potatoes to cook among the hot ashes. Jane looked, listened; warm, and with food to eat, they all enjoyed a sense of hope for a few hours.

She saw Sally, talking, sending a girl or boy off running. All done, they walked home in silence. Whenever she caught a glimpse of the girl's face, it was tight and strained. Fighting the pain. Jane stayed alert, remembering Mrs Shields's warning. But by the time she reached the house behind Green Dragon Yard, there'd been nothing.

John Bedford was dead. Three different people had seen the corpse. He'd picked a fight over a florin, gone up against the wrong man. Someone faster than him. A knife to his belly, left to bleed his life away while his killer vanished from Leeds.

Hard to feel any sorrow, Simon thought. Bedford had been a cruel man. Fate had caught up and punished him.

He wandered until late, but no sign of Erskine or Liddell. They were around, everyone said. Just not tonight. Even the prostitutes hadn't seen them.

Fog had clamped down during the evening. Thick, sooty, heavy enough to burn his throat as he breathed. He'd be glad to be indoors.

As he turned on to Swinegate, something made his head snap up. He brought out his knife, then the second from his sleeve. Stood still and listened. Had he heard something? The fog swallowed sound.

Simon was a handful of yards from Briggate, no more than two minutes from home. But someone was waiting. He felt sure of it.

One step forward, then another. Holding his breath as his eyes darted from side to side. Impossible to see any kind of movement in this. Simon let his boot scuff across the pavement, the hard sound of hobnails on stone. Let them come to him.

A flash and he turned aside just as someone crashed into his body. Moving saved him. He stayed on his feet. The attacker struggled for balance, stretching out a hand to steady himself against the wall.

Simon grabbed him by the collar and held the knife against his throat.

'You'd better throw your knife down,' he hissed, waiting until he heard the tinkle of metal as the man dropped his blade. 'Now you're going to tell me your name and who sent you.'

'He's not going to do that.' The voice came from behind him. Unruffled, someone used to being obeyed. 'If you want to make it alive to your bed, Westow, you're going to let him go.'

'Stab me and I'll kill your friend before I die.'

'Doesn't matter if you do.' He could almost hear the shrug. 'He's expendable.'

Simon believed the man. He wasn't acting. He'd allow his companion to die and never feel a thing.

'What do you want?'

'Let him go.'

Simon eased his grip, then pushed hard, sending the man sprawling to the ground.

The voice chuckled. 'Too obvious, Westow. Pity, I was told you could be subtle.'

Simon didn't take the goad, staying silent, trying to pick out a face, a shape in the murk. Nothing. He seemed more spectre than person. But whatever he was, the man had his measure.

'We didn't come to hurt you. Well, I didn't,' he added. 'Adam there might have other ideas now.'

'What do you want?' The air was damp but his voice was dust in his mouth.

'A warning. You were employed to complete a job and you walked away.'

'After that, the man who hired me threatened to sue me for slander.'

'You'd do well to take it seriously. Witnesses of good character can appear out of nowhere. No doubt you understand what I mean.'

An educated voice. Trying to sound reasonable, even friendly. But the threat was heavy as steel.

'Let's say I do,' Simon replied.

'That's a good fellow. I'm sure you've taken legal advice on the matter . . .'

'Go on.'

'You ought to understand that it's not worth a damn if the right people testify to you spreading lies.'

'I haven't done that.'

'You told one person.' He had to mean Porter. 'Your employer was quite specific: he ordered you not to reveal his name,' the voice continued. 'You betrayed that trust.'

'Three people have been murdered.'

'No matter.' Dismissing them as if they were chaff, not human. 'He has the reputation of his family to protect. He decided that a letter might not be enough to make sure you remained silent about him. I suggested a personal visit would carry more weight.' A pause. 'Tonight there's been no violence. If I need to return, you'll regret it.'

Silence. Simon stood for ten seconds, then ten more before he realized he was alone, not quite sure if he'd dreamed it all.

Why? Just when he'd hoped the lawyer's letter had been the last of Holcomb, there was this. What was so dark that he needed threats to keep it all quiet? Simon had given the name to Porter. He hadn't had chance to dig deeper yet. But after this, he'd make damned sure he did. If Holcomb wanted to warn him away, he'd failed.

The man who'd spoken tonight sounded too assured by half. But the type who could probably back up his promises. Military, probably an officer. The barracks lay on the far side of Sheepscar, and Holcomb would know men happy to do him a favour.

'Still thinking about Holcomb?' Rosie asked as they sat at the kitchen table in the morning. The boys were yelling as they played soldiers and Jacobites in the small yard behind the house.

He'd woken her when he came home, more shaken than he'd realized at first, and trying to make sense of what had happened.

'Impossible not to,' he replied through a spoonful of porridge. 'I'm damned if I can see the reason. Can you?'

'He's scared,' she said, then hesitated. 'No, it's more than that. He's terrified. He's hiding something important.'

'Then he's going the wrong way about it trying to keep it quiet.'

'Maybe threats are the only way he knows.' She stared at him thoughtfully. 'They wouldn't expect a woman to be looking for the clothes seller, would they? Janet Bristol.'

EIGHTEEN

Erskine and Liddell. They were the only names he had left. Someone had to know where they lived. But Simon's questions brought few answers. Hunslet, perhaps. Didn't Erskine have a house on Quarry Hill? Liddell lived on the Bank, a man was positive of that.

All guesses. Nobody knew. They were men who kept their distance. He spent half the morning going from place to place and growing more frustrated with each visit. Finally he leaned against the Moot Hall, sitting right in the middle of Briggate. Empty now, set to be pulled down once the coming winter had passed.

He didn't hear Jane until she was standing beside him.

'Nobody followed you.'

He'd gone to see her before he began work. Last night had worried him more than he told Rosie. Lying in bed, it had stolen his sleep, all the possibilities creeping around the edges of his thoughts.

For his peace of mind, he needed to be certain Holcomb hadn't sent anyone to trail behind him. Jane had listened and nodded, slipping on her boots, checking the knife in her pocket before arranging the hood of her cloak over her hair and buttoning it at her throat.

Whenever he checked over his shoulder, he saw no sign of her. But that was her special talent: to become invisible on the street.

He bought food for them at a stall in the market, oysters in a hot broth. She stayed quiet as they ate, listening when he spoke but saying nothing in reply.

'Is any of this bringing us closer to finding Harriet?' she asked once they'd finished.

'I don't know what else we can do.' He swept an arm around. 'She could be anywhere out there. Anywhere. People know. They've heard. They're searching.'

'I'm after two men. You want this Erskine and his friend. Are they the same pair?'

'I haven't seen Erskine in a long time, but he never used to wear a beard, and Liddell had ginger hair.' He glanced down Briggate. So many people moving about. A coach hurried along, the driver grinning as he cracked his whip over the heads of the horses and people scattered.

'Do you want me to keep watching you?'

'I should be fine now. Thank you.' She'd brought him assurance and calmed the worries that paraded through his head.

Sally's door was locked, no answer when Jane knocked.

She wandered through town, eyes sharp for the man with the beard and his companion, certain she'd recognize their faces the moment she saw them. Still no sign of Sally.

Jane was standing on the Head Row, deciding whether to follow Woodhouse Lane or Wade Lane, when the boy dashed up to her. Red-faced, breathless, he gulped in air as he gave her the message.

'Sally told us to find you. Tuppence to whoever got to you first. She's found them.'

When she gave him the coins, his face glowed as if he'd been handed a fortune.

'Can you take me to her?'

A nod and he turned away, taking a few steps before he looked over his shoulder to urge her along. She hurried to match his pace as he darted through town. Lands Lane and Kirkgate, down Steander to Hill House Bank.

'She went up there.'

One more penny and he ran off. A climb ahead, all the way to the top of Richmond Hill.

Close to the bottom of the hill, men were building new houses, blocks of cheap back-to-backs. Whole streets of them had risen in the few months since she'd last been here. Jane started trudging up the slope, eyes watching to the left and right, alert to any trouble.

Halfway up, she spotted Sally. Only a thin row of older buildings here, looking like they were desperately clinging to the ground. She'd discovered a place to shelter in a small grove of trees and bushes. Out of the wind, but still able to see.

'I thought Davey would find you. He can move through town like a greased pig.'

'Where are they?'

'Over there.' She pointed to a tumbledown cottage set well back from the street. 'I followed them from town.' With a sigh she stretched out her leg and gently pushed her palm against the ribs.

'Is it definitely them?'

'One of the girls pointed them out to me. She knew their faces.'

Jane breathed deep as she stared at the house. She was so close that she had the copper tang of blood running in her mouth.

Not yet, she thought. She needed to hold back a little and be cautious; this pair could lead her to Harriet.

'How long since they went in?'

'Long enough.'

The girl looked chilled all the way to the bone. No colour in her face, only thin clothes and a shawl that was long past keeping anyone warm or dry.

'Go home,' Jane told her. 'Do you still have any of that money?'

'Most of it.'

'Buy yourself some better clothes. Winter hasn't even begun yet. Put something hot in your belly, too. Go and see Kate the pie-seller. She'll feed you.'

The girl took a few limping steps and turned, pulling out a bright blade. 'I did buy a new knife.' A smile tinged with sorrow.

Jane took time to study the house properly. Smoke rose from the chimney; they were warm inside. Bare ground around the building, no opportunity to creep close and spy through the window without being seen.

Here she was hidden. She touched the tree trunks and wiped the moisture from her palms. The time of year when the ground was always sodden and she wondered if the world would ever be dry again.

A flicker of movement inside the building as one of the men moved past a window. Sally had done well to follow them to this place without being noticed. She had the skill.

Now came the hardest part: waiting.

The shank of the day, air growing colder. Simon hurried down a dirty ginnel, chasing after a tip; Erskine and Liddell had been seen in a beerhouse on Aire Street. He glanced up as he walked. Two figures blocked the way out. He slipped the knife from his sleeve, never hesitating.

'I hear you're looking for us.' Erskine's voice had always been loud, a bellow when a whisper would have been ample. A barrel chest, but the slim waist that was once his pride had run to a thick gut. No beard, definitely not the man the beggar or the homeless girls had seen. But still menacing, the type of mood that could change in a moment.

At first Simon didn't recognize the other man. Then he took off his beaver hat to show a shaved skull. No ginger; no hair at all. The gossip about it falling out must have been right; he'd decided to remove it all.

'I am.'

'Then you'd better ask your questions.'

Simon was close enough to smell the sour breath. 'Why don't we go where the rest of the world won't hear us?'

Yet another beershop. At least this one was clean, the floors swept, the lanterns bright and a warm fire in the hearth.

'I worry when people start asking about me,' Erskine said. He drained half the mug in one swallow. 'I think there might be some kind of problem and I don't like that.'

Liddell was quiet, sipping his drink, eyes shifting about the room, watching for any kind of waiting danger.

Simon held up his hands. 'Questions, that's all.'

A nod. 'What do you want to know?'

'About girls being snatched.'

The man's face hardened. 'You wouldn't be accusing us, would you?'

'No. But do you know anything about it?'

'Heard things,' he replied after a long silence.

'What kind of things?' He needed more than vague words.

'That there might be some important people part of it.'

The same thing Michael Day had told him. But what did that mean? On its own it was just another shadow. A tale. Simon repeated the question he'd asked then: 'More than one?'

'So I've been told. Been going on for a few years. Very secret.'

'Go on.'

'That's all I know for a fact.' He gaze hardened. 'We've never been involved. Never would be.'

'Who is?'

A shake of the head. 'I've not heard any names and I don't want to know. I keep my distance. Safer.'

'No hint at all of who it might be?' Simon could hear hope fading in his voice.

'Nothing. I told you, I'm better off not knowing.'

Without some evidence it seemed like nothing more than a grown-up version of the stories people used to scare children. Powerful men who moved behind the scenes. The same thing Mudie had found, years before. 'But that sort, they know people. They have power. They can make people disappear.'

'So can you.'

Erskine nodded. 'We have. I daresay we will again. Not the same, though.'

'How do they work the snatches?'

'They don't do it anywhere local. I know that much. Far enough away that people here aren't likely to hear about it.'

That fitted with Emma and Harriet. Tadcaster was fifteen miles from Leeds, a different world. News of a missing girl wasn't likely to travel that far. He'd need to see what Porter's letters to other constables brought.

'What about men doing the snatching?'

'Always going to find some scum.' Liddell spat out the words.

'Who?'

'I don't know their names,' Erskine said. 'Seen them once or twice. One of them . . . he just looks like he wants to hurt.' He cocked his head. 'Do you know the type I mean?'

Exactly what Jane had heard. *That* was real.

'Where do they live?'

'Couldn't tell you. Never needed to find out.' He finished the beer. 'Anything else, or are we done?'

'I appreciate the information.'

'For what good it does you.'

At least he was a little further on. A pity it only felt like an inch. Every hour that passed . . . what did it mean for Harriet? Since they'd started this, he'd been very aware that the clock was ticking. The urgency of it all. But things crawled along, and there was nothing he could do to speed them up.

'Are you sure they're in that house?' Rosie asked.

'Yes.' No doubt at all. Girls had told Sally. They knew. Then standing, watching, Jane was sure of it. She could almost smell them.

'We can't be sure they're the ones who took Harriet,' Simon said. 'We don't have any proof.'

'It's them.' Jane stared into his face.

She saw him nod. Good, he believed her.

'Then we need to make them tell us where they took her.'

'We will. After that . . .'

' . . . we'll go and find her,' Simon spoke before she could say more. 'Isn't that the most important thing?'

'Yes.' Killing that pair would remove some evil from the world. Only a moment's work with a knife. A little revenge for everything they'd done. Not the chivalry and honest combat she read about in *Ivanhoe*; her world wasn't as clean and straightforward as that.

'I'd like to see them, and we have to put together a plan to take them,' he said. 'If you go back and keep watch, I'll be there very soon.'

'All right.'

He opened the secret drawer in the stairs and took out his pistol. Loaded and primed it before slipping it into the pocket of his greatcoat.

Rosie looked on while he worked. 'Do you think you'll need it?'

'People keep telling me I need to watch myself.'

'They're right.'

'I'm being careful. Don't worry, I'm not going to walk away from Sophie Jackson.'

'I went over to South Market today. Janet Bristol, the clothes seller hasn't been back, according to the other stallholders. They haven't heard a peep from her.'

'What about her house?'

'Nobody at home. I took a look through the window. There was some dust on the table.' Rosie pursed her lips. 'I don't think she's been in there.'

'They inspector said no more female bodies have turned up.'

'Then she's still alive. Hiding somewhere, maybe, or run off.'

'Did the neighbours know anything?' he asked.

'No answer next door. Most people along the street were out at work. I did find an old woman, but her eyesight is bad. I don't think she'd know Janet Bristol if the woman was standing in front of her. Simon . . .'

'What?'

'It would be helpful to take a look in the house.'

'The inspector said the watch had checked.'

'Men,' she snorted. No need for her to say more.

He grinned. 'Do you remember how to use the lock picks?'

'I'm rusty.'

'Some practice would be good, then. Tell me when you're going back and I'll give the set to you. After last night, I want those papers more than ever.' Never mind shadows and figments of the imagination, Holcomb and his friends were a real worry.

'So do I,' Rosie told him. 'But I want you alive, and not in prison.'

As he walked, an image came into his mind. A young girl with fair hair. Terrified. Crying, but nobody would come to comfort her.

He could see a light through the window, and movement inside.

'Are they both there?' Simon asked in a quiet voice.

'Yes.' Jane never took her eyes off the house. 'They've been inside since I came back.'

He glanced up at the sky. Plenty of clouds to hide the moon.

'Can we get closer?'

'There's nowhere to hide.'

He started to move, but felt her small hand on his arm.

'I'll go,' she whispered, and suddenly he was alone.

Standing for so long, she'd studied the ground, each bump and ridge and dip. Now she moved light-footed and sure until she was around the side of the house. Jane realized she'd been holding her breath and exhaled. She gripped the knife tight in her fist, moving in a crouch towards the window.

A pause, long enough to be sure she hadn't been seen. The hood of her cloak covered her hair. She tugged it forward to shade her face and peered through the glass. In a moment she could make out the shapes. One sitting by the hearth. A small fire was casting its glow. A lantern burned on the table.

That was one man. Where was the other? She drew back in surprise as he passed the window but he never noticed her.

Two minutes; that was all she dare risk, but it was long enough. She crept back, sensing Simon come alert.

'One has a thick dark beard,' she said. 'He was pacing around and talking, but I couldn't make out what he was saying. The girls were right. Even through the window, I could feel something about him.'

'What about the other one?'

'He was in a chair, didn't raise his head. I couldn't see him properly.'

'We should tell the constable.'

'No.' He wasn't going to do that to her again. She wouldn't let
that happen. Jane wouldn't let him steal this from her. 'They're
ours.'

He nodded. 'Remember, we need information from them.'

'We'll get it.' Every scrap. She remembered Emma coming up
to her and gathering her courage to ask if they could find the men
who took her sister. They were one step closer.

NINETEEN

'We'll need to catch them when they're not expecting it,' Simon said. 'Very early in the morning, perhaps. We can overpower them before they have chance to put up a fight.'

'When?' she asked.

'Once we learn more about them.'

'Why wait? Harriet—'

'I know. Look, if we know who they really are, we'll be able to tell when they try to lie to us. You know they will, you can put money on it.'

'But—' she began but again he shook his head.

'I haven't forgotten why we're doing it. Believe me, we'll have a better chance of finding Harriet if we're sure we have the truth from them.'

He could see the frustration on her face. Given the chance, Simon knew she'd have already stormed in. He didn't blame her. He knew he was sentencing a young girl to another day of hell, if she was still alive. But this way offered a better chance of finding her.

'All right,' she agreed reluctantly.

'If they go out tonight, we follow. See who they talk to. Then we start asking those people about them. That way we'll know who they are when we confront them.'

'What do we do now?'

'The same thing we spend half our time doing. Wait. See if they go out.'

An hour. Jane rested her body against the tree, eyes on the house. She spotted movement inside, shapes passing to and fro by the window.

'Something,' she hissed as she stood upright, alert, twisting the ring on her finger, then pulling the knife from her pocket and feeling the comfort of it in her palm.

The lantern inside winked off. She tensed. Then the door opened and the two men emerged. The street was empty; they'd be easy enough to follow; no need to be close, not until they reached town.

'Wait a moment,' Simon whispered in her ear and disappeared towards the house, smiling as he returned. 'No lock worthy of the name. It won't give us any problem.' They began to walk.

'If they split up, which one do you want?' Jane asked.

'The quiet one.' Tall, easy to spot in a crowd.

The man with the beard seemed to talk without pause. His voice carried in the night. He was the one she wanted first. To take away that sense of power he seemed to carry with him. Even at this distance she could feel it.

The men stopped at the inns along Briggate: the Pack Horse, the Ship, Bay Horse, Talbot. Jane knew she couldn't go inside; Simon followed them.

Two hours of drinking before the men stood by the Moot Hall, talking. Jane on one side of Briggate, Simon out of sight on the other. Still people around, singing, shouting, threatening fights with each other. The same as most nights in Leeds.

The bearded man waved his arms as he spoke, then strode off. A fast, angry pace. Jane followed, invisible in the night with the hood of her cloak raised. From the corner of her eye she caught a glimpse of the other one ambling away, hands pushed deep into the pockets of his coat. Neither of them with the smallest sense they were being followed.

He was going home. She stayed behind him all the way to the bottom of Hill House Bank, then waited ten minutes in case he changed his mind. Nothing. It had been a long day. She was glad to make her way back to the cottage behind Green Dragon Yard. Sleep. Tomorrow they'd discover everything about this pair.

The other man weaved his way down Briggate, crossing over Duncan Street, towards the river. Going for the whores, Simon decided. Some drink, then finish the night with a little fun. As predictable as rain. The man seemed to be hunting for someone in particular, smiling happily as soon as he saw her. The clouds shifted for a moment and Simon saw her face in the moonlight.

Mollie. That was one of the names she used. A fixture down here for a few years.

Three minutes and the man was on his way again, Mollie touting for the next customer. Simon followed, but he looked to be on his way home. He lingered just long enough to be certain, then turned back towards Swinegate.

Rosie had already left for South Market, the slim leather wallet of lock picks in her reticule as she carried on her search for the clothes seller. Simon and Jane sat in the kitchen.

'The one with the beard seems to take charge of things. He talked to Richard Cottrell in the Pack Horse and John Hamm in the Talbot. Nothing likeable about either one. He knew them, so they should be able to give me his name.'

'When they split up, the bearded one went straight home. Marched just like a soldier.'

'Mine decided to go whoring. Ended up with Mollie, like he'd been looking for her.'

'I know her,' Jane said. 'I once chased off a man who was threatening her.'

'You talk to her, then. See if she knows his name,' he said. 'Let's meet back here at noon and see what we've discovered.'

The prostitutes came alive once night fell and slept in the day. Jane had to rattle doorknobs, disturb people, endure their anger until she learned where Mollie was living now.

The house stank, a filthy place off Skyes Row, rotting like a hovel, the flagstones around it weeping with shit and piss. She knocked on the door of the room. No answer. Tried again, then a third time, until a voice shouted.

'Get yourself to hell.'

'I need to talk to you.'

'Good for you. Come back later.'

'Now,' she said. 'It's important.'

'It had damned well better be.'

A key turned, the door was flung wide. The woman with the knife was large, wearing a face full of fury. It looked as if she'd tossed her clothes everywhere before going to bed. Her expression softened a little when she saw Jane.

'Come in, then.' She turned, found a small clay pipe on the table and lit it.

Mollie had full lips, three or four chins, and broad, pendulous breasts.

'You've found me, you'd best spit it out.' She took a swig of gin, sighing with pleasure as it went down her throat. 'Well?'

'You were with a man last night . . .' Jane began.

'I was with seven of them.' She chuckled. 'Not a single one took more than two minutes.'

'This one looked happy to find you. Seemed like he'd been looking for you in particular.'

Mollie gave a snort. 'Always one or two like that. Think I'll knock a little off the price.' She narrowed her eyes. 'Was this one a long streak of piss, doesn't talk much?'

She smiled at the description. 'Yes.'

'That's Gilly Harrison. Comes round about once a month, but God knows why. Half a second and he's pulling his trousers up.' She shrugged. 'Men.'

'Do you know much about him?'

'Depends.' She was suddenly suspicious. 'Why?'

Jane told her what she believed and saw the woman give a slow nod.

'I'd not put it past him. There's a man I've seen him with—'

'A dark beard?'

'Yes, and a look in his eye, like he'd do anything if there was a little money in it. Gilly's probably no better. What are you going to do to him?'

'Make him tell me the truth.' Complete certainty in her voice.

'I had a daughter once. She'll be thirteen or fourteen now if she's still alive. You do what you have to do, pet.'

'You mean Billy Wild?' Richard Cottrell asked. Simon had found him in the same place as last night, the Pack Horse, deep in serious conversation with Barnabas Wade. An interesting connection, Wade with his worthless stocks and Cottrell lending money.

'Thick, dark beard.'

A nod. 'That's Wild. I use him to collect when people don't want to pay. He was seeing if I had any work for him.'

'Did you?'

Cottrell gave a slow smile and tapped the side of his nose. He was a small man, wearing good clothes. But he could afford them. When times were hard, his business flourished, people needing a little to tide them over until they were paid.

'Not saying. That would be business.'

'Is Wild good at his work?'

'One look at him and people pay. If they can't, he makes them wish they had. This isn't a trade for the compassionate, Westow.'

'Who else does he work for? Do you know?'

Cottrell shook his head. 'No idea and I don't care. He comes around once a week, regular as a clock, to see if I have anything for him.'

He finally discovered John Hamm playing cards in the Unicorn on Nelson Street, winning the final hand of the game when Simon entered.

Content, Hamm stood drinks for the table. 'One for you, Westow?'

'No, but thank you.' He needed his wits sharp; Holcomb might send another man to find him.

'What can I do for you?' He took a satisfied sip of brandy.

'Billy Wild.'

He blinked in surprise. 'What about him? He only came to see me last night.'

'What did he want?'

'To see if I had any work for him.'

Hamm had money. Not rich, but comfortable. Simon had never found out what he did, but the man was never short.

'Did you?'

'No. It's rare that I need someone like him. Why are you looking? Has he done something?'

'You might want to find someone else to do your dirty work in future.'

Hamm raised his eyebrows and emptied the glass. 'I see. It's like that.'

'It is. What does he do for you?'

'What you'd expect from a man like that. He enjoys it.'

'So I've heard.'

'It's true enough. You'd do well to watch him, Westow. He's tricky.'

Simon smiled. 'So am I.'

'It's useful,' Rosie said as they gathered around the kitchen table. 'But it doesn't tell us anything about them that we hadn't already guessed.'

'We have their names now,' Simon answered.

'For whatever that's worth.' She glanced at Jane. The woman looked rapt in thought. 'Do you think it helps?'

'Names are power,' she replied. 'We know something they don't expect. It means they'll listen. Talk, too.'

They'd go into the house very early in the morning, long before first light. No need for an elaborate plan. Subdue the men and find out what they needed.

'The clothes seller still hasn't come back to South Market,' Rosie said. 'I managed to pick the lock on the back door of her house. Janet Bristol definitely hasn't been there for a while. There was mould all over the bread.'

'No sign of the package?' Simon asked.

She shook her head. 'I searched everywhere. She left in a hurry. Took a few things. Interesting, though. I found some neighbours today. They've seen a couple of men trying the door at different times.'

'Did they recognize them?'

'No.'

'What about the cart? Is it still locked up?'

'Yes. I went and looked.'

'The day you saw her at the market, did she seem frightened?' Simon asked.

Rosie rubbed her chin. 'A little, I suppose, once I told her someone was following Sophie. But no, not scared enough to vanish.'

'What about when you followed her home?' he asked Jane.

'She looked around a few times, but that's all.'

Then it had to be the discovery of the bodies in the beck that made her flee. She'd sensed danger even before she knew who was dead. Perhaps she'd guessed at it.

After the things Holcomb had done, Simon wanted those documents. First, though, they had to find Janet Bristol.

TWENTY

'You look a little better.'

Jane was standing near the top of Briggate, listening as Davy Cassidy the blind fiddler played. She saw Sally weave through the small crowd. The limp didn't look as bad today, and the constant cloud of pain was gone from her face. The cut on her cheek had scabbed over and her bruises had reached high colour. The girl had done as she suggested and bought a thick brown woollen dress a size or two too large and a heavy cloak. Better boots, too. Good winter clothes. Nothing colourful to attract stares.

'A little.' She said nothing until Davy had finished his slow air. 'What about those men?'

'Very soon.' She explained. Sally's gaze burned.

'I can help you.'

'No.' The girl was still recovering from her beating. She was young, too small, not strong enough to stand any chance against men like these. She and Simon were used to working together; a stranger would only be in their way during a fight.

'You'll need to make them talk.'

'They will.' She was certain of that.

'I can do that.'

Jane looked into the girl's face and believed her. All those years of being hurt, all that pain. She'd take it and use it, exactly the way Jane had when she began. Sally would make sure that honest answers came. But she wasn't ready to agree. Not yet.

'Let me think about it.'

'I found out where they lived. I took you there.'

'I know.' Jane owed a debt; that's what Sally was saying. But how much was it? 'Show me your knife again.'

The girl drew it out. Still a faint sheen of oil on the blade. If she knew how to use it properly, it would keep her alive.

'Meet me by the church. Four in the morning. I'll tell you then.'

A flash of frustration, then a reluctant nod.

* * *

Jane settled in bed as Mrs Shields moved around the kitchen. A few hours of rest before tonight.

She had to make up her mind about Sally. This time, she was the one in charge; Simon had agreed to that. She'd always done what he decided. Now she was carrying all the responsibility, and she couldn't afford to fail. Harriet's life depended on finding the right answers. She'd use anything that would bring them the truth.

Perhaps Sally was right. She could help. Unleash her with the knife and her years of fury and the men would talk.

Smiling, her decision made, she settled to sleep.

Fog had come down again during the night. Jane waited at the foot of Hill House Bank, Sally two paces behind her. Simon came out of the mist, walking lightly, pausing as he noticed Sally.

'She'll come in after,' Jane told him. 'When the fighting is over.'

She wondered if he'd object, but after a moment, he nodded. They moved in silence, the fog growing thicker as they climbed.

Not a glimmer of light showing from the house. Whispered instructions to Sally to stay hidden outside for now. Jane waited beside the door, scarcely daring to breathe, as Simon took out his set of picks.

Gentle movements as he felt the lock give. Trying to avoid any sound that might alert Wild and Harrison. Simon eased the door open with one hand as he drew the knife from his belt.

He'd been wary when he saw the girl, relieved when Jane told her to wait until they overcame the men. He knew how Jane fought, knew he could trust her.

Simon eased through the door, sensing her right behind him, then stepped to the side. The fire had burned low, only a few embers throwing out a dim light from the hearth. They couldn't afford to blunder round. No warning. Surprise was going to be everything against a brutal man like Billy Wild.

A few seconds to let their eyes adjust to the gloom. No sound; they must be sleeping in a back room. He edged forward. If they were awake . . .

No. The door was ajar. He could hear the soft, rasping breaths of men sleeping. Very carefully, he slipped through the opening. He could smell them now. The ripe sourness of sweat and alcohol and stale tobacco.

Jane was in the room, moving to the other side. Two pallets on the floor. Simon waited until he could pick out the shape of the man lying by him, then brought the blade down hard. Through the blanket, deep into the muscle.

A yell, cut to sudden silence as he knelt on the man's chest. Simon felt him struggling. He pressed down harder and drew the edge of his knife against the man's throat. No pressure behind it, just enough to trace a thin, tender line through the flesh and draw blood. That made him hold completely still.

Shouts from the other bed. A blow followed by a grunt. For the smallest moment Simon hesitated and the man under him tried to push up again.

'No.' He stabbed the hand reaching to gouge his eyes. Another shout and the figure fell back. The fight had gone out of him very quickly. Easier than he'd expected.

Something slammed against the wall. No sound of pain; that had to be Jane. Simon bunched his fist.

A hard blow to the temple and the man on the bed sprawled back, unconscious. Simon scrambled across the room. He sensed a figure and wrapped his fingers around a thick neck. Billy Wild, he was sure. It took the man by surprise. Simon pulled, using his strength, dragging the man backwards, off balance.

Strong fingers took hold of his wrists and tried to pry them away. More powerful than Simon expected. He pulled at the man again. Felt him begin to topple.

That gave Jane the opening she needed. She plunged her knife into his thigh. Enough to disable him. Panting, Simon let go and Wild fell to the floor. Jane drew her boot back and kicked him between the legs. Once, twice, three times. All her strength behind each one, until he was curled over on his side, sobbing as he gasped and tried to protect himself.

She was ready to make the killing blow. Her eyes flared madly as Simon put his arms around her shoulders and drew her away. He'd expected a battle royal and barely found a skirmish. Catching them asleep had worked. The hard men hadn't proved so deadly. All too human, he thought.

Jane bent over, rubbing the places he'd hit her. She wiped her knife on Wild's blanket before sliding it back into her pocket.

'We need to tie them,' he said.

He lit a pair of lanterns. Harrison was still unconscious, Wild was hurting too much to put up any kind of resistance. Blood oozed from the cut on his thigh. No walking for a while, but it wouldn't kill him.

Simon had brought rope, and tied strong knots until the pair were helpless and immobile. Harrison began to stir, moaning and moving. Wild kept straining against his bonds, cursing under his breath. He knew he was caught and helpless, beaten. But even bound tight, he still gave off that air of danger. Too late now. Simon glanced down and saw the hatred on the man's face. Much too late.

'How do you want to do this?' Simon asked.

Jane stared at the pair in front of her. In a straight, steady voice she said, 'Sally and I will talk to them. I'll come and tell you what they said in the morning. Nobody will ever know we were here.'

He'd been dismissed. Simon took a final look at the men before he walked outside and felt the fog cold and clammy against his skin. Sally limped past him into the house. He knew Jane had just given Wild and Harrison a death sentence. For just a second, he considered turning back, then the door closed with a soft click.

He felt as if he'd barely slept. Rest had never come, as worries and fears cartwheeled and tumbled through his mind. His eyes were gritty as he blinked awake. Every movement was slow and muddy.

Simon stood by the coffee cart, sipping the liquid, letting its heat run through his body. People were talking, gossip flowering. Someone mentioned a fire and he turned.

'Where did you say it was?'

'Hill House Bank. Why?'

'Nothing. It doesn't matter.'

He drained the cup and began to walk. Suddenly he felt very awake.

The same house. Hardly anything left of it now. A few fallen beams, charred and cracked. Mounds of ashes. He was one of half a dozen gathered to stare. Once someone began sifting through it all they'd discover the bodies. A few burned bones. Nothing to say who the men had been when they still breathed. That was what he hoped. Jane had said there'd be no trace she or Simon had been here. It looked as if she'd kept her promise.

He couldn't find any sympathy in his heart for Harrison or Wild. They'd traded in violence and pain; now they'd died that way.

None of it helped his sombre mood.

Little rest, but she was completely calm. No raw edges scraping in her mind. She sat in Simon's kitchen, feeling him watching her while Rosie stirred a pot on the range. But she'd be listening, too; she was a part of this.

'Wild handled everything,' Jane said. 'He arranged all the jobs and took the money.'

Simon thought of the men he'd talked to; Wild had been the one looking for work. That fitted.

'What did Harrison do?'

'Whatever he was told. Didn't matter if it was hurt or kill. If Wild ordered him, he'd do it.'

'Did they take Harriet and Emma?'

'He didn't want to say.'

'But?' Rosie asked the question.

After Wild had refused to answer, Jane let Sally work. The girl had been coldly efficient, brutal in the way she started and paused as Jane pushed again and again until she was satisfied they had every detail. 'He hired a wagon and went looking for a girl to take,' she said. 'Always from good, clean families, and never too close to Leeds. Those were the orders.'

'Always?' Rosie said.

'This was the third time they'd done it in two years.' Her voice was flat, not letting any emotion seep among the facts. 'He thinks there were others before them.'

Simon gazed straight ahead, jaw set, then turned to look at her.

'Where did they deliver them?'

'A farm on the road to Wetherby, he said. Three miles from Leeds, as close as he could judge.'

'Who owns it?'

'He didn't know the man's name. Didn't want to.' She thought of Wild trying to scream, but Sally stopping it in his throat. 'I believe him. They were hired by a man called Carpenter. He'd come looking for them whenever a new girl was needed.'

'What happened with Emma and Harriet? How did they find them?'

'Blind luck. That was what he told me.' Wild had been crazed with pain when he spoke, gritting his teeth as Sally's hands moved. 'They delivered them. When the man rejected Emma, they needed to do something with her.'

'Not kill her?' Rosie's voice was sharp. 'Easier to dump her in Leeds. Even if she told people, nobody would ever believe her.'

'Until you.'

A nod. 'They knocked her out first as a precaution.' Jane raised her eyes. 'Exactly as Emma said.'

She'd forced him to describe the man who'd bought Harriet. Wild had been reluctant, but Sally had kept going until he gave in, sobbing like a child between sentences that were shattered into fragments. A tall man, he'd said. Bald on top, thick white side whiskers. Thin legs, pigeon chest. Well dressed, the few times he'd seen him. He insisted again that he'd never heard a name. She'd kept asking until she was certain he wasn't lying.

'How good were his directions to this farm?'

'Very.'

'As soon as we find the place . . .' Simon began.

'We get Harriet out of there,' Jane's voice rose over his. 'Wild said there's no dog. I asked.'

Simon took a breath, then nodded. 'What do we do about the man who bought her?'

Her reply was a stare. Why ask when he knew the answer?

'We can't,' Rosie told her softly. 'He's obviously someone who has money. When important men die, others start asking questions. It's safer to tell the constable, let him go in and search.'

'Once we have Harriet away from there,' Jane said.

'Yes,' Simon agreed.

'The law won't touch him,' Jane said. 'You know he'll destroy whatever there is to tie him to all this.'

'Maybe,' he said. 'He might miss some things. Anyway, as soon as Porter starts, word will spread. Whoever this man is, his life might as well be over. Everyone will be after his blood.'

Jane thought. She didn't like it. There was nothing final about it. No real ending. No justice. But Rosie was right; if she killed him, there would be questions. She wasn't going to hang for someone like that. Safer to do it this way.

'Carpenter. The one who arranges things.'

'I've never heard of him.' She saw Simon glance at his wife; Rosie shook her head. 'I'll start asking. We can hire a gig. Go and find this place.' He gazed at her. Jane's face was drawn, exhausted. 'We both need to sleep first.'

* * *

After Jane left, Rosie turned to him.

'I wonder if the men were alive when they started the fire.'

'I'm not sure she'd have told us. But she discovered what we needed to know. Her and that girl, Sally.'

He didn't want to think about it. If he started, he'd have to wonder how far he'd have been willing to go to find the truth, and what sort of justice he'd have meted out. Not questions he wanted to ask himself. And Sally . . . she was barely older than his boys, but she was hardened in a way he hoped Amos and Richard would never know. Another Jane.

'I'm going to look for Janet Bristol again,' Rosie told him. 'There's too much we still need to know there.'

'I'll see if anyone had heard of a man called Carpenter.'

TWENTY-ONE

'Carpenter?' George Mudie frowned as he worked, fixing type into the blocks. His fingers moved quickly and confidently. Simon watched, transfixed by his assurance. 'No,' he said eventually, 'I don't know anyone with that name. What's he done?'

'You're better off if I don't say, George.' When Mudie gave him a curious look, Simon continued, 'I'm not making light of it. Some things shouldn't be said in good company.'

'All right,' he agreed reluctantly. He thrived on news and the gossip.

'You'll learn it all later. Everyone will.'

No luck there. No luck anywhere, it seemed. Finally, standing in the coaching office, one of the clerks raised his head.

'Did you say Carpenter, sir?'

'Yes.' Simon felt a surge of hope. 'Do you know him?'

'There's a gentleman called Carpenter who sometimes sends a package on the coach to London.' He blinked behind his spectacles. His right hand was curled like a claw from holding a pen each day and his shirt cuff stained blue with ink. Middle-aged, with hair beginning to pull back from his forehead and turn grey, he looked like a sober, honest man.

'A gentleman?' That was a jolt. He'd expected someone dark and furtive.

'He's always mounted. A good animal, too.' More blinking. 'I grew up on a farm, sir. I know a little about horses.'

A horse . . . They needed space. The countryside.

'Can you tell me anything else about him?' Simon produced a shilling. 'Where does he live?'

The clerk's face flushed. His fingers fidgeted together as he eyed the money and considered his reply.

'I don't know. I never had any need to ask. He's definitely not a rich man, I can tell you that. Always wears the same clothes when he comes and they're a bit worn. But his face has the look of spending a lot of time in the weather.'

'A farmer?'

The man shook his head. 'No, I don't believe so.' He blinked again. 'I'm not sure why, sir. He doesn't seem like one, that's all.'

'How old is he? What does he look like?'

When the clerk hesitated, Simon added another sixpence.

'Probably close to forty, sir. Around my age. A long face, and a large nose. Fair hair, but there's not too much of it left. He's short, probably not much more than a few inches over five feet.' A hurried, nervous smile. 'You learn to judge height in this job, sir. How many people can squeeze inside a coach.'

'Very good. You're observant.' He handed over the money. 'When was he last here?'

The clerk pursed his lips and thought for a long time. 'It's been a while, sir. Early autumn, I think.'

'Thank you.'

Sheer luck. If the clerk hadn't overheard, he'd still be groping around. But sometimes luck smiled. He felt sure this was the right man. Not what he'd expected, but it worked with what they knew. Now they had to find this place.

Jane bought two pies from Kate and strode over to Sally's room. The girl unlocked the door and sat silently as she ate.

'How's your hip?'

Sally shrugged. 'A little better. Still hurts.'

'Any regrets about last night?'

She lifted her head, astonished by the question. 'Why would I? I made sure they told you what you wanted to know.'

'You did.' Jane felt no guilt. The men had deserved it all.

'What are you going to do now?'

'Find that place where the rich man lives.'

Sally nodded. 'Harriet's there.'

'We'll bring her out.'

'It's country, you might have to search plenty of ground.'

'Then that's what we'll do.'

'I can help.'

'Do you want to come? Can you manage?'

'Yes.' A hesitation before she asked: 'What about the man who bought her?'

'We don't hurt him.' Sally's eyes widened and she opened her

mouth, but Jane shook her head. Rosie's words had carried wisdom.
'Not even a cut.'

At first the fog seemed like more of the smoke and soot that always
blanketed Leeds. Nothing more than a few shreds drifting through
the air. But as the gig moved through Sheepscar, past the toll gate
and up the Roundhay turnpike, it started to thicken. Another mile
and he could barely see ten feet on either side of the road.

'We'll never spot the place in this,' he said.

Jane was turning her head from side to side, straining her eyes
to stare into the gloom.

'It might ease as we carry on,' she said.

But it didn't. The opposite; it was thicker still. Somewhere around
three miles from town Simon pulled on the reins and the gig creaked
to a halt.

'It could well be somewhere round here, but we're never going
to find it in this. It's taken too long to come this far and it's growing
darker, too.' He turned to Jane with a sad, defeated look. 'We're
blundering around. I'm not even certain how far we've come. We
could have passed it or we could still have a mile to go. It makes
sense to try again in the—'

But she was climbing down to the ground.

'Take the gig back,' she said. 'I'll walk home.'

Simon glanced across at Sally. The girl had arrived with Jane,
squeezing on to the seat as they left the ostler's yard. She began to
move, but Jane laid a hand on her arm.

'Go with Simon. You're still limping. I'll move faster by myself.'

Jane didn't hurry. She knew what she needed to see, a pair of stone
gateposts leading to a rutted drive that Wild had described through
his pain. She'd been watching carefully as the gig bounced along
the road; they hadn't passed it yet.

She moved through a silent world. No traffic on the road, no
carriages or carts, nobody on foot. All alone, caught in the fog and
the creeping night. She followed each track that led off the road for
a few yards, hoping for gateposts, and finding nothing.

Jane tried to gauge how long she'd been walking. Half an hour?
She couldn't tell; it was as if time didn't exist out here. She trudged
on. A little farther, a little farther, the fog cold and clammy against

her face. Under the cloak, she gripped her knife tightly. She'd keep going a while longer to try and find Harriet.

Around a corner, then, to her left, a broad path with a pair of stones to mark it. They were wet under her touch. She tried to peer ahead, but couldn't see more than a few yards.

Each step was hesitant. Halting, listening, but the fog devoured every sound. Maybe a hundred yards until the track broadened in front of a house. Lamps burned in the windows. Without thinking, she drew back, although no eyes would ever be able to spot her in this weather.

Jane eased her way around the building. The cobbles in the yard glistened in the light from a kitchen. She circled around, keeping away and saw a small building. Brick, with a door that barely fitted in the opening. She pushed. It creaked open under her hand. Jane looked around, expecting someone to shout. Nothing. She waited, ready, her heart beating a tattoo in her chest. But there was only silence around her.

Two steps inside, whispering Harriet's name. But the man would never leave her somewhere she could run off.

Another building. This one was larger, made from stone. She breathed in the heavy scent of a horse, a mix of clean, fresh hay and stinking shit and felt her way along to the door. It was closed with a heavy padlock. Jane rattled it, but nothing gave. Emma had remembered a stable. She slid her knife between the hasp and the wood of the door, but it didn't help. If she pushed any harder, she'd snap the blade.

Harriet was in there. She knew it. She could sense the girl behind the walls. But she couldn't get past the door.

Jane circled the stable, hoping for a window, some way in. She saw one, but it was too high for her to reach. Her fingers explored the wall; no footholds that would let her climb.

She stood for a long time, thinking, trying to find some kind of plan.

In the end she had to admit it.

She'd failed.

They'd return tomorrow, when they could see, but it meant the girl would have to endure one more night here.

To come so close, but not enough.

She heard a coach coming along the road as she walked back to Leeds and faded into the undergrowth as it passed.

In her head, Jane knew there was nothing more she could have done. That didn't satisfy her heart. She berated herself, rubbing the skin under her sleeve to feel the ridges, the old scars where she used to cut herself, the punishment for her failures.

A long time since she'd felt the need to use her knife for that. Now they were pale reminders, tiny bumps on the skin. She'd done it to relieve the guilt and the pain. The same things that hurt her now. This time, though, the blade wouldn't touch her flesh.

Once she'd passed Sheepscar Beck, Jane felt easier. The fog was still thick, the darkness complete, but this was familiar ground. Her feet knew it without thinking, carrying her home.

Mrs Shields fussed about her, draping her dress and petticoats with their sodden hems by the fire, then stuffing her boots with old newspapers and setting them next to the hearth. Jane relished the warmth as it soaked into her bones. But then she thought of Harriet in the cold and damp and darkness.

'Drink this, child.' The voice pulled her from her thoughts. She sipped. Something warm, sweet. Jane looked up, grateful.

'Thank you.'

'You need to sleep.' Even as the old woman said it, she felt the weight behind her eyelids.

He watched Sally, but she barely spoke on the journey back to town. She kept glancing over her shoulder as if she expected to see someone behind them. Most of the time she kept a sullen, brooding expression on her face.

The girl winced as she climbed down from the gig, stretching out her leg and hobbling a few steps before she turned.

'Tomorrow?'

'As long as the fog lifts.'

'I'll be ready.'

He returned the vehicle and marched home. Driving always left his back sore, and concentrating on the road in this weather had drained him. He'd be glad to be in his own kitchen, out of the dampness and mist.

But as he entered, he saw Rosie standing by the range with her knife in her hand and a bruise just beginning to blossom on her cheekbone. Her skin was swelling, left eye beginning to close.

'Christ.' Simon pulled her close, feeling the anger roar inside. 'What happened?'

TWENTY-TWO

'I was out looking for Janet Bristol,' Rosie began. She sounded hoarse, voice fluttering by his ear. 'Someone had told me about a woman who might be able to help. It was coming on dusk, I thought I'd have time go there and still manage to be home before Amos and Richard finished with their tutor.' She hesitated. 'It's my own fault. I wasn't paying attention.'

'Who was it?'

'He came out of nowhere.' Her voice was barren. Shock. 'The first thing I knew, he was right there in front of me. I never heard him in the fog. He pulled his arm back and punched me. I didn't have time to take out my knife. All I could do was turn my head.' She raised her hand and gently touched her cheek.

'Was he on his own?'

'No. There was another man. I never saw his face.'

It had to be the same pair who'd threatened him. 'Was he the one who talked?'

'Yes. He said he'd spoken to my husband, and now he'd leave me with a mark as a warning to keep out of business that was none of my affair.' She looked at him questioningly. 'How could he have known what I've been doing?'

'I've no idea.'

But he'd find out and make sure they paid. Simon examined the bruise. It was ugly; at least the damage was only superficial. A few days and it would be gone.

'The one who spoke. Did he sound educated?'

'Yes. Said we'd do best to drop it all and make sure we said nothing about the man who employed you.' A short silence. 'The boys will be wondering what we're doing. They looked terrified when they saw me. I sent them upstairs to play. I wanted them out of the way if the men came back.'

'They won't.'

He saw the determination in the set of her face. She wasn't going to let herself cry. She wouldn't give them the satisfaction.

'I'll go and talk to Amos and Richard,' he said. 'Then we'll all come down.'

She smiled. Not back to normal. Nowhere close; she'd feel this long after the bruise had gone.

The fog had vanished, the morning was grey, damp and dreary as he walked to meet Jane and the girl.

The night had been a clamour in his head, trying to understand how Holcomb's friend could have known what Rosie was doing. She was going out again today, following the hint she'd been given. If the man believed he'd scared her away, he didn't know Rosie. If they returned, she'd be prepared.

There had to be something very dark in those papers. Holcomb would have done well to burn them when he had the chance. Much too late now.

'I found the house,' Jane said. 'We hadn't gone far enough.'

She explained about the lock on the stable and Simon borrowed a crowbar from the ostler. Back in the gig, they bounced about on the turnpike. No mist to hamper them today. Past the barracks, then trotting out into countryside.

Plenty of dense woodland beside the road; fine opportunities for the highwaymen who used to roam around here. She pointed out the gates.

'The first thing we'll need to do is look around,' Simon said. 'I'll hide the gig in the woods.'

'The stable . . .' Jane said and he nodded.

It wasn't a farm. Not even a smallholding. Probably the land rolling off into the distance had once been part of the property, but stout fences separated it now. Simon crouched behind a bush and stared at the house. Old, maybe a century or more, but kept with pride. The paint was thick on the door and window frames. With the nearest dwelling more than a quarter of a mile away, it was perfect for hiding a stolen child. Nobody could hear the screams and cries.

Jane pointed out the small broken building, then the stable with its stout lock.

Through the window he could make out a pair of figures in the house. Two men. Too far away to make out their faces through the heavy glass in the mullions.

'We'll need a distraction so I can break the lock on the stable door,' Simon hissed.

She nodded, tapped Sally on the arm and they vanished into the undergrowth. Off among the bushes and trees and tall, wet grasses, she was invisible in the green cloak.

He waited, breathing softly, crowbar in his hand. A useful weapon if he needed to fight, but Simon sensed there'd be no battle today.

Glass shattered on the other side of the house. He stiffened, ready to move.

Jane threw the stone and watched it crash through the window. A few yards away, Sally picked her target. Another hit. Two more, then they began to push through the undergrowth to the back of the house.

It was a simple idea, easy to carry out. No shortage of stones. An attack out of nowhere. Damage and confusion. The men inside would panic and wonder if the world was ending. Going from one direction to another would baffle them, keep them occupied.

Another rock, enough weight to it to do some damage. More glass breaking. A quick volley or two from Sally, the panes glistening as they shattered. Then they were moving again, back to where they'd been before, the girl hurrying awkwardly and unevenly with her injured hip. The opposite side of the house to Simon. Give him chance to work.

The girl was poised, ready for more, but Jane shook her head. Wait. Let them wonder what was coming next.

A few whispered words and Jane ran off, leaving Sally. She wanted a spot where she could lob stones at the front of the house. Try to draw them out that way.

Three of them, one following the other, and the sharp, jubilant sound of glass breaking again. A pause. She was breathing hard, grinning with childish pleasure and excitement at the destruction.

The heavy front door opened a few inches and she was gone.

A shot cracked open the air. Nowhere near her, but Jane ducked. Instinct. It would take time for the man to reload. Chance for more damage and to buy Simon time to rescue Harriet.

If she was in the barn.

For the very first time, Jane felt a twinge of doubt. This was the right place. She knew that. She felt it in her bones. It was exactly as Wild had said. She'd been so certain the girl would be there. But the house would have a cellar, too, empty rooms; plenty of safer places to keep someone. Angry at herself, she picked up a stone and hurled it at a window.

The hasp was screwed tight to the door. It took three pulls with the crowbar to force out the screws. Simon pushed the door back, letting in the light.

A horse began to whinny in its stall. Not pleasure, this was fear as it scented a stranger. Simon drew out his knife and took a few paces into the barn. The smell of shit and hay. Something else, too. Too faint to make out.

'Harriet.' He said the name softly. He didn't want to shout. She'd hear him. 'We've come to take you home.'

For a second he thought he heard a whimper and moved towards the sound. The stall at the end.

'Please, don't be scared. We want to take you out of here.'

Another noise. Someone trying to stifle tears. Definitely the far stall. It had a gate as tall as him, a heavy bolt to keep her inside. He slid it back.

She was huddled in dirty straw. Clothes torn. Shuddering with fear and cold, looking up at him with terror.

'You're going to be safe now, Harriet. I promise.'

Simon reached for her, but she inched herself away into the corner.

'Please,' he said, then reached down and cradled her against his greatcoat. He didn't have time. No knowing how long Jane and Sally could keep the men occupied. She hammered at him with fists and feet, but he barely felt it as he strode back out to the daylight. She weighed nothing.

As he reached the gig, he let out a long whistle. Harriet was still struggling and squirming, trying to break free. He hoped to God that seeing Jane and the girl would calm her. Taking her to Leeds was going to be a trial otherwise.

There was a cut on her face. Bare legs covered in scabs and bruises, her shoes and stockings gone. But strangely, someone had bathed her. She was clean. It had to have been the man who wanted a girl from a decent family. In its own curious way it made complete sense.

He kept talking, a low, even voice as he tried to reassure her.

Smile. As gently as possible. Simon raised his head as he heard the noise of feet hurrying through the bushes.

Jane appeared, face flushed, startled and happy as she saw Harriet. Sally came hobbling behind, not trying to disguise the pain on her face as she pressed a hand to her side.

'In,' he said, handing Harriet to Jane once she'd clambered into the gig. He helped Sally up, then took the reins.

For five minutes he pressed the horse until it was flecked in sweat. Glances behind to make sure no one was pursuing them. By the time they reached the toll booth at Sheepscar Beck he felt easier. They'd done it. He smiled to himself as he exhaled slowly. They'd rescued the girl.

Turning on the seat, he saw Jane was cradling Harriet under her cloak, keeping her warm as she and Sally kept their heads together in urgent whispers.

He stopped on Swinegate and led the way into the house. Rosie was hanging up her cloak in the wall. One look and she swept Harriet her arms, carrying her through to the warmth of the kitchen.

'We'll send someone to tell your parents where you are,' she said. 'They're going to be overjoyed to see you again, just as happy as you'll be to go home with them.'

The child gazed around, silent, sucking her thumb, eyes still filled with fear. But who could blame her for that?

'I'll go and tell Porter,' Simon said. He inclined his head for Jane to follow. Sally moved slowly behind them.

'We need to leave it to the law now,' he told her. 'We'd agreed on that.'

Not happy, but she nodded. 'It'll all be cleaned up by the time the watch arrive.'

'Maybe so,' Simon agreed, 'but they'll be rushing. They're bound to overlook something. The rumour alone will ruin the man.' He shook his head. 'We don't even know who he is.'

'We should have killed them.' Sally's voice was bitter. 'We had the chance.'

'No.'

'They deserve it.'

'They do, but this way will serve better. You have to believe me about that. The stones . . .' He smiled. 'That was an excellent idea.'

* * *

'I've sent a fast rider to Tadcaster. The Caldwells should be down here soon. My men are on their way to search this place. How did you find her, Westow?'

'Luck. I was out on the road and spotted her in the bushes. She must have escaped.'

The constable raised his eyebrows and stared. 'You're telling me you just happened to be in the right place at the right time.'

'That's exactly what I'm telling you.' His expression showed nothing. He doubted Porter would say more, happy to let that truth remain buried, down where it belonged.

'Come along. You can show me this place.'

'What do we do now?' Sally asked as she watched Simon walk into the courthouse.

'Nothing,' Jane told her. 'We've done it. Harriet's safe. Her mother and father will take her home.'

'Those men . . .' Her voice was low, an angry hiss.

'I said. We're going to do nothing.' It was the agreement she'd made. Maybe the law would hang them. Or it might turn its head away and ignore justice. But they'd released Harriet. She'd done what Emma asked and found her sister, felt the small, quivering body against hers on the journey back to Leeds. Seen the silent tears on the girl's cheeks. Her skin had been as cold as the dead; Jane had rubbed the arms gently to warm them.

But now there was nothing more for her in this. It had become Simon's business. The constable's business. Men's business.

'What should I do?' Sally sounded lost.

'Go and sleep. Heal. Do you still have money?' A nod. 'Buy some food. A quiet day and plenty of sleep will help you mend.' Jane heard the words as they came from her mouth; she sounded like Mrs Shields. 'I'll come by to see you tomorrow.'

'Do you promise?' Sally sounded very young and lost. But she was exactly that.

A smile. 'I promise.'

TWENTY-THREE

They took the turnpike at a slow, steady trot. Simon had never felt comfortable astride a horse. The animal scared him. What if it shied or reared? The drop to the ground was long.

The watch had been marching steadily, the inspector at their head. Simon and Porter caught up to them a little shy of the house. The constable leaned in his saddle and talked softly to the inspector. The man nodded and hurried away.

'Is this definitely the right place?' Porter asked as they halted by the gate.

'The girl came out of here.' At least that much was fact; she had. Just not by herself.

Another sceptical look, then Porter dismounted and led his horse along the drive, stopping as soon as he saw the house with its windows smashed. An ocean of glass spread across the ground. He glanced doubtfully at Simon.

'It looks like a mob has been through here. I don't suppose you know about that, Westow?'

'Nothing at all.' He hadn't seen any mob.

The constable detailed two of the men to search the buildings and tethered his horse to a post. He loosened his sword in his scabbard. 'Let's go and see who's inside.'

Empty. Everything abandoned in a hurry. Nothing left in the strongbox in the corner of a bedroom. Clothes tossed across the bed. The men here had realized what would happen and decided to flee. How much of a start did they have? Two, three hours at the very most. Long enough to cover a fair distance.

Porter stood by the head of the stairs. He picked his words carefully. 'Whatever went on here has stirred up something.' He turned his head to gaze at Simon. 'Sure you have no knowledge of it, Westow?'

'Why would I?'

The man shrugged. At the front door he looked around and shook his head. Dismay? Disbelief?

He was talking to the inspector by the time Simon emerged.

'It seems the house is owned by a man called Thomas Wise.'

'I've never heard of him,' Simon said.

The inspector picked up the tale. 'According to a farmer down the road, he lives here with a manservant. Inherited a lot of the land, but he had no interest in farming, so he leased most of it out. Hardly ever shows himself in public, but the man said he's heard some peculiar noises here at times.'

'I remember him,' Porter said. 'Important man in his day. I saw him dining with Magistrate Holcomb once. Years ago.'

That caught Simon's attention. Most probably it meant nothing at all; the rich all knew each other. He stayed quiet, turning his head at a shout from the barn. The inspector took off at a run.

'Small world, isn't it?' Porter said.

'We both know what Leeds is like. No better than a village in plenty of ways.' The right families socialized together, of course. Met at the assemblies, danced together, intermarried.

'Aye.' It came out as a sigh. 'It is.'

The constable ran a hand over the broken hasp. At the stall where Harriet had been kept, a man from the watch was showing things.

The horse had gone. Simon said nothing. After all, he'd never been here.

'This must be where they kept her,' Porter said.

He finally had the chance to examine it properly. Filthy straw, a stinking bucket in the corner. It was a cell, nothing more than that. No heat. How much longer could Harriet have survived if they hadn't freed her?

'How could someone do that to a child?' the inspector asked.

But people did. This and worse. Sometimes in the name of love or God.

A cry from outside. Feet running.

'Sir.' The man's face was the colour of ash. 'You'd better see this.'

Small bones, a few scraps of cloth still clinging to them. A shallow grave, no more than three feet deep. Which one was she? Simon wondered. What was her name?

'Dig up the whole area,' Porter ordered as he stared at the remains. 'We need to find out if there are more.'

He walked away.

'Christ Almighty, Westow. What have we found?'

A phrase came into Simon's head. One the vicar had used in Sunday services when he was a child in the workhouse. 'A charnel house.'

'I'll put out a notice to arrest them. For the love of God . . .'

*   *   *

It was long past dark when Simon unlocked his front door. His body ached from driving the gig, then riding. The certainty of home was solid and welcoming when his heart was so full of sadness.

Rosie was sitting in the kitchen, working by the light of an oil lamp, nib scratching as she filled out their accounts. As soon as she saw his face, she rose, took his hand and led him to the table. A glass of brandy.

'Is she asleep?' he asked as the first sip burned some life back into him.

'It took a long time. Everything terrifies her.'

'Hardly surprising.' His voice hardened. 'They were keeping her in a stall in a barn.'

'The skin around her wrists is still raw. They must have had her tied for a while.' Rosie pawed at her eyes, pushing the tears away before they could begin. 'She's so tiny.'

'Four years old.' He hesitated, then said: 'The watch have dug up a body. Another child.'

She couldn't speak for a long time. 'Who did all this, Simon?'

'The man's name is Thomas Wise. He and his manservant have fled. Porter said he knew Holcomb's father.'

Her eyes blinked wide. 'We need those documents.'

Simon nodded. 'Any luck with your lead today?'

'She'd gone to the market at Wakefield. Tomorrow.'

'At least Harriet's parents will be here soon.'

'They'll need to give her plenty of love.'

The family arrived a little before eight. The night had turned colder and they arrived bundled in furs and wool, filling the kitchen. Emma was still frightened, curtseying shyly to Simon and Rosie before ducking back behind her mother.

He watched their faces as his wife led Harriet into the room. Washed, hair brushed, but with nothing to fit her in the house, she was still dressed in the same rags she'd worn at the farm. A moment, then Emma was holding her sister tight, apologizing over and over as she wept.

The mother knelt, arms around both her daughters, hands moving and stroking their backs, the assurance that this was real, that her terrors had finally ended.

Mr Caldwell watch them with a smile Simon couldn't read. When he knocked on the door, his face had been tight with fear. Now that had drained.

'Thank you, Mr Westow. You can't know what you've done for our family.'

'The person who deserves the credit is Jane, the woman who works with me. The same as with Emma.'

Caldwell bowed. 'Then she's a remarkable woman. I'm deep in her debt. I hope you'll tell her how grateful we are.' He waited as his wife drew the girls out to the carriage. Emma curtseyed again; Harriet was too overwhelmed to know what to do.

'How badly was she hurt, Mr Westow?'

He told the man the little he knew, seeing his horror grow with each second.

'Who did this? Has the constable arrested him?'

'He's vanished.' Simon weighed giving the name. Caldwell could spread it across the county. 'He's called Thomas Wise.'

Harriet's father extended his hand. 'Thank you again, Mr Westow.' He looked at Rose, around the room. 'All of you. I don't think I'll ever be able to express just what my wife and I felt when we received the note today. You've given both our daughters back to us when we were starting to lose faith. You bank at Beckett's? Excellent. I'll send a draft on Monday. Believe me, you've more than earned it.'

Simon stood in the doorway as the coach trundled down Swinegate. Richard's sleepy voice floated down the stairs: 'What's all that noise, Papa?'

Jane rose early, up with the first light on the horizon. She checked on Mrs Shields, stoked the fire until it was throwing out heat, and dressed by its light. During the evening she'd read more of *Ivanhoe*, happy to lose herself for an hour or two in the past.

The roofs were white with the first frost of the year, the paving stones slippery underfoot. She saw Simon at the coffee cart on Briggate, hands wrapped tight around a steaming tin mug.

'Harriet's gone home,' he told her. 'She's safe now.'

But Jane knew a truth he could never understand; the girl would never feel completely safe again. The fear would always be there, lurking, waiting at the back of her mind. She could still feel the little hands clinging in the gig, the pleading in her eyes.

All around, people were talking about the young girl who'd been held in a stable and the remains discovered in the ground. Full of outrage and anger. She watched Simon cock his ear towards a conversation.

'Come with me.'

They approached a pair of men who paused to eye her with suspicion, as if a woman had no place in their company.

'What were you saying?' Simon asked the one who'd been speaking.

'I saw a carter who was unloading his wagon earlier. He claims somebody told him a man had found a pair of bodies last night. When I asked him where, he didn't know. Said it was just what he'd heard.' He shrugged and gave a short laugh. 'Who knows, eh?'

'You think the bodies could be Wise and Carpenter?' Jane asked Simon as they walked away.

'I'll go and see Porter. The watch will be out at the house again today, seeing how many more bodies are there.' He shook his head to try and rid his mind of the thought. 'Why don't you ask around, see what people know about these bodies the carter is supposed to have mentioned.'

Some work for Sally, too, she thought. The girl could pass the word among the children. They heard more than people imagined. She looked relieved to have something to do.

'We'll meet at noon,' Jane told her. 'By the Moot Hall.'

She talked to Kate the pie-seller, Dodson, looking smart in his greatcoat, even Davy Cassidy the fiddler. None of them had heard anything new about Wise and his companion, no rumours flying on the wind. Everywhere she asked she received shakes of the head. It seemed like a tale somebody had made up to pass an empty hour.

Sally was waiting, limping in small circles.

'Nothing. Words,' she said.

A nod. 'Still, worth finding out.'

'What do we do now?'

Jane smiled at the girl's eagerness. 'I told you. There's nothing else for us to do. Not on this, anyway.' Sally seemed to be walking a little more easily today, but she kept pressing a hand against her side. 'You still need time to heal. Rest again.'

A nod and a quick smile, but as she watched the girl walk away, Jane knew she wouldn't do it. She'd be counting the days until the rent ran out on her room and wondering what came after that.

TWENTY-FOUR

'I saw that report about two bodies,' Porter said after Simon told him the rumour. 'But it was an old man and his wife, all natural at home. Not our friends.'

'No word on them yet?'

'No.' He took a paper from the top of the pile on his desk. 'I've started to hear back from those letters I wrote, about missing girls from good families. Read this.'

Simonetta Hopkins from Ilkley. Five years old, vanished eighteen months earlier, no trace ever found. No other girl taken with her. A description, but that would be no use with her body mouldering in the ground.

'There'll be more,' Simon said.

'No doubt about it. We're going to be digging that ground for a while. I've had volunteers offering to help. Men with daughters of their own.'

He was happy to leave it all with the constable. Simon had done his job. He'd returned Harriet to her parents. Now he needed to protect himself and Rosie, to find Holcomb's documents and discover what was so dark it meant blows and talk of suits for slander.

Rosie was out, tracking down the woman she'd tried to find yesterday. Simon buttered bread and thought where he might go next. There was still the question of the man who'd followed Sophie Jackson, the servant who stolen the papers. It had to be his body that had been found with hers. But he'd never been identified. Put a name to the man and he might have a direction to follow.

As Simon turned on to Briggate, he heard a shout. Porter, red-faced as he hurried along, trying to dodge between people on the pavement. People turned to watch.

He grabbed Simon's arm and led him into the cramped dark tunnel leading to a court, panting as he caught his breath.

'We found them.' No need to say who. The man's face should have been blazing with triumph. Instead, he looked . . . baffled.

'Where?' It had to be good news, surely.

The man took a long breath before he answered. 'In the house—'

'What?' They'd searched the entire place, from attic to cellars. It was empty, Wise and Carpenter vanished in a panic.

'They were laid on their beds, wrists tied behind their back, throats very neatly slashed. One of the men decided to take another look inside this morning, then came haring back here like the devil was on his heels. I'm going to take a look. Do you want to come?'

He was drawn. No denying that. Any thief-taker worth his salt would be. But he needed to attend to other business.

'I'll leave that for you. The question is who'd want to kill them.'

'Someone who wanted to make sure they never had chance to talk and give us some more names.'

'Wise must have run to one of them, expecting help.'

'He got cold comfort, then. Leaving them like that has to be a message.'

'I'm sure it is,' Simon agreed. 'Who for, though?'

The news rippled quickly around Leeds. Jane heard a garbled version as she shopped at the market, buying carrots, onions, parsnips and potatoes to make a stew. Enough fragments of gossip flew from mouth to mouth for her to piece together three different versions of the tale. All with the same ending: the pair of child snatchers has been found in their home, bound, throats cut, and good riddance to them.

She thought of the door opening, a man standing and firing his fowling piece. She could never mourn men like that. They'd received the end they deserved; she wished she'd killed them herself. But Rosie had been right. Let someone else feel the law after them.

From the corner of her eye she caught a glimpse of a girl who could have been Sally in her new cloak, going down Wood Street with a child scurrying after her. No matter, Jane thought with a smile. No matter at all. Now she needed to buy some mutton, then home and start cooking.

Wherever Simon went, talk about the dead men raced before him. People asked him questions, as if he might have the answers. He smiled, told them to talk to the constable and started with his questions about another corpse.

Finally, close to six, long after lanterns had been lit and people blew on their palms to keep themselves warm, he sat in a beershop that had no name, just the far side of Timble Bridge. The man he was seeking should arrive soon, just as he did every day.

The door opened. He seemed to slide in, more shadow than anything solid, going to the far side of the room, hidden from the firelight. But when he saw Simon approach, the man made no move to leave.

'I wondered when you'd come around.'

'Did you?' Simon asked in surprise. 'I'm only here because I'm out of other ideas.'

Robert Jordan smiled. He was a man who preferred to stay clear of attention, to duck away from the light. He was earnest and intelligent, a young man who earned his money in a radical bookshop selling the magazines and the newspapers. But in his other life he knew the people behind the words, the ones who risked arrest under the Six Acts that Parliament had passed to quell protest. The men and women who risked the same sentence of transportation that Holcomb's father had given the machine breakers.

'I'll give you a start,' Jordan told him. 'We know about the papers that were taken from Captain Holcomb. Thomas Deacon contacted me before he was murdered.' He held up a finger. 'In case you were going to ask, no, we had nothing to do with that.'

'We?'

'Come on, I know you're not a fool,' Jordan told him with a small, frustrated sigh. He ran a finger between his neck and a stock grubby with soot. 'Let's not pretend you need it all spelled out. Call it groups with an interest in justice and leave it at that. Deacon knew those documents included a great deal the magistrate had written about his corrupt decisions and bending the law. He offered to sell them to us. The problem is, we don't have the money he was asking. I told him so. The next thing I knew, someone said he was dead. I went to look. His woman and the papers had gone.'

'You went into their room?'

'Surprised, Mr Westow?' Jordan grinned. 'Quite a few people pass us information. That was how we spotted Miss Jackson. One of our people offered to follow her.'

'A night in an abandoned building. He never tried to take the bundle.'

The man pursed his lips and nodded thoughtfully. 'You had someone there, too, did you? Theft isn't our way. He saw Sophie pass over the papers, then he followed her all day. She seemed to be searching for someone, but we don't know who.' He stared at

Simon. 'The next morning, he and Miss Jackson were found. I've no idea who did it or why.'

'Why were you following her?'

'To keep her and the papers safe.'

'Now she's in the ground and the papers have gone, along with the woman who was looking after them,' Simon said as the man gave a slow nod. 'Your man, what was his name?'

'Tim Loftus.' A hesitation, then regret. 'He'd become a good friend. He was no fighter.'

'You've no idea at all who's behind any of these killings?'

'For a while I suspected Captain Holcomb—'

Simon shook his head. 'He'd have taken the papers and been done with it.'

'—but I wasn't convinced. I had a feeling we weren't the only people Mr Deacon had contacted.'

'People who could blackmail Holcomb?'

'Probably. Deacon might have believed he could sell them the papers and they'd do all the work. Does that answer your questions, Mr Westow?'

'For now.' He started to rise, then sat again. 'What did you intend to do with the information?'

'Publish it. The magistrate transported Deacon's uncle. Were you aware of that?'

'I was. I understand he died on the voyage.'

'Thomas Deacon wanted revenge. But I suspect he craved money more.'

That sounded like the young man who'd been described to him.

'Now we have three dead, a missing woman, and the documents could be anywhere. Are you looking?'

Jordan cocked his head. 'Listening for any word.' He narrowed his eyes. 'I was told you'd stopped working for Captain Holcomb.'

'I did. I have my own reasons for wanting to find things out now.'

Jordan gave a short laugh. 'You know, you've done a very fine job of getting me to talk and saying little yourself, Mr Westow.'

He smiled. 'That's how it's going to have to stay. Some things I want to keep quiet.'

'If you find the papers, what will you do with them?'

'You can have them.' Simon frowned. 'Maybe not all; it depends what's in there.'

Jordan's eyes narrowed, suspicious. 'Why? Holcomb would pay for their return.'

'I daresay.' He stood again and placed the hat on his head. 'I told you: I have my own reasons, and I'd prefer you didn't say anything about this conversation. Goodnight to you.'

The third corpse had a name now. That was some small consolation. Maybe the Radicals had spirited his body away for a proper burial. Every soul deserved to go into the ground carrying their own name. A stupid superstition – why would the dead care? – but curiously comforting.

Time to go home and see what Rosie had learned. The confrontation wouldn't have stopped her, not even caused her to pause.

'I found the woman,' Rosie said as they sat at the kitchen table. He'd played two games of draughts with the boys, making sure they each won, then finished with a story about a giant. How long before they grew too old for that? Every day, it seemed, they were larger and stronger.

'What did she have to say?' Simon asked. 'Is . . .?'

'Janet Bristol is still alive. That's about the only thing she *would* tell me. Nobody has her.'

Simon felt a rush of relief. 'Some good news, at least.' He'd be dreading another death in all this. 'This woman knows where she is?'

'Yes, but she's not saying. I explained who I was, that I'd talked to Janet at South Market. I said I'd like to see her. She told me to come back tomorrow.'

'Does she still have the papers?'

'"What papers?" That was her answer. Looked at me with a blank expression. She has us over a barrel, Simon.'

He pressed his lips together. This was out of their control.

'We don't have any choice, then. Go and see her tomorrow and see what happens. Nobody followed you?'

'I made sure of that.'

He had little doubt; Rosie would be on her guard. 'She'll be seeing Janet Bristol. Let's hope the woman's willing to talk to us.'

TWENTY-FIVE

I t was a night she couldn't settle to the hearth or the page, a night when all the demons decided to taunt her. After Mrs Shields had settled down to her rest, Jane laced up her boots and put on her cloak. She'd walk the devils away from her thoughts.

No destination, simply wherever her feet carried her. Fearn's Island. The ferry. Back along the Calls with its warehouses. Over the bridge, into Hunslet then out as far as Thwaite's mill, back along the road and over into Holbeck, wandering the streets. She recognized the locked yard where the clothes seller kept her cart.

As she moved, from the corner of her eye she glimpsed a figure slipping through the darkness. Jane stood completely still, curious, invisible in the night with the hood covering her hair. She watched as he climbed over the fence, into the yard in a moment. Curious, and very agile. Soon enough he was back, hands empty. He hadn't found whatever he wanted to steal.

The man was cautious, as if he was expecting to have someone behind him. Halting, circling back on himself to make sure no one was there. That was enough to raise her suspicions. This seemed like a gift, somehow. Maybe it had nothing to do with the clothes seller or the documents, but it gave her a focus. Her devils had been sent packing.

She wasn't going to let him evade her as he made his way to one of the new terraces rising up by the pottery on Jack Lane. A tap on the door, a short wait for someone to open up, then he was inside.

She remained. This wasn't his home, not if he had to knock for entry; he'd be leaving again. Five minutes later he was back outside, heading up Meadow Lane with brisk strides that rang off the paving stones, walking like a man without worries.

Over Leeds Bridge, and into the town. The man strode along the small ginnel and to the Pack Horse. Jane had to make a decision. He could easily slip out through the yard at the back. But if she stood there she wouldn't see most people coming and going.

A quiet spot across Briggate instead. Most passed without noticing her. A few men offered her money. She ignored them. One drunk became insistent, but hurried off as soon as she showed him her knife.

Not to be noticed; that was the key. For eyes to pass over her as if she was part of the building.

Almost an hour later he emerged with someone else. Not enough light to see the face, but she thought she recognized the second man's walk. Everyone moved in a slightly different way, a signature they could never disguise. Not familiar enough to place him, though.

Down the street, then into Hirst's Yard. She couldn't follow there, they'd see her in an instant. Should she wait or would she be wasting her time? There were houses and rooms in the yard. It was growing late. Jane decided on home. Warmth and sleep. The walk had done its job, and much more.

Near the top of Briggate, past the tumbledown building of Middle Row, up close to the market cross, she sensed someone close and spun round, knife ready.

Sally.

'I saw you standing outside the Pack Horse,' she said.

'I'm done for the night.' Jane looked at the girl and saw the loneliness that touched her face. 'Why are you out?'

'I needed some company. People around me.'

As Jane began to walk, Sally fell into step, along to the crest of the Head Row. Still with a slight limp as she moved, the hand against her side. A slight movement in a doorway caught the girl's eye. A pair of children, huddled together under some rags.

Sally knelt, talking softly to them, her voice filled with concern. For a moment, Jane stared, then turned away, too weary to linger when it was only a few more yards to her bed.

Her thoughts were filled with what she'd seen, wondering what it all meant. She wasn't paying attention.

They were waiting in the entrance to Green Dragon Yard. Two of them, grabbing hold of her before she had chance to hurt them. Her own fault. She wasn't ready. Jane heard her knife clatter on the stones, then a sudden, sharp blow to the face stunned her and forced her off-balance. For a second she tasted blood in her mouth. Then a fist hit her again and there was only blackness.

Jane blinked. Very slowly, she tried to move her head from side to side. Sharp pain seared through her. Everything was blurred, watery,

not a thing clear in the world. Stop. Take your time. Use your brain.
Don't panic. Work it out. She began to remember, the tiny fragments
knitting together in her memory. The men. Sour breath. Pain.

She tried to move. To stand. Couldn't. Something was stopping
her.

Think.

Slow, even breathing as she tried to steady her mind. To make
sense of what was happening.

Where was she?

She turned her head. Small movements, but each one enough to
send pain lancing through her skull.

A room. A lantern hung from the ceiling. There was a bare table
in front of her. She tried to reach out for it. Impossible.

Another moment, pausing to gather her thoughts. She looked
down, eyes fogging for a second; panic as she felt she might pass
out again. Small, quiet breaths until her head cleared. She was sitting
on a hard chair in a room, with a table in front of her. That was
something. A start.

Her wrists were tied to the arms of the chair. Ankles bound to
the chair legs.

Stay quiet. Don't shout. That would only bring someone.

Jane drew together all the shards of her strength. Quietly, she
began to strain against the bonds. Testing the knots and the
firmness.

Everything was tight. No hope of escape. The ropes rubbed against
her skin. But the rawness, the pain of it was good. It made her come
alive. Broke through the bolts of agony that flared inside.

Behind her, a door opened. She tensed as she felt cold air on her
neck. Then something crashed against her head and there was
nothing.

When she came to, she saw two of everything. All she could do
was close her eyes again, not sure how long had passed before she
could slowly open them once more. A deep, throbbing pain shot
through her skull where she'd been hit.

A man was standing, watching her. She raised her head, trying
to see his face, but the image kept slipping and shifting. Did she
know him? She wasn't sure. He was staring at her with no mercy
in his eyes.

'Billy Wild was my brother,' he said. His gaze never wavered.
'You remember him?'

One of the pair who snatched Emma and Harriet. The man who'd told then where to find the girl, once they forced the truth from them.

'Do you?'

Jane felt herself breathe, the rise and fall of her chest. She tried to hold his look, but she couldn't. He slid in and out of focus. Think, she told herself. She needed to think. How could he have known she was responsible for his brother's death?

She would never allow him to see her fear. He could wonder. A sudden thought: did they have Sally, too?

She felt so, so tired. She couldn't keep her eyes open. The noises inside her head were drowning the world, everything kept moving away. She felt unmoored.

She sensed his words rather than heard them. 'You won't be leaving until I've finished with you.'

Then there was just emptiness.

Jane lurched forward as she came to, straining again the ropes.

'You're in time for the fun,' he said, as he placed a battered leather bag on the table and took out a pair of metal shears.

'See them? Of course you do.'

Her vision was blurred. Everything wavered. He'd planned all this. Her heart was beating hard. He wanted her to suffer.

She passed out again, and the world turned upside down as she was unable to hold on. By the time she blinked it all back into shape, he was forcing the little finger on her left hand back.

Slowly, deliberate. Relishing his power, the way each drop of pain flowed through her body.

She didn't have the strength to fight it. Jane let the blackness carry her away once more.

Somewhere far off, Jane heard the sharp click of metal. Slowly, she stirred. She knew what he'd done and tried to gather in her chest. She opened her mouth but he put his hand over it, letting her gag from the smell of grease and dirt on his skin.

Cold. She began to shiver. The man took hold of her hair and tugged her hair back, pushing an old kerchief into her mouth to stifle her.

'We're nowhere near done yet. We have all night ahead of us, and I'm going to enjoy every minute of it.'

Behind her, she heard the door close. Just the silence of the room now. Jane stared at her left hand. At the stump of her little finger.

She tried to move her tongue, to push the rag out of her mouth, but he'd forced it in too tight. But trying was something. It stopped her feeling the agony, the roiling in her stomach. The hopelessness in her heart.

She turned her wrists, seeing if she could loosen the ropes. No. Her gaze shifted around the room. Was there any way to escape? She had to stop this.

He'd be back soon. What then? People lost fingers every day in the factories and the mills. It wasn't that rare. They lost hands, arms. Dodson the beggar had lost a leg. They survived.

But Billy Wild's brother wanted everything. He was never going to let her leave this place alive.

Think.

Her head dropped forward. He'd stolen her will when he took her flesh.

TWENTY-SIX

S imon heard the sound of feet running off into the night. One of the bastards had escaped. The other had his back against a wall, hands raised, disarmed. He'd already pissed himself as he stood there, terrified. Sally stood guard over him, blade in her hand and murder in her eyes.

He reached for the handle of the door in front of him, turning it cautiously as he gripped his knife. The lantern swayed gently on its hook, sending strange shadows swirling around the room.

He called her name. Jane didn't stir and he felt a chill in his blood as he reached out to touch her neck. A strong pulse. She'd passed out.

Simon sliced through the ropes. He lifted her left hand and saw the remains of her finger. Christ. The shears sat on the table, still smeared with blood. He gathered her up, no weight to her at all, just the way he'd lifted Harriet Caldwell. Jane began to stir and pull away from her.

'It's me. You're safe now. It's all over.'

He'd been in bed, sleeping when Rosie shook him awake.

'Someone's at the door.'

He opened his eyes, mind still clouded, and heard the pounding. Constant, hard. Urgent. Simon held the knife by his side as he turned the key in the lock.

Sally. Wild-eyed, panicked.

'They've got her. We were walking. I stopped. She turned a corner and I heard her knife fall. Two men. They had her. I followed them.' A torrent of words. Her hand tugged at his sleeve and she turned to leave. 'Come on. Now. Please.'

He followed her, running through the darkness, through streets, courts, until she stopped in front of a house.

'This is it,' she whispered.

Nothing to distinguish it.

'Are you certain?' he asked, and in the small light of the moon he believed her. Simon stood back, raised his leg and brought his boot down on the lock. Wood shattered and splintered as the door flew back.

He was inside, the girl right behind him. A man, standing and smoking. Another already disappearing towards the back. Follow him? No. If Jane was here, she was going to need help.

The man threw down his knife and lifted his arms in surrender.

'Watch him,' Simon told her.

'I will.'

Sally's eyes moved to them.

'What did they do?'

'Cut off her little finger.'

The girl's body tensed; Simon expected her to start attacking the man. Instead, she asked: 'What should I do with him?'

His thoughts rushed one after the other. 'Find out who they are. What they wanted.'

A nod. 'After that?'

She made it sound so easy. She'd probably make sure it was. 'Don't kill him.'

'Why not?'

'Ask yourself if it's worth risking the noose. That's the reason.'

He carried Jane out into the night.

Where could he take her? Not back to Mrs Shields. Not when she was like this. The old woman didn't need the scare of a knock on the door in the middle of the night. He had to take her home; Rosie would tend her. That finger was going to need care. Jane was still only half-conscious. Delirious. Muttering so softly that he couldn't hear the words.

By the time he reached Swinegate he was starting to feel her weight. His shoulders ached and muscles complained. Simon hurried into the house, pushed the door closed behind him and carried her up to the attic.

'What happened?' Rosie asked, kneeling by the bed. He told the little he'd been able to work out from what he'd seen. Jane was coming to, trying to pull her hand away as Rosie examined it.

She stroked the young woman's face. 'You're with us now. It's Rosie and Simon. It's over.' Rosie turned to her husband. 'Bring me a bowl of water and a towel.' A moment's thought. 'One of those clean rags from the dresser, too. She's going to need a bandage on this.'

As Rosie worked, Jane blinked her eyes and began to talk. Halting, jumbled sentences as she tried to fit things together, finding some order in it for herself as well as Simon. Being hit in Green Dragon Yard. Trying to free herself from the ropes in the room.

No mention of being terrified. But she'd never admit to that.

'He said he was Billy Wild's brother.'

Simon was stunned. How could anyone have known Jane had been involved in Wild's death? They'd been careful. Simon would swear that nobody had seen them go into the house and overpower the two men.

In a sudden panic, Jane tried to sit up. With gentle hands, Rosie eased her back down.

'You need to rest.'

'Mrs Shields . . .'

'As soon as it's light.' Very lightly, he squeezed her right hand. Her knife hand. At least the man hadn't hurt that. 'Better than waking her now.'

'Yes,' she said as her voice began to waver. 'Yes. I'll go home early.'

Jane's eyes were beginning to close. Rosie tucked the blanket around her.

'At least it's a clean cut,' she said when they were in the kitchen. 'I've washed it, but Catherine Shields will have some ointments. She'll heal.' A sigh. 'What about this man?'

'We'll find him. There were two of them. I left Sally to question the other one.'

'You know Jane's going to want him for herself.'

As soon as she was able, she'd start hunting. He'd help, and this time he wouldn't try to hold her back.

His mind was churning too fast, too deep for him to sleep. Instead, he tugged on his greatcoat again and began to walk.

First, where the man had held Jane. Empty now; only the tools and bag remained. Sally had kept her word; no bodies. He wandered over by Green Dragon Yard, peering through the hole in the wall to see if any lights were burning in the small house. All dark. Good, Mrs Shields was asleep.

From there, he drifted around and about, seeing what rose from his mind.

Wise and Carpenter. They'd become the constable's business and Simon knew he was well clear of it. People had warned him it was dangerous. They'd been right.

The clothes seller, Janet Bristol . . . he had to hope she'd be willing to see Rosie, and that his wife could persuade her to give up the documents. It was the only way Sophie Jackson would ever see justice.

He knew he was trying to balance too many things. Simon was trying to draw all his thoughts into some kind of order when he sensed someone close and moved into a crouch, pulling the knife from his sleeve.

Sally.

'How is she?'

'Sleeping. You should be, too.'

'Sometimes I can't,' she said. 'Nights when the memories come. Walking helps keep them away.'

She was another one who'd never reveal much about herself. Like Jane, she'd developed a shell, her armour.

'What did he tell you?'

'Someone recognized Jane when she was watching the house where Wild and the other man were living. Seems he never noticed me.'

'He told Wild's brother?'

She nodded. 'His name's Paul. He wants to pay her back. Kill her piece by piece. It's become . . .'

'An obsession?'

'He has to do it. For his brother.'

'What about the other man?'

Sally looked into his face, showing no expression. 'He was alive when I left him. Nobody saw me go.'

She worded that very carefully, Simon thought. But he had no desire to learn more.

They walked in silence, over the river, to South Market and back. As they reached Duncan Street she turned to follow the road.

'Thank you,' he said as she left. If she hadn't come for him . . . he wouldn't let his thoughts dwell on that. Not in the empty hours when small imaginings could grow into stark nightmares.

The watch were out, patrolling in pairs. One moved towards him, but his companion drew him back with a pair of quiet words and a friendly nod towards Simon. Leeds was calm. On the surface.

No talk of Jane or anyone named Wild at the coffee cart. The bodies of Wise and Carpenter and the discovery of the graves still gave them plenty to chatter about as they drank. The night had chilled him, and the hot liquid warmed his belly.

At home, Jane was sitting in the kitchen. Her left hand lay flat on the table, the little finger with its dressing and bandage. She gazed at it, lifting her head as he entered. But she seemed lost somewhere and he wondered if she saw him.

The pain had woken her. Not physical; that had passed quickly; it was little more than an ache now. But the memory. Of shame. Of being beaten. She was shivering, bitterly cold even under the blanket. Her head was full of panic.

As soon as she closed her eyes, the feelings crowded and clawed at her until her eyes snapped open again. The man was going to kill her and she was powerless to stop him. All her fault. She'd given them the opportunity when she lowered her guard for a moment. Her wrists were rubbed bloody, trying to free herself from the ropes. She'd always carry the rancid taste of the gag in her mouth.

Sleep would be a torment for a long time.

'Before . . .' she began, as Simon settled across from her.

'Before?'

'I was out walking . . .' She told him about the man she'd followed from the locked yard in Holbeck. It seemed to have happened to someone else, as if she was recounting a hazy tale she'd heard. As she finished, she glanced through the window. A low band of daylight lay along the horizon. Jane began to rise.

'You said his name.' She lifted her hand. 'The one who did it.'

'Paul Wild. The one who was with him told Sally.'

She'd never be able to forget it. Jane looked around the room, then into Simon's face. 'Thank you.'

'Sally heard them take you. She followed them and fetched me.'

She pressed her lips together and gave a small nod. A few seconds later she was out in the day, feeling the cold pressing against her face as she walked along Swinegate.

Mrs Shields had only been up for a few minutes. Dressed, coal on the fire starting to throw out some heat. But she hadn't brushed her hair yet, pale grey wisps that fluttered around her head.

'Here you are.' She bustled through from the kitchen, smiling, relieved. 'I was worried when you . . .' The words tailed to silence as she saw the bandaged hand. 'Oh child, child.'

She inspected everything and rubbed on an ointment that stung. Another for Jane's bloody wrists.

'That will help everything heal quickly and properly,' the old woman said. She mixed up a tonic for Jane to drink, a lingering taste of summer berries to try and rinse the ugliness from her mouth. But the hatred remained inside. She wanted to keep it there, to hold it in her belly. To let it build. She needed to feel it. The constant reminder. It wouldn't vanish until she found Paul Wild.

'Porridge.' The old woman held a bowl in her hands. She ate without thinking, suddenly aware that Mrs Shields was staring at her.

'Child, this life is going to kill you.'

'No,' Jane answered, 'it won't. I promise.'

In that moment, at least, she was certain of it. It couldn't. Not yet. She had to finish this.

The boys were busy with their tutor. Rosie had gone to seek out Janet Bristol's friend, hoping for good news.

In the courthouse, Constable Porter cupped his chin in his hands.

'I've heard from more towns about girls who went missing and were never found. Two of them, both close enough to have ended up with Wise.' He took a breath and wiped tears from his cheeks. 'For the love of God, Westow, how could someone do that?'

'I wish I knew.'

'If he were here . . .' He balled one hand into a fist and opened it again. 'The men are out at the property again, digging. Can you believe there's a part of me that hopes they don't find anything? If there's nothing, it means those other girls might still be alive somewhere.'

His eyes showed that he knew the truth: everything he said was wishful thinking.

'Wise and Carpenter,' Simon said. 'Why take them back to the house?'

'I've no idea. The people who did it are never going to tell us, are they?'

'Then what are you going to do?'

'What I can. Pass the word all around. People are outraged. Let's see if that sparks anything. There must be servants who know. Maybe one of them will be willing to talk.'

'Perhaps.'

'Help us if you like. You're the one who pulled all this into the light.'

Simon shook his head. 'Too much on my own plate.'

Holcomb, that dangling threat of a lawsuit, the possibility of violence. Maybe justice for Sophie Jackson. The girl had been a fool, but she'd done it for love. She deserved better than death.

'Then you can wish me well, Westow. God knows, I'd rather have an honest crime.'

'Good luck to you.' He needed to pursue the man Jane had spotted breaking into the yard with the clothes seller's cart. The one who ended the night in Hirst's Court. That man had a story Simon wanted to hear.

TWENTY-SEVEN

Jane wanted to settle. Her body was exhausted. But her thoughts kept spinning, refusing to slow down. She picked up *Ivanhoe* and tried to read. It might calm her mind. She put the book down again after she'd read the same page four times and couldn't recall a single word. Chivalry and honour didn't feel as if they had a place in her world. She was drained, wearier than she'd ever felt, but terrified of the dreams that would appear if she managed to sleep.

Hunting. That was the only thing that could make her feel better.

She was ready to leave, desperate to start, to stop the thoughts creeping and the memory of the night before piercing her when the old woman inspected her and said, 'Wait.'

Jane heard her rummage through the chest at the foot of her bed. When she returned, she had a day dress and two heavy petticoats draped over her arm.

Her tiny fingers plucked at Jane's sleeve. 'Just look at yourself. That thing you're wearing is only fit for rags. There's blood all over it.' She glanced down, seeing the smears across the fabric. 'If you're determined to go out, at least put this on. I used to wear it. It was made by a very good seamstress. Fine wool, I remember selecting it. There are years left in it yet.'

'But you're smaller than me. It's never going to fit.'

That sweet smile. 'Believe it or not, I used to be as tall as you, child. I've shrunk. We all do as we grow older.' Her eyes shone. 'Who knows, maybe I'll become tinier and tinier until there's nothing left at all and I disappear. But you can get plenty of wear out of this. It's cold out; the petticoats will keep you warmer, too.'

Jane owned a good gown, one she'd had made in some moment of madness. But she'd never wear it for work. This, though . . . it was plain brown. No trimmings. All very ordinary as she gazed in the mirror. It smelled of rosemary and lavender, soft, comforting scents.

She did feel warmer as she strode down Briggate, with the two thick petticoats rustling against her legs and the old green cloak on top. For a few minutes as she put on the clothes and adjusted them, she managed to forget everything that had happened. That was something. Her fingertips stroked the gold ring Mrs Shields had given her long ago to keep her safe. It hadn't worked last night. Or maybe it had. She'd been found. She was alive, she'd only lost a single finger. That was something.

No knife. She'd lost it when they grabbed her. She tightened her right hand, imagining a grip on the hilt. She'd need to buy another and hone the blade until it was sharp enough to satisfy her. She was going to use it very soon.

Paul Wild. She was going to find him. But she wanted him to know she was looking, to live with that fear until it was time.

She knew Sally would come. Soon enough the girl appeared out of the shadows on Vicar Lane, moving like a wraith. Jane held up her hand. Mrs Shields had rubbed on more ointment and insisted on a fresh bandage.

'Can you still feel it?'

'Yes.' She moved her fingers. In her mind, the missing one waved with the rest of them. 'You saved my life.' She watched the girl shrug, as if it had been nothing. 'Thank you. He wanted to kill me.'

'He ran off as soon as we arrived.'

'I'm going to find him.'

'I can help you.' She reached under her cloak and produced Jane's knife. 'You'll want this.'

'Yes.' Relief as she caressed the handle, the shape so familiar and comforting. She slid the flat of the blade across her palm, calmed by the chill of the steel. With this she possessed some power again. It completed her. 'Thank you,' she repeated. 'Have you had anything to eat yet?'

Kate the pie-seller frowned, craving details. Jane shook her head. The woman thrived on gossip, but she simply wanted to try and forget. Memories had never been a friend to her.

She couldn't describe Paul Wild. He'd been no more than two feet from her, staring into her face, but she couldn't remember him. Only a pair of dark, bitter eyes . . . the rest was a blur in her head.

Sally went to start the wild children looking for the man, happy to have something to fill her time. Jane walked. Even the music of Davy Cassidy's fiddle couldn't soothe her. A minute, a coin in his cup and she moved on.

'Paul Wild,' she said to Dodson as he stood, propped up by his crutch. 'Do you know the name?'

He shook his head. 'I heard someone called Wild died in a fire. Was that him?'

'His brother.'

He pressed his lips together. 'Why are you looking for him?'

She held up her hand with its bandaged remains of the little finger. Dodson was missing a leg, shot away during the war with Napoleon. He'd understand.

'This.'

A slow nod. 'I've never heard of him at all. What does he look like?'

'I wish I knew.' She placed a coin in his cup. 'It doesn't matter. I'll find him.'

'I've no doubt you will. Something you should know. About the finger.'

'What?' she asked.

'You're going to find times when you'll believe it's there, that you only imagined it all.' His face fell. 'But it's always gone. Just something in your mind trying to put things back to the way they were.' He paused, trying to find the words. 'To try and make all the parts fit the way God intended.'

Another coin and Jane wandered off, hands hidden under the cloak, a tight grip on her knife. She'd never be caught unawares again. There were others she could ask about Paul Wild. Time to find them.

Most of the night watch were out digging around Wise's house. Only the old ones had been left in Leeds, a presence that would never manage to keep order if trouble arrived. Richard Fetterman had to be close to seventy, a man who ambled around slowly and saw the town with rheumy eyes. But he'd been the watchman covering lower Briggate for the better part of two decades. He knew every cobble, each paving stone.

Simon found him outside the Old George, standing and pressing fingertips against the small of his back.

'Tired, Dick?'

The man peered, trying to fix Simon in his gaze and his mind.

'Never gets any easier,' he replied, watching his breath bloom as he spoke. 'Especially with this cold. It does for my joints.'

'I don't suppose Porter pays you enough.'

'Grudges the little he hands over, more like. Even when he knows there's nobody knows round here like me.'

Simon smiled. 'That's why I wanted to talk to you.'

Fetterman listened while he told what he knew of the man who'd gone into Hirst's Court.

'Someone used to being followed,' he added.

That made the old man laugh his way into a damp wheeze, showing off his yellow teeth. 'Oh, he's in Hirst's Court, right enough. The place towards the back with the dirty white door. Name of Jack. Surname changes, depending who's after him. Last I heard, it was Dyson.'

'Who does he work for?'

'Whoever pays him. Not picky. Never been able to catch him with anything stolen.' He tapped the side of his head. 'He's a sly lad.'

'Young?' Simon asked.

'Seems it to me, but he's been doing this for a few years,' Fetterman told him.

'What about friends? Does he have many?'

A wide grin. 'Anyone who'll stand him a drink. If you want him, he's probably at home now. His lordship rarely rises before noon.'

A shiny silver sixpence, but the man had earned it.

Simon checked his knives and marched down the court towards the grubby white door. Banging his fist against the wood, rattling the handle and shouting the man's name loud enough to wake the dead.

He drew one of the knives as he heard the bolt being drawn back, then barged against the door as it began to open. The man inside stumbled back, flailing as he tried to keep his footing. Too late. Simon slammed the door behind him.

'Hello, Jack Dyson. You can answer a few questions for me.'

'He stared at me like I'd climbed up from hell.' Simon laughed and Rosie grinned. 'I terrified him, appearing like that. He thought I was there to drag him back to the devil.'

'What did he have to say?'

'Admitted he'd been in the yard and Janet Bristol's house but didn't discover any documents. He couldn't understand how I'd found him.' He grinned. 'No need to tell him it was Jane.'

'Who paid him to do it?'

'He claims it was someone who called himself Mason.' He ran his tongue over his lips. 'Here's where it becomes interesting. Dyson thought the man was a soldier. Something about the way he spoke and carried himself. But from the description, it might have been one of the pair who came after us. Not the one in charge; the other one, the man who thought he could use his fists.'

'Really?' Her eyes widened and she rubbed the bruise that still showed on her face.

'It makes me wonder if he might not have something going on his own account, a chance to make some quick money. This man Mason told Dyson how to contact him if the search paid off. We could leave a note and arrange to meet him . . .'

Rosie's eyes began to sparkle with anticipation. 'He might not enjoy that.'

'No,' he agreed. 'But you would.'

'Oh, yes. I'd like that very much. Now, do you want to hear what Janet Bristol's friend said to me?'

Simon used his fingertips to count in the darkness, feeling the roughness of each stone in the wall. The small gap was exactly where Dyson had promised; the man hadn't been lying. He folded the note and pushed it deep out of the weather. He'd made certain nobody had spotted him. Mason would find it in the morning. He'd be looking, Simon had little doubt of that.

Now he had to hope that the man's greed was strong enough to put himself in a trap.

Set back from the other side of the road, Chapeltown barracks was still lively with noise, the clatter and tumult that happened when men were together. As he walked back through the night to Leeds, he saw that someone had turned part of their home into an alehouse for the soldiers. Doing good business from all the laughter inside.

'Done?' Rosie asked as he settled next to her in bed.

'Now we have to be prepared for him.' He'd looked in on the boys, the way he did whenever he was out at night. Hearing their soft, even breathing was a comfort. Something stable in the world. What did they make of their father's work? he wondered. They understood it, he'd taken care to explain it to them. Perhaps it just seemed normal to them, the way other children might accept a father who went off to work as a clerk or a machine operative every day.

Maybe.

He pulled his wife close and kissed her.

'The friend's name is Caroline,' Rosie had told him earlier. 'She talked to Janet. She remembered me.'

'In a good way?'

'It must have been. She was willing to let me know where she's been hiding.'

He sat up straight, giving her all his attention. A sly smiled played around her mouth and her eyes sparkled.

'Go on.'

'In the house next door to hers. Apparently it's been empty for months, and the people who lived there had given her a key.'

Very clever. Close enough to see who came around. Safe, too; no one would think to search there. Janet Bristol had a clear head on her shoulders.

'Well,' he said.

'She's willing to see me in the morning. She trusts me that far.'

'You've done a good job.'

Rosie shook her head. 'Janet has. She's cannier than the rest of us. I'll take her some food. A little tea. She probably needs it.'

'What about the papers? Did you ask again?'

'No point. Nothing's likely to happen before morning.'

Waiting. Always so much waiting.

The day seemed to slip away from her. Twice Jane needed to find somewhere to sit for a few minutes, to stop her mind from racing. She looked down at the hand again; her eyes strayed there every few minutes. Wild had taken a part of her and done it with pleasure. He'd have taken everything if he'd had time, cutting her life away piece by piece.

Nobody claimed to know him, but she'd passed the word, anyway. *Tell him I'm coming for him.* She wanted him scared, looking over his shoulder every moment, expecting her. He might run, leave Leeds. But she believed he'd stay. He was tied to her now, whether he liked it or not.

'How is it?' There was concern in Sally's voice. Jane had felt her close by, but she didn't raise her head. Too tired, yet the thoughts weren't going to allow her any peace.

This life is going to kill you. Mrs Shields's words, and maybe she was right. But she'd returned to it. Now, though, there might always be a sliver of fear to hold her back, to make her hesitate. She had to discover whether she could still trust herself.

'I'll be all right.' She stood. 'Found anything?'

'Not yet.'

'I'll track him down.' She began to walk, nodding towards Sally's leg. Hardly limping at all today.

'Almost better. My side still hurts. If I cough I can feel it right through me.'

'Mrs Shields says broken ribs take weeks to heal. At least you have a room.' Better than having to live outside in the cold and the damp.

Jane sensed the hesitation before the girl asked the question on her mind: 'I have to find work. The rent you paid has almost run out. Do you and Simon need someone else?'

'I don't know.' When it was over, the job done . . . it would be time to leave all this again, to try and forget. If she was still alive. Sally could be an ideal replacement. She was fearless. She'd never hesitate. She could be ruthless. Able to follow. Small enough not to be noticed. All the things the work demanded.

'I went to a mill to ask about a job. Someone told me they were looking for people. But the man said I'm still a child so I'd make less money. It wouldn't be enough for the room and food.'

Jane had seen the way the little ones on the street followed the girl and trusted her. She looked after them. If she had her letters and her numbers, Sally would make a good teacher. But she'd already said she didn't see any point in learning. Jane had been like that, too. Long ago, in another life.

'I'll talk to Simon.' She couldn't promise more than that. It was his decision. Jane could say she was still willing to work on bigger cases. Maybe he'd see the advantage in it. The girl would need some training, but she had the boys and the girls on the streets willing to help in a way Jane had never managed.

'You mean it?'

'I do.' The girl had saved her life. She could do nothing less. 'Now we need to make sure Paul Wild knows the hunt is after him. What about that other man who was with him?'

Sally shook her head. 'He's gone.'

'Gone where?'

'Nobody's ever going to see his face again.' As Jane opened her mouth, the girl quickly added, 'I didn't kill him. He was still breathing.'

No need to ask what she'd done.

'I'll talk to some of the whores,' Jane said. 'They're good at passing things on.'

'What about Simon? Can he help?'

'This is mine.' Her voice was hard.

'I'll do what I can. I told you that.'

'Go around the homeless. Talk to them. Get everyone passing the word. I want Wild to know I'm coming.'

Night had grown around her by the time Jane finished talking to the women on Briggate. Her body was drained, thoughts finally starting to slow. But she stayed alert as she walked home. Gripping the knife tight in her good right hand. The hand that was whole.

Jane hesitated, breathing deeply before she turned the corner into Green Dragon Yard. Nobody waiting for her this time. Her heart thumped as she passed through the hole in the wall that led to home.

Home.

Tonight she would be able to rest. The demons could come. The man's leer, the stink of his breath. Her powerlessness. She'd face them down and win her sleep.

TWENTY-EIGHT

S imon was brushing down his coat, his weekly cleaning of the stains and the dust and making it look presentable as the boys disappeared into the front room to start their lessons with the tutor. A knock on the door.

Lawyer Pollard, frowning hard as he followed Simon into the kitchen.

'You don't look like a man with good news,' Rosie said as she wiped her hands on a rag.

'I had another letter from Holcomb's attorney this morning. The captain has set out his demands. If you don't comply, he will file suit for slander. We have today to comply.'

'Today?' Simon echoed the word.

'Today.' The lawyer's voice was grave.

'You said any judge would toss it out of court.'

'I did.' He hesitated. 'That was before they sent a list of names who'd claim they heard you defame Captain Holcomb.'

'But I—'

'Hear me out, Simon. He has three officers from the barracks and two gentlemen willing to testify.'

Panic was scratching at him. It was all lies, but . . .

'When is this supposed to have happened?'

Pollard brought the letter from his jacket and unfolded it.

'". . . on various and sundry occasions". It's a phrase that means nothing and everything. With people like those speaking for him, he'll win. Every word will be a lie and the judge will find in his favour.'

'That's—'

'Unjust? Corrupt?' He raised his eyebrows. 'You know how the courts work in this country. He'll be able to ask a great deal in damages from you.'

Simon's anger was beginning to boil. A few breaths before he could make himself speak in an even voice. 'You said he had demands.'

'An advertisement to go in the *Mercury* and the *Intelligencer*.

They sent the wording they require you to use. In essence, you apologize for statements you made about the Holcomb family which you knew to be untrue and request their forgiveness. Your name must be prominent at the bottom.'

'What else?' he asked.

'That's all. It's meant to humiliate and discredit you.'

'Anyone who knows Simon will know there's something wrong,' Rosie said.

'I daresay,' Pollard agreed. 'But most people in town don't know him. That's the point.'

'It could make them reluctant to employ me.'

'Or even trust you.' The lawyer sighed. 'You said you were working for Holcomb then announced to him that you were stopping.'

'He wouldn't tell me everything. I was trying to do the job half-blind. Three people were dead and he refused to let me give his name to the constable.'

'You didn't insult him?'

'Never.'

'He obviously took very deep offence at whatever you did. I have no idea why. There could be so many reasons. I'm sorry, Simon, but you should swallow your pride and publish this apology. If you don't, you're going to end up paying damages and legal fees. It's a battle you'll lose, believe me.'

'Those witnesses would perjure themselves,' Rosie said.

'And the judge will gladly let them,' Pollard agreed.

'It's—'

'I'll do it.' He could hear the emptiness in his own voice. Defeated. But better than the alternative of losing everything.

'You'll need to go to the newspaper offices. Have it run in both papers on Friday, three days from now. I'm sorry, Simon. If I thought we had a chance, I'd say fight it. There might not be much honour in doing it this way, but you'll keep all you have.'

He managed a half-smile. 'Except my pride.'

'You'll be the butt of jokes for a day or two.' Pollard shrugged. 'Then the next thing will come along and they'll forget about it. There's much worse, believe me.'

'I know that. I think I do, anyway. Thank you. I'll do what you suggest.'

The lawyer looked relieved. 'It's for the best.' A nod to Rosie and he left.

She took her husband's hand. 'He's right. By next week people will have forgotten.'

'I won't.'

'Don't start thinking about revenge. Please, Simon.'

'I promise.'

'What about Janet Bristol?' she asked. 'Should we drop that?'

'No,' he answered after a little thought. 'Now I'm more curious than ever to see the documents that are causing all this.' He looked at her. 'Aren't you?'

'Yes, but—'

'No buts. We're going to meet this man Mason, too. We'll have Jane with us.'

'Do you think she's ready?'

'She will be.' She'd welcome this, a chance to prove herself; he was sure of it.

'Why? If it's just him . . .'

'It might not be. He thinks Dyson is bringing the documents. He might decide it's safer not to leave anyone alive who can tell the story.'

Very gently, he rubbed the bruise the man had left on her cheek. She owed him a reckoning for that.

'All right,' she agreed.

'Isn't it time for you to go and see Janet Bristol?'

'I'll make certain nobody follows me.'

He gave a sour smile. 'I'll go to the newspaper offices and debase myself.'

It was done. He watched the clerks' faces as they read, eyes widening, and he paid his money. Set for Friday. He'd need to be ready for the ridicule.

He stopped at Mrs Shields's house to look for Jane, but she'd already left. He found her at the corner of Briggate and Duncan Street, talking to Kate the pie-seller. Her finger wore a clean bandage, but she held her hand down, as if she was trying to keep it out of sight.

Her face was drawn, deep shadows haunting the space under her eyes. No surprise after what had happened, he thought. He flexed his fingers.

'You watch out for her,' Kate said quietly as he paid.

As they began to walk, Simon explained what he wanted.

'I'll bring Sally as well,' she said, and he glanced at her doubt-fully, not sure why she wanted to include the girl.

'She's small.' He couldn't spend his time keeping an eye on her.

'Yes.' Jane's agreement caught him off-guard. 'But she's fast and she's dangerous.'

That was true. He'd already seen it.

'All right,' he agreed.

'She let me in.' Rosie unpinned her hat and hung it on top of her cloak in the hall. In the kitchen, she settled on the bench. 'She was grateful for the tea. I said I'd take more next time.'

'What about the papers?'

She shook her head. 'As soon as I mentioned them, she changed the subject. She's seen people come around to her old house.' Rosie looked up at him. 'She's scared. She doesn't know what to do. But she'll need to trust me before she'll do anything, Simon. I told her I'd go back tomorrow. It's going to take a little while.'

He sighed. Time. He had to hope there was enough of it.

Sally was nervous. She kept shifting from foot to foot as they stood near the turnpike in Sheepscar, pressing a hand against her side. She'd settle as soon as things began to happen, Jane decided.

In the twilight it was an eerie place. A few carts heading away from Leeds. A coach speeding along the road, its driver cracking his whip above the horses.

'I've never been round this way before,' Sally said in a low voice. 'There's never been any need. These days I like houses and people around me. I feel safer that way.'

Jane understood. She'd lived her entire life in Leeds. She under-stood it. Out here there were too many open spaces. Animals to worry her. But she'd learned to do it when it was necessary.

'Someone's coming,' she whispered, and they faded back into the undergrowth.

A pair of men, backs bent under heavy packs, making their slow way north. Five more minutes and she heard Simon's familiar foot-steps, someone else with him.

Rosie.

'Amos and Richard are staying with the neighbours tonight,' she explained as she saw Jane's quizzical look.' She touch her bruised face with a fingertip. 'I wanted to be here.'

Simon's plan was simple enough. Once Mason arrived, he'd show himself. If the man brought company, the women would cover them. If he arrived alone, they'd surround him so he had nowhere to run.

'He's a soldier, so he'll know how to fight dirty,' he said. 'Be careful.'

Watching, alert to all the strange noises of the countryside. She sensed the movement of animals, scenting people and keeping their distance. But no men. Not yet.

The man would arrive soon; Simon told her he'd collected the message. He'd never see them until they were ready.

Jane lifted her head. The nerves fluttered in her belly. She had to do this. Someone was approaching. On his own, trying to keep quiet and failing. She crouched, knife in her hand, ready.

There was a clear sky and a half moon, enough for him to recognize Simon as he stepped out from behind a tree.

'Well, well. Something to sell, Westow?'

'If I had, it wouldn't be to you.'

'At least I can even the score for what you did to me the other day. The lieutenant laughed at me all the way back to the barracks.'

'You're not the only one wanting to settle scores.'

Rosie had appeared to stand behind him, a blurred outline in the gloom. Mason turned quickly, drawing a long blade.

'Two of you? Doesn't matter. I've taken care of more than that before.'

Jane stood and glided forward. On the other side, Sally did the same.

'Four,' Simon told him.

'Women? A girl? Is that the best you can manage?' The man spat and sneered.

'Go ahead and try them if you think you can win.'

'You seem to enjoy hitting women,' Rosie said. 'Care to do it again?'

Mason's eyes flickered around, searching for the easiest way out. Simon's voice stopped him.

'Are you working for anyone else?'

'Anyone else?' he asked in disbelief. 'Who? The lieutenant? I wouldn't give him the steam off my piss. This is my chance to make some money. The army pays nothing.'

'I wonder what would happen if he learned about it.'

He hid it well, but Jane saw worry flicker across the man's face. 'He'd never believe you.'

'Maybe I'll give him the chance to find out,' Simon said.

Mason moved without warning, darting towards Sally. He was a big man; he probably believed he could knock her to the floor. But she stood her ground with her knife poised. Any closer and she'd impale him.

Jane was swift, coming up behind him. She saw Rosie and Simon move forward. No escape for Mason and he knew it. He raised his hands in surrender.

'What do you want, Westow?'

'Give this up, or your lieutenant will learn about it, and so will Captain Holcomb.'

For a moment Jane wasn't sure what the soldier would decide.

'All right,' he agreed.

'One other thing,' Rosie said. As he turned, her fist lashed out. She put every scrap of her anger behind the blow. It sent him staggering backwards, barely keeping his balance. She stood, daring him to come again.

A small nod, an admission of defeat.

'Nothing more,' he said to Simon.

'No comebacks. I don't want you appearing with some comrades.'

'This is the end of it.'

Too easy, Jane thought as they watched him walk off into the night. She didn't trust a word of it.

Rosie was grinning and merry as they walked back into town. She'd had her revenge. She'd understand when Jane took hers against Paul Wild.

She flexed her left hand, feeling the little finger that was no longer there. The ghost to haunt her. Dodson had been right.

'He didn't scare you,' Simon said to Sally as they all stood at the corner of Swinegate.

'Why would he?' she asked. 'He's only a man.'

Mrs Shields looked up from her book and smiled. The room was warm and cosy. It was home.

'Is your business all done?'

'This part of it.' The rest of all that would be Simon's affair. She had her own concerns.

'Let me put more ointment and a fresh dressing on that finger.'

Later, in bed, with the comfort of a sachet of dried lavender under the pillow, she set her thoughts free. Read for a few minutes, slipping deep into the world of *Ivanhoe*. Tomorrow she'd talk to Simon and Rosie about Sally. Tonight the girl had proved herself, shown that she didn't flinch, that she had no fear.

Tomorrow she'd be back to her own hunt. That one would end in blood.

TWENTY-NINE

Simon listened closely as Jane talked about Sally. Rosie was standing by the range, arms folded.

'She's very young,' Rosie said.

'So was I when I started.'

'How old is she? Eleven?'

'I don't know. Maybe a little older.'

He was thinking. The girl had given a good account of herself so far. She'd found Wild and Harrison, followed them home without being noticed. Discovered the answers they needed to free Harriet. Kept her head when Jane was taken and led him to her. Last night she hadn't shied from a fight.

'Do you think she can do the work?'

'She still needs to learn things, but she's good. She's a survivor. You can teach her the rest,' Jane replied.

Rosie gave a thoughtful nod. 'You're doing a lot for this girl.'

'I suppose so.' But she said nothing more. No explanation.

'You said she has a room. How can she afford it?'

Jane stared down at the floor. 'I've paid until tomorrow. If she starts working for you, she'll be able to cover it herself.'

'What if we say no?' Rosie asked.

'I don't know.' She raised her head. 'Sally can do most of the things I do . . .'

'What about you?' Over the years he'd learned to trust her when they worked together. Even after the splintering between them, he didn't want to lose her completely.

'If you really need me in future, I'll help.'

Jane had made up her mind. He knew better than to try and change it.

'Give us ten minutes,' he said.

She pulled her cloak around her and left.

'Well?' he asked. 'What do you think?'

'She was good last night,' Rosie said.

'I agree.'

'My only worry is her age.'

'She's been out there. Jane said it, she's a survivor. That takes something.'

'If she works for us, I want her living here, Simon. In the attic. It's bound to be better than the room she has now.'

He hadn't expected that. 'Are you sure? With us?'

'Yes. If she's willing to do that, we'll take her on. Jane's made it clear what she intends to do when this business is over. There are plenty of people Sally can talk to that I can't. All of those without homes. The children. The way Jane used to.'

Less than an hour and Sally was living with Simon and Rosie. The attic was sparse, but better than the room he visited, where the window had rattled in the smallest breath of wind and dark mould covered the walls. No matter; someone else would be eager for it.

Five minutes for her to settle, eyes as wide as if she'd stumbled into a palace. Then he sent her off with Jane. Rosie left to visit Janet Bristol, to try gentle persuasion for the documents.

Simon buttoned up his greatcoat and strode up Briggate.

'That's what Holcomb demanded?' George Mudie asked. He turned the printing press as they talked, glancing at the quality of each sheet as it emerged. 'A printed apology?'

'Very precisely worded to make it look as though I'd defamed and libelled him.'

'If you refuse, court?'

He nodded. 'With a list of names happy to lie through their teeth for him.'

'I'd say you've got off very lightly, Simon.' He squared the printed sheets and tied them into a bundle with practised fingers.

'Why?'

'A few people will talk. Give them a day or two and they'll forget. People like you and me, we're not important. Most have no idea who we are, and they don't care. They're too busy trying to get by. All you're paying is the cost of the advertisements. That's a damned sight cheaper than lawyers and damages.'

'And my pride.'

Mudie gave a snort of disgust. 'If you worry about that, you're a fool, Simon. It's not worth a fart. Now go away and let me work in peace. I have the chance to make some money for once.'

The man put it in perspective. He'd refused Holcomb and now he was going to pay for it. But the price was small. Inside, he understood that, even as he hated it. Probably the captain believed it would be enough to deter him from delving deeper.

He arrived home to Rosie's horrified face.

'She's gone. Didn't answer when I knocked. The back door wasn't locked. Things had been tossed all over the place.'

His heart started to race. 'Has she run or was she taken?'

'I don't know. I couldn't tell.'

'We'd better go and look.'

She was right. Someone had done a thorough job. If the woman had hidden the documents here, they were gone now.

'What about her clothes? Hairbrush, things like that?'

'I don't know what she had. Not much. Every time I've seen her, she's always worn the same dress, thick grey wool.'

He went next door, to the woman's old house, picking the lock. Inside was the same story. Whoever had been searching knew what they were doing, all the places to look. But no answer to what had happened to the woman. Or the package Sophie had taken from the Holcombs.

What in God's name could be so important about these diaries and letters of a dead man? The only way he'd ever answer that would be to find them.

'What now?' Rosie's voice dragged him away from his thoughts.

'I wish I knew,' he admitted. There was nothing here to offer a hint. They were back to the beginning.

Jane took the girl around, introduced her properly to Kate the pie-seller, Dodson and the other beggars who sometimes had information for her. Davy Cassidy the fiddler rosined his bow as she told him about Sally, then turned his sightless face to her with a smile.

'I've heard you. You're always with the children.'

Her mouth opened in astonishment. 'How—'

'When one sense doesn't work, the others grow sharper,' he told her. 'I have keen ears.' A small, merry laugh. 'Handy for music.' He tucked the violin under his chin and started to play a slow, melancholy air, swiftly carried off by the music. Jane dropped a coin in his cup and they moved on.

'Paul Wild,' Sally said.

'Have you talked to the children today?'

'Just after it was light. They didn't have anything.'

'Remember, I want him.' She held up her hand.

'I know,' the girl agreed. But Jane could pick out the blood lust in her eyes.

'I hear you've agreed to grovel and make your apology, Westow.'

The voice was behind him. Close enough to feel the breath on his neck. Quiet, mocking, smug. The lieutenant. Simon started to turn.

'No, keep walking and look ahead unless you want a knife in your back. Is all this going to teach you a lesson, do you think?'

The man was gloating, relishing every moment of this. 'Yes.'

'Good. But just in case, we'll be keeping an eye on you to make sure you behave. Your involvement with those documents is over.'

Who had taken them from the clothes seller?

'You understand me, Westow?'

'I do.'

'Good fellow. Oh, and I'm quite aware of Mason's attempt at a little enterprise. Admirable, perhaps, but he won't be repeating it.'

Silence. Simon turned, but the man had vanished.

'The men have finished digging at Wise's house,' Porter's voice was bleak. 'Three bodies in the end.'

'Christ.' If they hadn't rescued Harriet, she'd have become the fourth as soon as the man had finished with her.

'Dr Hey's examined them. What he can, anyway. He's convinced they're all girls. His guess is they're probably no older than six.' He shook his head. 'Do you understand how someone can do that, Westow, because I'm damned if I can.'

'No.' Evil didn't seem like a strong enough word. 'Nothing about the ones who killed Wise?'

'Not a peep.' He let out a long, low sigh. 'I'm offering a reward, but . . .'

'Nothing.'

The constable shook his head. 'Not yet, and I don't know what else to do. By tomorrow, everyone in Leeds is going to know exactly how many bodies there were and they'll expect me to arrest people. I'm hunting thin air.'

'I wish I knew something to help you.'

Porter gave a weary nod. 'So do I. We're not going to give up on this. We can't. My men are angry.' He stared at Simon. 'If you hear anything, will you let me know?'

'Yes.' It was the constable's job to bring justice in this, not his. Simon had done his work by freeing Harriet. But how many nightmares would plague her in her life? 'I don't imagine Holcomb has been willing to talk to you about those other three murders?'

'Pigs might fly first. I've sent him notes. He ignores them. I've had my hands full with this other business. But don't you worry, I haven't forgotten him.'

Robert Jordan shook his head. Evening, cold, the promise of frost in the air. The same beershop where Simon had found him the last time.

'Nothing to do with us,' he said when Simon had finished his tale about the missing clothes seller. 'We asked if she'd be willing to give us the papers, but she refused.'

'When was this?'

He pursed his lips. 'Probably the day after Sophie Jackson and Tim Loftus were murdered. I didn't even know she'd left her house and gone next door.'

Should he believe the man? Jordan always seemed honest and sincere; that was his manner. There was nothing to show he wasn't telling the truth. But anyone involved in radical politics needed to be able to lie well to save his own skin.

A little more talk and Simon left. Full night, and the blurred shape of the moon showed through the haze that always blanketed Leeds. He kept his hand on his knife as he walked, ears cocked for footsteps. Holcomb's lieutenant friend probably wouldn't return soon, but there might be others after his life.

He was listening, but he still didn't hear Jane until she was beside him on Kirkgate. One of her talents, to appear as if she'd just been conjured out of the air.

'No Sally?' he asked.

'She's helping me.'

'Tell me honestly: can she do this work?'

'Yes.' She stared at him with eyes full of certainty. 'She was born for it.'

'Any luck finding Wild?'

'Not yet.' Her mouth was set. 'By now he'll have heard I'm after him.'

'What if he leaves?'

'He won't.' Jane shook her head and held up her bandaged hand. 'That was just the start. He won't be satisfied until he has it all.'

He believed her. She was the one who'd seen the man's face and heard his hate. He might attempt to complete what he'd begun, but she'd never allow him a second chance.

'The clothes seller has vanished,' he told her, sketching in the few things they knew before they reached Briggate. He noticed her eyes constantly shifting around, searching. The tense, taut way she held herself, always ready. Would Jane always be like that now?

'Did you hear about the bodies at Wise's house?'

'Someone said three,' she replied.

Simon nodded. 'That's right.'

He watched as Jane turned away and vanished up Briggate, into the night.

'I might have something on Wild,' Sally said. Friday morning, not long after dawn; she must have slipped out of Simon's house before it was light. Jane stood on Leeds Bridge with the girl as carts and coaches rumbled by. People walked, bent under baskets piled with vegetables to sell at the market. 'A girl called Elspeth claims she's heard something about him.'

'What did she say?'

'Come and talk to her yourself.'

She looked to be nine or ten, scared and cold, standing on Dock Street as a frigid wind howled between the buildings. No coat, just a man's ripped, frayed jacket, far too big for her body, covering a thin cotton dress.

'You know something about a man called Paul Wild?' Jane asked, and the girl nodded, as if she couldn't completely trust herself to speak. 'What is it you know?'

Elspeth glanced towards Sally, asking permission.

'It's fine. Tell her what you said to me.'

'I was trying to get closer to the fire in the building down there.' She turned to look at the shell of the burned boat yard. 'I was behind two women. One said that if the weather grew any worse, she'd have to go and see a man she knew who'd pay for her body. You know,' Elspeth said, and quickly gazed at the ground.

'I do,' Jane told her.

'The other one didn't believe her. Down here, people lie and make things up all the time. But she insisted it was true. Said his name was Paul. But she only went when she was desperate, because he liked to hurt her.'

'There are plenty of men named Paul.'

Elspeth nodded. 'That's what the other one told her. But the first woman said, no it was all true and she could prove it. His name was Paul Wild and he lived near Steander. At least his room was warm, she said, and if she let him go a few times, she could stay all night. Then they started arguing about something else.'

Steander. Not much more than a stone's throw from Hill House Bank, where they found Wild's brother. Now she had a start.

'You've done very well.' She placed four silver coins in the girl's dirty hands. 'Thank you.' With a shy, grateful smile, Elspeth darted away. Jane looked at Sally.

'Let's go and find him.'

For once, he wasn't too early to the coffee cart. Simon considered not going at all. Friday, both the *Intelligencer* and the *Mercury* publishing, with his apology inside. But if he'd stayed away . . . that would be cowardice.

Instead, he tried to act normally. Some of the men had jibes and taunts for him, but he took them in good part. Nothing as bad as he'd imagined as he smiled and tried to laugh it off. The words all stung, but they didn't pierce deep and draw blood. Finally, he wandered off. More to come during the day, no doubt, but the worst was over.

Mudie and Pollard had been right. Most people didn't care. He wasn't as important as he'd always liked to believe, and this time he was glad. He'd built it up in his head, imagined his reputation wrecked and his world in shreds. The truth was, there hadn't been much humiliation at all. Simon smiled to himself: now he could crack on with some proper work.

A woman who ran one of the small corner shops believed she'd heard of a man called Wild. No idea where he lived, she said; her mind was a-tangle today. All she remembered was someone might have mentioned the name a week or so before.

Not much, but a start. Jane tried the other two shops in the area,

Sally standing behind her, listening and taking it in, learning. But the name meant nothing.

No matter, they had a scent of the man. Faint, but it would grow.

'What else can we do?' the girl asked as evening fell. She was huddled in her cloak, face pale from the biting November cold.

'I'll come back tomorrow and keep trying. He won't be going anywhere,' she said with certainty.

They hurried to Swinegate. Just Simon and Rosie in the kitchen, the boys already in bed. Jane stayed long enough to warm herself, then home to the cottage behind Green Dragon Yard.

Alert, nervous, keeping a grip so tight on her knife that her fingers hurt. Listening for every sound. But it was a peaceful walk. The cold kept people off the streets, even on a Friday night.

Home. She checked on Mrs Shields, happy to see the old woman comfortably asleep. A breath of a kiss on the papery cheek, then in her own bed.

She tried to read, to let go of the day, but the words danced on the page. Jane put the book aside and blew out the candle.

Paul Wild. He wasn't going to escape.

THIRTY

Simon stared out of the kitchen window. Rosie was ladling porridge into bowls. Sally smiled at Richard and Amos, then asked them a few questions. Not much of an age gap between them, he realized, but such different lives. They'd been shy, quiet as they learned she'd be living in the attic. He heard them now, voices falling over each other as they opened up to her. The girl had an easy, natural manner with children. That could be useful.

He turned to his wife.

'I'm starting to think the clothes seller is dead.'

Rosie cocked her head. 'I hope she's not. Why? What makes you believe it?'

'You saw the way that house had been searched. It was thorough.'

'She might have run.'

He nodded. 'Possibly. But she trusted you, didn't she?'

'As much as she trusted anyone, I suppose,' she answered after a little thought.

'Nobody knows anything about her. I asked all over yesterday. She hasn't been in touch. She could have sent a message.'

'Maybe.'

'It feels like the only explanation to me.'

'Just don't go thinking there can't be any others,' Rosie warned and he nodded.

'I won't.'

'Did many people talk about your apology yesterday?'

'A few.' It was done now. By Monday, nobody would remember it had ever happened. He turned to Sally. 'You can work with me today.'

She beamed, and he was surprised by the eagerness on her face.

'Before we go, though . . .' He reached into his waistcoat pocket, brought out banknotes and coins and placed them in her hand.

She looked up at him in disbelief, as if it was some kind of test. 'What's this for?'

'Harriet's father employed us to find her. He paid his fee. This is your share – one-third.'

'But—' she began, then couldn't find more words. He knew it was more money than she'd ever been able to imagine; Caldwell hadn't stinted on his reward.

'Hide it in your room,' Rosie told her. 'Before you go to work.'

As they walked, she moved easily, all traces of the limp gone.

'Your wife strapped my ribs tighter,' she said. 'It feels better.'

'Why don't you call her Rosie?' he said. 'She works with me, too. Before the boys it was just her and me doing this.'

'She's kind.'

He chuckled. 'She's deadly in a fight. I want you to follow me today. Not too closely, I don't want people to know. Make sure nobody else is behind me.'

'Is that all?'

'Act if there's any trouble.' He'd be prepared for the lieutenant. 'I'll warn you now, most of what we do is boring.'

He stopped at the coffee cart. A few more gentle insults. A question or two about the young bodies dug up at Wise's house. He didn't have much to give them, none of the bloody detail they craved, and soon enough they drifted away.

Simon swallowed the rest of the drink and put the tin mug back on the trestle as Sally brushed by him.

'Someone's been watching you,' she whispered.

He acknowledged her words with a blink of his eyes, thrust his hands in his pockets and began to walk away. Simon never looked back, gave no hint of anything, but moved into the maze of small streets, the courts and yards that ran between Briggate and Vicar Lane. Plenty of places to stop and confront any follower.

Simon strode on, not slowing, until he turned a corner and waited. The knife was out of his sleeve, ready by his side. A soft tread approached on the ground; someone was trying to be very quiet. Now he had to hope that Sally was behind the man and wouldn't run off if anyone came at her.

The man came around the corner and jerked to a halt. He saw Simon's blade and lifted his arms.

'See,' he said, 'no weapon. I'm no danger.'

'I'm glad to hear it, Mr Jordan. Now why are you skulking around like this? You could have sent a note.'

When he'd seen the man in the beershop, Robert Jordan claimed to know nothing about the clothes seller's disappearance or where the missing documents might be. Something must have changed.

'I needed to see you, and make sure it was all done quietly.' With a pair of fingers, he reached inside his coat and drew out a piece of paper. 'Read that.'

'Very well.' He glanced over the man's shoulder. Sally was a few yards away, knife poised. 'No need to worry,' he called. 'This one means no harm.'

Jordan turned, eyes wide. Working with radicals, he was used to secrecy. But not violence and definitely not young girls.

The paper was old and musty, with ink fading from blue to brown. Cramped writing, but still legible.

'Magistrate Holcomb,' he said as he passed the page back to Jordan.

'It must be,' the young man agreed. 'It doesn't mention machine breakers, but talking about transporting fifteen people this way, it has to be him. We know that's the number he sent to the other side of the world for the crime.'

'Where did it come from?'

'A boy brought it to the bookshop late yesterday. Said a man had paid him to deliver it, but he didn't know his name. No note with it.'

Someone had the bundle of documents. Who, though? And what had happened to Janet Bristol? It looked as though he might have been right. Hardly good news.

'There's nothing especially incriminating in what you've just shown me,' Simon said. 'We knew about this, you just said so.'

'It proves he has old man Holcomb's papers. I expect we'll be hearing from him soon.' Jordan gave a sad smile. 'Things haven't changed since poor Tommy Deacon tried to sell them to us, though. We still don't have the money to buy. Doesn't matter how little it is.'

'Let me know. Too many people have died over what that man wrote.'

The courthouse was busy. The clerks who ran Leeds were scratching away with their nibs in the offices, a steady flow of people coming in and out of the building. The constable's room seemed like the quietest of all, just Porter and one man writing a report with clumsy ink-stained fingers.

'Information for me, Westow?' The look on his face was pitted with hope, falling when Simon gave a shake of his head. He had deep moons of shadow under his eyes.

'I wanted to ask if you'd managed to learn anything more. Those bodies are still the talk of the town.'

'As well they should be.' He ran a hand across his skull and motioned for the secretary to leave. Once they were alone, he continued: 'They visit me in my sleep, you know. They come and ask me to find out where they belong.' A breath. 'But no, I haven't found a damned thing. Half the council have been badgering me about it. I've had the men out talking to servants from all the big houses, but absolutely nothing yet.'

'Killing Wise and his servant . . . that was a message.'

Porter nodded. 'I'm sure everybody who needed to listen has heard it. You know the galling thing, Westow? It won't stop. Maybe for a year, until the waves settle. Then they'll be back at it, the same bloody evil as before.'

'The rich.'

'They hold the purse strings, they control us all. At least we've helped pause it for a little while. Maybe that's an achievement.'

'It's not enough, though, is it?'

'I'm not giving up.'

'I didn't think you would. Not on this.'

Porter sighed. 'You and I, we've had plenty of differences. But all these things, Holcomb and the murders, and the girls, they've changed things.'

'A little,' Simon agreed with a smile.

Sally was waiting for him, following as he strode along Boar Lane and out past West Bar. More buildings out here than the last time he'd taken this road: factories and workshops. Chimneys pouring their smoke into the sky to add to the pall across Leeds. There was money here for some. But who knew what the cost would really be?

He'd heard that a man he wanted to see was working out this way, in the office of Wormald's Engineering. There were dozens of firms like it these days, designing and building the machinery that others used. Business was obviously good; men were scurrying all over the place. He signalled Sally to wait and entered the building.

The noise stopped him for a second. Banging and crashing, a scrape of metal that made his teeth ache. Nobody else seemed to notice; they carried on with their work.

A clerk directed him to Jacob Sterling. The man was bent over a table, examining a drawing through a magnifying glass. Middling age, ordinary looking, moderately well dressed, hair receding, he was the type nobody noticed. Being anonymous had proved very useful in those days when he'd been a Radical.

They were long behind him now. He'd become respectable, remade himself as an engineer and found himself good employment.

He straightened, stretched out his back and saw Westow, eyes opening wide in worried surprise. He glanced around nervously.

'What do you want?'

'To talk.' Sterling opened his mouth, but Simon continued. 'Not now. When you finish for the day.'

The man considered it, looking around again, scared like a rabbit caught in a light.

'A little after six o'clock.' He kept his voice low, speaking hurriedly. 'I'll come to your house. Now go, please, before someone sees you.'

A minute and he was back outside, ears still ringing from the din. The building had thick stone walls; on the road, the cacophony was muted. Sterling probably wouldn't have much to tell him, but all those years before he'd been on the edge of the group of machine breakers that Magistrate Holcomb had arrested. Not caught himself, not even named, he'd stayed free. But he'd be able to say more about what happened. At this point, anything might help.

'Where are we going now?' Sally asked.

'Home,' he told her. There was little more he could do out here for now.

Jane was back on Steander. Walking, watching people, talking to some of the children she saw playing on the street. Working alone, she felt freer. Sally was good, she learned quickly. Jane saw a little of herself reflected in the girl. But what she saw was someone she used to be. Most of the anger that forced her through life had dissolved and she didn't miss it. Most, but not all. She flexed her hand and felt the soft cloth of the bandage. The need for revenge was still very strong.

Twice she stopped to talk to children playing in the street. No pavement or cobbles here, nothing more than mud turned solid and rutted by the cold, but they were still out with their games in the bitter weather. Too young to work, everybody else in the family labouring in the factory or the mill.

Children noticed things. But she had no proper description of Paul Wild to offer. The man she'd seen in that room where he cut off her finger would always be stark in her mind, but she couldn't conjure up a clear image of his face or body, how he held himself. Only the eyes of a devil, and that would mean nothing to anyone out here.

Two more shops, with no better luck; they didn't know the name. No choice but to keep on walking. As she passed a front door, an old woman was wrestling with her key in the lock. She stared beseechingly at Jane.

'You've got young fingers. Could you turn that for me, pet? My hands are too stiff.' They were curled like claws, the joints gnarled and awkward with age.

A deft twist and she pushed the door open, handing the woman her key.

'Thank you, lass. Come in and warm yourself up. You look frozen. It's perishing out there.'

Jane perched on the edge of the chair. Only meagre heat from the few coals on the fire, but it was welcome.

'You must be looking for something. You've been all over round here. I've seen you through the window.'

'A man.'

She gave a flicker of a smile. 'Has a name, does he?'

'Paul Wild.'

'Paul.' The way she spoke the name made it obvious she knew him. 'Spent half his life living right around here.' Jane felt the woman's eyes assessing her. 'He's not the sort someone like you should be after. What's he done?'

She held up the bandaged hand and watched the woman's eyes widen.

'I knew he was a bad sort. Him and his brother both. I'd never pictured him for anything like that, mind. You heard about his brother Billy?'

'I did.'

'He was a nasty piece of work, but Paul looked up to him. Him dying like that might have done something to his mind.'

'Does he still live around here?' Jane asked.

'He does.' The woman's eyes flickered to the damaged hand. 'What are you going to do if you find him?'

'Make him pay for this.'

'I see,' she said finally. 'Well, I've no time for any man who'd hurt a woman. If my Jack had raised his hand to me, he'd have been out of the door before he could draw a breath. But you want more than a finger of his, don't you?'

No point in trying to lie about it. That face had already seen the truth. 'Yes.'

The woman sighed. 'I daresay there won't be many who'd miss him. He tried to pull my lad astray. Might have succeeded if Willie had lived, too.' For a moment she was silent, thoughts turned inward, remembering her grief. 'He's a lot bigger than you.'

'I'll win.' No doubt about that.

Another look. 'Are you certain this is what you want to do?'

Jane nodded her head. 'I have to.'

'Right. Since your mind's made up, go along the road. Almost to Water Lane and turn right. There are some buildings back by there.'

'I've seen them.'

'He's in one of them. Don't go asking me which, I don't know.'

'I can find him.'

'You look after yourself.'

Jane smiled. 'I will. Thank you.'

With the hood of the cloak raised over her hair, she wandered along the street. Three possible buildings. She drifted by them. One was a workshop, doors closed against the cold, but she could hear hammering and the sound of conversation. Two left and no sign of Wild.

Jane discovered a small space between a pair of walls that offered a view of the front doors. It was going to be a cold wait.

He never showed himself during the day. Nothing moved in or out of either house. By the time darkness fell, and the bells had finished ringing for evening service at the Parish Church, her joints were stiff and her legs numb with cold. She believed she could feel the missing finger and move it. Visited by ghosts, she thought as she walked home.

She stayed alert, gripping her knife, senses sharp, especially as she turned from the Head Row into Green Dragon Yard. Nothing, and she felt her body sag as the entered the small house and the warmth of the fire reached her.

THIRTY-ONE

Ten minutes past the hour and Simon picked out the timid taps on the front door. He led Jacob Sterling into the front room. The fire had been burning for an hour, and a bottle of brandy and two glasses sat on the table. The man poured himself a drink and sipped gratefully.

'They don't like anyone visiting us at work. You were lucky; nobody saw you.'

Simon dipped his head. 'I'm sorry. It was important.'

Sterling's eyes narrowed. 'Important? How?'

'You remember Magistrate Holcomb.'

His expression twisted in disgust. 'How could anyone forget that bastard? He hasn't risen from his grave, has he? I wouldn't put it past him.'

'His papers have. Did you hear they'd been stolen?'

The man shook his head. 'I lead a different life these days. I've stayed clear of all that for years. Too dangerous for me. I learned I'm not a brave man. Who took them?'

'His son was keeping them. A maid and her lover stole them. They're both dead now, along with another man. Murdered.' He thought about the clothes seller. 'Possibly another woman, too.'

'Christ Almighty.' The shock was real. He definitely knew nothing. 'What's in them?'

'That's a very good question,' Simon replied slowly. 'How corrupt was Holcomb as a magistrate?'

'I don't believe he took bribes, if that's what you mean. He didn't need to. He was part of that class that runs things, and he knew his job was to make sure nothing altered that. They all took care of each other. Were you aware that none of the men who were sentenced did any damage to a factory?' He waited until Simon nodded. 'They weren't even that close to the place when they were arrested. The testimony of the officer who took them was twisted to make the men seem guilty of all manner of things.'

'No hope for them?'

Sterling shook his head. 'None. We all knew what kind of man

Holcomb was. He was never going to take time to hear any defence. Guilty verdict and you know the rest.'

All familiar, but to hear it from someone who'd been on the edge brought it close to home.

'Was that when you decided to move away from the Radicals?'

'I was in court, and I saw them hold their heads high when the sentences were read out. I knew I could never be like them. They made me feel ashamed.'

'People do what they can.'

A flicker of a smile. 'That's true. But I hope you didn't want me here just to rake up the past.'

'Holcomb's son wants the papers back. He feels that what's in them could destroy his family's reputation. Do you know of anything the magistrate did that was bad enough for that? Any rumours?'

'Nothing,' Sterling began, then stopped himself. 'No, wait. I suppose it must have been eight or nine years ago now. I heard he'd helped cover up something for one of his friends.' He pressed his lips together as he tried to remember, then shook his head. 'I'm sorry. I don't know the name. Or even what it was. It was only a passing word. I recall thinking that nothing about him would surprise me. That was it.' He shrugged.

'It all helps.' It was one more thing, if he could find someone with some details. 'Another tot of brandy?'

The heat of the kitchen was welcome after the walk down from Green Dragon Yard. The smell of loaves baking in the oven. Outside, a thin, icy drizzle was falling, feeling like winter already. Any colder and they'd have frost and ice, Jane thought. She listened impatiently to Simon's account of the day before, and told what she'd discovered in a few sentences.

'Are you ready for him?' Rosie asked.

Ready? She been waiting to settle this score since the moment Wild cut off her finger.

'I am.'

'Do you need Sally today?'

The girl sat silently on a stool in the corner, paying attention to everything being said.

'No.' Easier to hide if she was on her own.

She slipped out of the door, walking briskly out to Steander and

Water Lane. The church bells were ringing for the service, and she saw couple strolling down Kirkgate arm in arm. It was going to be a cold, wet wait for the man. But worth every minute when she took her revenge.

Simon was late to the coffee cart. Sunday morning, only a few customers with nowhere better to be. Always worth a stop. Someone might have a nugget of gossip of information he could use.

Nothing worth his time today as he drank from the tin cup and listened. On Swinegate he'd told the girl: 'Just like yesterday. Stay behind me.'

She'd nodded and dropped back. Jane had done well to find Sally. Once she had more experience, she'd be valuable. She seemed happy to spend time with the boys, too. He'd seen her playing with them after supper. Not a duty, she genuinely enjoyed it, and he wondered what stories about her lay hidden beneath the surface.

Mudie's printing shop was closed, the windows dark. No matter, he knew where the man lived.

The man raised his eyebrows in surprise as he opened the door. 'Sunday and here at my home. It must be important, Simon.'

'Information.'

He gave a short laugh. 'Isn't it always? You'd better come in.' He spotted Sally a few yards away. 'Is she with you?'

'Keeping watch.'

'What do you want to know?' Mudie asked. He stood with his back to the fire, hands clasped behind his back and the tails of his coat raised to feel the warmth.

'You said you heard things about Magistrate Holcomb covering something up for one of his friends when he was a magistrate. It must have been a year or two after the end of Napoleon.'

'I told you before. Things that floated around. When I looked, I couldn't find a damned thing.' His gaze sharpened. 'Why, what have you heard?'

'Nothing more than that, really. I don't suppose any names slipped back into your mind?'

'It definitely wasn't Wise, if that's what you're wondering. I'm sure of that. That would ring a bell. I don't even recall that there was a name.' His mouth turned sour. 'Tell me something: are all these stories about what happened out at the house true?'

'Probably. The bodies of young girls buried in the ground. Wise and his man ran off before Porter could arrest them, then turned up in his house again murdered.'

'What the hell is happening in this town? What's it become? We never used to have anything like this.' His voice was soft, sorrowful.

'We probably did, but it never came out into the light.'

He took out his pocket watch. Time to stride out if he was going to meet the man. Three weeks to the day since he'd stood on Pitfall waiting for Captain Holcomb. Time to confront the man again. Hard to believe so much had happened in that time.

'Stay well back,' he told Sally. 'Make sure you keep out of sight.'

A nod. She moved quietly, flowing over the ground. The limp had completely gone. He had to hope she possessed Jane's knack for being invisible.

Woodhouse Ridge, looking down into the valley that led to Meanwood. He'd been careful in choosing the place. The area was well wooded, no opportunity for Holcomb to ride too close. The man would come, he was certain of that. After the threats and printed apology, he'd wonder why Simon had sent a note wanting to meet. Simon had to hope that curiosity would get the better of him.

The captain was late. Five minutes, then ten, and he began to wonder if Holcomb had chosen to ignore his note. Then he heard the sound of hooves coming over Woodhouse Moor towards the crest of the hill and he smiled to himself.

'Are you down there, Westow?'

'Over here.'

The man was dressed for riding, with shining boots, a thick, short cape, and a sword fastened to his belt. He limped towards the small clearing, watching his footing on the uneven ground.

'You're the last man I expected to hear from,' Holcomb told him when they faced each other. His voice was even, but there was fury in his eyes. 'First you decide you don't want the job I offer. I threaten you with a lawsuit, make you apologize in print, and now I get a scrawl pushed under my door to say you've found something. Why do you want me here? Some revenge, is that it?' He offered a smile. 'I've been trying to make sense of it.'

Simon shook his head. 'I was shown something. I thought it would interest you.' He'd gone to the beershop the evening before and persuaded Jordan to let him have the page in the magistrate's hand. He put his hand inside his coat. Holcomb tensed and started to reach for his sword.

'No need for that.' He produced the piece of paper and held it out.

The captain read, frowning, then stared at Simon. 'How did you get this?'

'It was sent to a man who showed it to me. Just that page, no note or explanation with it.'

'Why should I believe you? You could have had the papers all along, ready to sell to me.'

Time for Holcomb to hear some truth and stop being so pig-headed. 'I've endured a great deal because of you. Three people, maybe more, have died because of your father's writings. One of them used to be your maid. As I understand it, the constable is still waiting to talk to you about those deaths and the reason for them. Whatever is on those pages is tainted, Captain.' He paused, looking to see if the words had hit home. No sign of it. 'You sent someone to threaten me and my wife—'

'If you're out of my business, you should stay out of it.'

'It seems to keep following me around.'

'What do you want, Westow? I have no wish to stand here all morning wasting time with you.'

'After you employed me to find them, you said those papers could ruin your family's reputation. But you never would tell me why.'

'You had no need to know. As I recall, we went over this. It's the reason you walked away.'

'Have you changed your mind?'

Holcomb straightened his back, standing a little taller. 'Give me a good reason.' He seemed genuinely offended by the question. His arrogance hadn't changed at all. 'What is the point of this meeting?'

'I wanted you to see that page.'

'I'm still waiting to hear how much it's going to cost me to buy all the papers back from you.'

'You'd better to listen to me again, Captain. I don't have them, I thought I made that perfectly clear. I don't know who does. One thing I didn't mention was that they sent that page to one of the radical groups in town.' He saw the captain's face tighten with sudden fear.

'What will they do if they receive all the documents?'

'Publish them, I imagine. But it doesn't matter. They won't ever have them. Never more than a page or two.'

Holcomb's eyes narrowed. 'What makes you so certain?'

'Whoever has them will be looking to make a handsome profit for their effort. The radicals don't have the money. Deacon, the young man who was your maid's lover, offered to sell them the documents, were you aware of that? They'd love whatever dark truths exist about your father to come out, but there's not a hope in heaven that their pockets will be deep enough.'

'Then what?' Holcomb asked. Simon tried to read his face, but there was nothing. Whatever he was thinking, the man kept it well concealed.

'No respectable newspaper would pay for that material. They'd certainly not print it. The person who has them will likely approach you to buy the papers back.'

'You still haven't given me a reason to believe you're not behind all this.'

Simon shook his head. 'It would be a very elaborate way of doing things, Captain. I'm more straightforward than that.'

'I don't trust you, Westow.'

'You're free to believe what you want.' He shrugged. 'There's nothing I can do about it. I have no reason to trust you either, do I? But if I were you, I wouldn't be looking in my direction.'

'Oh really? Then where?'

'Ask yourself who else knows all about this, then start thinking about them.' He gave a nod. 'I'll wish you good day.' Simon turned and began to walk away.

'A moment, Westow,' Holcomb called. 'Why are you doing this? You can't feel you owe me anything.'

'I don't. I'd as soon see you damned in hell. But too many have died.' He stared at the captain. 'Maybe I consider it a matter of honour to see you learn the truth, even if you never tell it yourself.'

'Is it honour for you?'

He laughed. 'Surprised I'd have an idea like that? After all, I'm a low-born-man.'

'What should I do if someone offers to sell me my father's papers?'

'You were willing to pay me to retrieve them. From everything you've done since, I know there must be something very bad in there. I imagine you'll dig in your coffers to give them the money.'

Holcomb rested a hand on his sword hilt. 'I could kill you out here. Nobody around to see.'

Simon drew the pistol he'd put in his pocket before leaving home. 'You could try. Captain,' he said kindly, 'it's time you talked to Constable Porter.'

'We'll see,' he replied.

At least it wasn't an outright refusal, Simon thought as he followed the tracks to the Otley Road, then back into town. He'd crossed the Head Row before Sally appeared beside him.

'There was a man watching you the whole time. He was waiting out there, then followed you most of the way back here. He only left two minutes ago.'

'What did he look like?'

'Tall. Well dressed, a shine on his boots. One of those fancy coats with all the short capes. His hat was too low to make out his face, but he had a dark moustache.'

'Which way did he go?'

Sally blinked. 'Down the Head Row. Why?'

Time to see if he was right.

'There's a toll booth for the turnpike by Sheepscar Beck. If he doesn't have much of a start, you can probably overtake him if you run. See if he goes into the barracks.'

No questions. She simply hared away, out of sight in a moment.

THIRTY-TWO

J ane stood for ten hours, hearing the church bells peal, every single one of them. Her legs felt rigid as she tried to move, her hands stiff and clumsy. But there was a pain like fire where Wild had taken her finger. That was enough to keep her there until long after the early darkness fell.

She saw a flicker through the window and took a tighter grip on her knife. The light flared and settled as he trimmed the wick in the lamp. Through the glass she could see a face and suddenly she remembered him very clearly. The sharp features, the dark eyes. It brought back all the memories of being in that room. Tied, helpless, feeling his breath in her face. The devil in his stare and his pleasure as he hurt her.

All the fear. Her heart began to race and breathing became harder for a moment. Unbidden, she began to sweat. Her palms were suddenly damp, a cold trickle on the icy skin of her back.

A minute of watching and swallowing, of beating down the panic raging in her mind. She had to overcome that. Finally, it began to subside and slowly she pushed it away, into a vault where she could close the door and turn the key on it. No more.

From there, she felt the tide begin to rise. An urge to march over and hammer on his door. He wouldn't be expecting her, she'd have chance to take him by surprise with her knife. Kill him before he knew what was happening.

For a moment it almost overwhelmed her. No. Wait, do it where nobody might see, where the body could vanish. Where there was no risk of Porter and his men coming to ask questions and accuse her. She'd been in the gaol once. Never again.

Now she knew beyond doubt that he was in the house, she could be patient and pick her time.

Jane slipped out of the shadows and began to walk. Home, warmth.

Simon was playing with the boys in their room. A physical game, wrestling, tickling. Soon enough, they'd be too big for this; enjoy it while he could.

He heard the front door close and left Amos and Richard to put everything back in order.

Sally had taken off her cloak and stood by the range to take in its warmth, sipping from a bowl of broth.

'How did you know?' she asked.

'Know what?' Rosie asked. He hadn't told her about the man who followed him. Waiting until the girl returned to see if he was right.

'That he'd go to the barracks.'

'A good guess,' he answered, and turned to Rosie. 'The lieutenant.'

'The one who threatened us.'

'Holcomb must have wanted him there for safety. Did he see you?' he asked Sally.

'No. I stayed out of the way. He just marched along, never looked around once.'

That fitted. The man had sounded utterly self-confident, as if nothing could touch him. Maybe he was right. After all, he'd hinted that he'd killed Mason, a small, casual boast.

'With Sally, we could take on more business,' Rosie said after she'd vanished upstairs. 'Her, Jane, I'm becoming involved again . . .'

He shook his head. 'Jane made it clear the other day. Don't expect her to do much in the future.'

'She might change her mind.'

'I don't believe she will.' She'd given her word to help with the bigger cases and that was it. All because he'd tried to keep her alive earlier in the year.

Footsteps, Sally's light tread. She seemed embarrassed as she peered around the door.

'I need to go out. Not for long.'

'Lock up when you come back,' Simon told her.

'You know where she's going, don't you?' Rosie said. 'She's giving money to some of those children she used to live with.'

As he lay in bed, he heard Sally arrive. The security of the key turning in the lock and the bolt sliding home, then the creak of the third step and she climbed quietly up to the attic. Jane had definitely done them proud when she brought the girl to join them.

* * *

Monday morning. The bitter weather seemed to be easing a little. Around the coffee cart, men looked less glum, talking and joking. Simon stood and listened. Plenty of gossip, but nobody was talking about him any longer, and he didn't care about rumours of seductions and infidelities. He was about to turn away when he heard someone speak a familiar name: Holcomb.

'The captain?' he asked.

The man shook his head. 'His bloody father.' He spat on the ground. 'The bastard.'

'What about him? He's been dead for a while.'

'Some are saying that there are going to be a few secrets coming out. Things he did.'

'What? Who said it?' He felt the urgency gripping his belly.

'I don't know. Just talk, but I can believe it. He was a devil, that man. Sent my brother-in-law's cousin off to Van Diemen's Lane for poaching a coney to feed his family. Holcomb had evil in his heart.'

A hint here, a nudge there. A slow start, but it would feed on itself and start to ripple across Leeds. Who was behind it? Why were they doing it? Who stood to gain?

'That man's here again,' Sally hissed as she bustled past. Without a backward glance, Simon ambled off into the courts and yards.

Robert Jordan's face was creased with worries.

'You've heard what's going around?'

'Secrets to come out, you mean?'

He nodded. 'When I went to the bookshop first thing this morning, this note had been pushed under the door. Read it.'

> By now you have had chance to examine the small sample you were given. You will have realized it was written by the late Magistrate Holcomb. A rumour has been planted in town that there are a number of revelations about to appear. People will be eager to hear them.

Simon glanced at Jordan. The man was staring intently, hands fidgeting as he waited.

> You have the means to publish these papers, and the money you'll need to pay to obtain them is very reasonable. Not free, of course, as too much work has gone into securing these. Place a sheet of paper in the window of your office to show

you're interested and you will receive all the details of amount
and payment, and where the exchange will take place.
   Yours &c

No signature, of course. But a flowing articulate hand, someone
who'd been taught penmanship when young. He folded the letter.
   'What do you think we should do?' Jordan asked. 'It doesn't
matter how little he's asking, we can't raise it. Then there are the
people who've died for this . . .'
   'Believe me, I remember. Every one of them.'
   Why did the man want to sell to the radicals? It could only be
to humiliate and ruin the reputation of the Holcomb family.
   'Put the paper in the window. Agree to pay.'
   Jordan's eyes grew wide. 'But—'
   Simon held up a hand. 'Once you have the details of the meeting,
pass them to me. That will be the end of your involvement.'
   'What are you going to do?'
   He grinned, a sense that things were finally pushing ahead. 'I'll
take care of it. That's all you'll need to know.'
   'Can I trust you?'
   A thoughtful smile. 'Would you have come to me in the first
place if you didn't? Just tell me when you hear.'
   'What's going to happen now?' Sally asked. She'd stayed out of
sight but close enough to hear.
   'I'd say it's all going to be over soon.'
   'What are we going to have to do?'
   'With a little luck, nothing at all.' Luck, always luck. Suddenly
he felt weary. 'I'm going home. Why don't you go and see if Jane
needs some help today?'

She was tying the leather laces on her boots. Not quite as cold
today, but she still wore two pairs of stockings and the pair of heavy
petticoats under the day dress Mrs Shields had given her. Standing
for hours was a chilly business. A shawl around her shoulders and
the cloak on top, fastened at the neck.
   Jane paused as she heard the tapping on the door. A flicker of
fear in case it was Paul Wild, come to finish the job. She felt her
chest tighten as she reached for her knife, then wrenched the door
open.
   Sally.

'Simon sent me to work with you.' She sounded apologetic. A little scared, perhaps.

'Come in. We'll leave in a minute.'

Mrs Shields made a fuss of the girl, watching her walk to be sure the hip had healed, then strapping the ribs again.

'They're healing,' she said, 'but it'll be a few weeks yet before everything's mended.' A glance at the bruises, a satisfied nod. Then Jane kissed the top of the old woman's head and ducked through into Green Dragon Yard.

'You've found where he lives, haven't you?'

'Yes,' Jane replied. The girl would see soon enough.

'What are you going to do?'

'You know.'

'I'll help.'

She shook her head. 'This is for me.'

It was how she'd expel the demons. From all this, but also reaching back to the spring when Simon had stolen her satisfaction from her.

Nothing to do. It was a curious feeling, as if he was forgetting something important. Simon walked around town, stopping to see George Mudie and Barnabas Wade, simply to pass a few idle minutes. A visit to Constable Porter; he still had no leads on Wise's murder, coming to realize that all the chances were slipping through his fingers like dust. He read the frustration on the man's face.

Food from Kate the pie-seller. The woman was desperate to talk about Jane and her missing finger. But he'd learned; she didn't want anyone else to discuss her business. Better to smile, plead ignorance and walk away.

At home again, Simon settled in the kitchen and spread the *Leeds Mercury* across the table. Rosie was at the market. The boys were learning their lessons. Soon enough, he felt drowsy, trying to shake it off. But his eyes kept slipping shut. Like an old man, he thought. Like a bloody old man.

They'd been standing for two hours before Wild came out of the house. He glanced around to see if anyone noticed, then locked the door and set off at a brisk pace into town.

Jane followed, Sally beside her. She never took her eyes off the man, happy to be moving, to work a little warmth into her legs. Her fingers turned the gold ring, for luck, to stay safe.

'When are you going to take him?'

'I'm not sure yet.' He'd need to be alone, and it had to be a place where she could make his corpse vanish, to turn him into a mystery without any answers. Not a fire; they'd done that with his brother.

The chance would come soon. Deep in her heart, she knew that.

Wild went to the inns and the beershops. She couldn't follow; heads would turn if a woman walked into places like those.

'We have to be patient,' Jane said. 'Keeping still and quiet. We need to be sure we're not seen or remembered.'

'Why don't you ask Simon to help?'

'No.' Her voice was firm. 'This is my battle.'

'Then why not use some of the children? They could follow him,' Sally said. 'Nobody ever sees them.'

That was the truth. She pressed her lips together, annoyed she hadn't thought of it herself. But revenge had crowded so much out of her head, even sense.

'How long would it take you to find some?'

'Only a few minutes.'

Wild had only just gone into the dram shop.

'Four or five of them. If I'm not here when you come back, look for me. I doubt he'll have gone far.'

Alone, watching men arrive and leave, she knew Sally's idea was sensible. They could watch, tell her when Wild gave up and turned for home.

That would be the time. He'd have drink in his belly, his mind fogged. Jane would have the advantage. She just needed to find somewhere quiet for it.

'Has he moved?' Sally asked. She had four children trailing behind her. The youngest was probably six. A bit older than Harriet, Jane thought. But this one wouldn't have a family aching to have her home again. She was ragged and dirty, but sharp-eyed and alert.

'No.'

'I'll stay. I can point him out when he appears. Where will we be?'

We. Like it or not, the girl had forged herself a role in this. She'd earned it, thinking of using the children. And the end would still be just her and Wild. No one else. 'Either with the pie-seller or the blind fiddler,' Jane said and the children nodded. 'Come and tell us every time he moves on.'

Two pennies for each of them. Some hot food, maybe even a night's lodging out of the weather in a cheap rooming house.

'Simon Westow was here earlier,' Kate said. 'I asked him what had happened to you but he wouldn't say.'

Good. It was her story to tell. She glanced at Kate as she ate. The woman's eyes were close to pleading. She'd been a steady friend over the years. Fed her when she had no money. Listened on those few occasions Jane wanted to talk. Probably only Mrs Shields knew her better. A long moment of hesitation then she gave Kate the tale.

'He put you through it and no mistakes,' she said after hearing it all. She stared at the hand, the little finger neatly bandaged. 'I'd ask what you're going to do, but it's written all over your face.'

'I have to,' Jane said.

'Yes,' Kate agreed. 'You do, pet. He has a price to pay. Just watch out for yourself. He might be better than you think.'

Maybe. He'd have size and fear on his side. But she had fury and fire to keep her alive. It never occurred to her that she wouldn't win.

They were still talking when Sally arrived. Jane tensed, thinking it might be time, but the girl shook her head and ordered two pies. Together, they strolled toward the sound of a fiddler's jig at the top of Briggate. Davy's breath clouded their air, but his bow seemed as if it could strike sparks from the strings, music lively enough to warm the chilly day.

Sally leaned her head towards her, speaking softly into her ear. 'Simon gave me money. He said Harriet's father had paid him.'

He'd come to the small house, too, passing over Jane's share.

'It's not a gift. You earned it.'

'But . . . that much?' She shook her head in disbelief. 'Is it always like this?'

'Depends how much we make. But he's fair. He won't cheat you, that's one thing about him.' Even if he might let her down in other ways. 'Save as much as you can.'

'Why?' She looked puzzled, the way Jane had been when she began doing all this. When you'd had nothing, when you might not see tomorrow, the idea of putting any money away, believing in a future, felt wrong. It had taken a little time, but she'd learned.

'Do you remember what you told me? The bargain we made? You wanted to stop living on the streets.'

'Of course I do. You did what you promised.' She looked down at the ground and kicked a pebble. 'I'm working for Simon. I'm living in his house. I'm grateful to all of you.'

'There's good money in this, believe me. Put enough of it aside and you'll be free to do anything you want.'

'Is that what you're doing?'

She had plenty hidden in Mrs Shields's house. Enough to last her for years. All earned working for Simon.

'Maybe,' she said with a distant smile. Her foot began to tap in time with the music.

Jane saw Sally turn as small hands tugged at her cloak. A boy, his young face serious and urgent. The girl bent, listening to him, and gave some instructions before he hurried away again.

'Is Wild going home?'

'He's moved to the beershop at the top of Boot and Shoe Yard.'

Maybe the man had settled in for a full day of drinking. That would make him an easy target on his way back to the little house on Water Lane. More waiting while he warmed himself by a fireside, but that felt like a small price to pay.

'You don't have to stay,' she said to Sally, but the girl shook his head.

'The children know me.' A faint smile. 'I owe you.'

Late afternoon. The light was just beginning to fade when Simon heard a faint scrape against the tiles in the hall. Not loud enough to be the girl. Was someone trying to come in? He took the knife from his belt and glanced at Rosie. She'd heard it too, standing with her own blade in her hand.

Slowly, softly, he opened the kitchen door. He was holding his breath, only feeling his body ease when he saw the piece of paper. From Robert Jordan.

The man with the documents would meet them on Wednesday, the day after next. Nine in the morning, up on Woodhouse Moor. All very open, it offered few places to hide. They had to bring the money; in return, the man would hand over the packet of papers.

But there would be no money. No more than a small, tied sack stuffed with torn paper and a few coins. He passed the letter to his wife.

'Not long until it's over.'

'No.' Now he had to decide who to involve.

* * *

Davy Cassidy had packed up his violin and gone home. The weather was turning too cold for his fingers to move properly, he told the people listening. He emptied the tin cup into the pocket of his coat, pleased with the weight of the coins.

Kate the pie-seller was done for the day, all her wares sold. Night was coming, the temperature falling. Sally looked at Jane expectantly.

'We wait.' This could be her chance; she wasn't going to let it slip away.

Almost half an hour before a girl came running up, breathless. A few rushed words and she pounded away again, dirty hair flying out behind her.

'Wild's left the alehouse.' A long pause. 'Another man is with him.'

'We'll follow.'

'They'll probably be close to the Parish Church now. That's what she said. Going slowly.'

Unsteady was more likely with all that ale inside him, she thought. But this other man could be a problem. Whoever he was, she had no cause to harm him. If he stayed with Wild all the way home, she'd have to wait and try again.

The men had just turned down towards Crown Point and New Causeway. Jane motioned Sally to the other side of the road. With their dark cloaks, hoods raised, they were more shadow than human as the darkness grew.

They kept their distance. Wild and his companion weaved along the streets. On to Steander, still together. She felt the weight growing in her heart. It wasn't going to happen tonight. All the way to the house. The key turning in the lock. A moment, then she saw the flare of a lantern through the window.

'They won't be going anywhere else. Time to go home and sleep.'

Everything inside her head had been ready. This would have been it. No matter, she told herself. The chance for revenge would still come. But it seemed as if the word hadn't reached him. He didn't look scared.

They stayed silent until they passed the church.

'When you began working for Simon, did you like it?'

She tried to remember. Like? She'd never thought of it that way. It was a chance to survive, better than scrambling and fighting to stay alive through each day and night, She'd earned silver pennies then, simple tasks, nothing more than following people at first, then more and more over time.

'I did it.'

She'd kept living on the streets. Almost a year passed before she gave in to Rosie's pleas and moved to the attic where Sally now lived. Simon had insisted it made sense to have her close. She understood that. But it was never more than a place to sleep. They might stop needing her, tell her to leave. The first place that was anything like home had been Mrs Shields's cottage.

'He hasn't wanted me to do much yet.'

'Learn while you can.'

They parted at Briggate. Jane watched as the girl melted into the night. Sally was one who'd always make certain she swam, not sank. She had that air about her.

THIRTY-THREE

Jane read a few pages of *Ivanhoe*, but tonight the words couldn't tempt her to step through time. The fire lulled her towards sleep and she settled under the blankets in her bed.

The idea came in the night, between the bad dreams that woke her. She was up early, working at the note. Resting the steel nib on her tongue before dipping it in the ink. Every word considered, slowly and painstakingly penned. Wild would never imagine that a woman like her knew how to write. Could he read? If not, he'd find someone to do it for him.

It took an hour until she was satisfied. She'd never been fully taught how to make her letters; she'd watched and learned through trial and error. But that made it more convincing. Well before dawn she stole out of the warm house and into the night, pulling her cloak tight around her.

There was barely a soul around. People were keeping out of the weather. Even through the haze of smoke that hung over the town, she could pick out the light of a few stars. The hard cold had returned. Muddy roads had become solid ruts. Frost covered the pavements and crackled across the window of the houses she passed.

Along Steander, around the corner to Water Lane and follow it almost to East Street. No lamp burning in his house. Wild would be lost in ale dreams for hours yet. Still, at the door she hesitated, pulling together all the threads of her anger and courage before slipping the paper between the wood and the stone of the entry, pushing it all the way to be sure it was inside.

A final glance around to make sure nobody had seen her and she hurried away. Her heart pounded, every nerve tingling. By the time she turned from Briggate on to the Head Row she was smiling to herself.

The men gathered around the coffee cart looked disappointed there were no new scandals to occupy their tongues. Breath clouded the air as they warmed their hands on the tin cups and passed idle gossip. Who'd been seen with whom, which woman's servant had delivered a message to a man's house. Nothing to concern him.

But it was Simon's routine to start his day here. All too often he'd learned things that had pushed along his investigations.

Sally stood a few yards away, half-hidden by the archway to the yard of the Bull and Mouth. Every few minutes coaches roared in and out, drivers taking pleasure in scattering people.

Her eyes flickered to the side. Simon followed her gaze and saw Robert Jordan ambling up the street. He took his time following, knowing Sally would be watching in case anyone followed.

The young man lingered on the far side of the old market cross, huddled in his greatcoat against the wind.

'He sent another note to confirm it,' he said. 'Tomorrow morning.'

'Good.'

'Are you sure you don't need me to do anything?' He was nervous, tense. The man was used to working with people whose politics brought them in conflict with the magistrates and the government, but this was something different. He understood there was going to be violence.

'Not a thing.' Simon gave him a smile. 'You set it all up. That's more than enough. I'm grateful.' He thought for a second. 'You might consider staying out of sight for a day or two.'

'Yes.' Jordan nodded, happy at the idea. 'I'll do that.'

'Don't worry.' That was his job.

'Janet Bristol still hasn't appeared,' Rosie said as they ate porridge for breakfast. Amos and Richard sat at the table, cramming facts from their schoolbooks into their heads before the tutor tested them later.

'No one's found a body,' Simon told her.

'Then we can still hope.' There was only bleakness in her smile. 'You know she wouldn't have given the papers up willingly.'

He had no idea what had happened to the woman, and no way of finding out. They couldn't search all of Leeds, and his wife knew it.

'Let's go and look at the houses again.' He glanced down at his sons. 'As soon as these two prove that they've learned a few things.' He tousled their hair.

Nothing to indicate the woman had returned. Dust covered the furniture, everything had an air of neglect. No notes to indicate where she might have gone. They weren't going to solve this without a heavy stroke of luck.

'There's nothing more we can do,' he said to Rosie. 'I'm sorry.' She was searching through everything, hopeful for some sign that might tell them if the woman could still be alive somewhere.

'I know,' she said with a sigh. 'I just . . .'

He looked at her and nodded. The unanswered questions: these were the ones that hung longest in the mind.

'There's something else I need to see. To make sure we're prepared for tomorrow.'

Jane was waiting, already wearing her cloak. At the first tap on the door, she slipped outside to join them. She didn't want Mrs Shields's house full of the sound of talking, making the room feel too small. The day was cold, the air stank, but outside was space.

They followed the road to Headingley, Simon and Rosie ahead, her arm through his as they walked. Jane stayed behind them, Sally at her side. The girl was quiet and she was happy with the silence. Again and again she worked through her plans for Wild, examining everything, hunting for flaws. She touched the gold ring. Safety.

At the bottom end of Woodhouse Moor, Simon stopped. The trees had all shed most of their leaves, the branches reaching stark and black to the sky. He pointed to one that stood alone.

'That's where I'll be meeting whoever has those papers,' he said.

'You don't look much like Robert Jordan.' Rosie stared at him.

'I'll hunch over and make myself smaller. Wear an old coat and a hat like his. By the time this man realizes he'll be close.' A grin. 'Too late then.'

It was a broad, flat space. Small copses of trees dotted around with thick bushes and empty trees. But each one stood at least thirty yards from where Simon would be.

'Nowhere very close,' Rosie said as she surveyed the area. 'What if he attacks you as soon as he realizes he's been cheated?'

'I'll have my pistol,' he told her. He gave her shoulder a reassuring squeeze. 'Don't worry, I won't be afraid to use it.'

'I'll be here,' she said. 'The tutor can come in early.'

Jane glanced at Sally, then said, 'Where do you want us?'

'Hidden. The pair of you together. Come out as soon as he starts talking to me. As if you're taking a stroll up here. Just be ready.'

He saw her nod, then move off to find a spot that would keep them out of sight. Sally followed.

'What about me?' Rosie asked.

'The same as them. Where he can't see you as he approaches.' A tight smile. Even as he said it, Simon knew it wasn't a plan. So threadbare you could see through the holes. The man had chosen this place with care. Very open, so he'd be able to spot anyone approaching. Simon would have to play the hand he'd been dealt.

'There's going to be trouble, isn't there?'

He took a breath. 'I hope not.'

'Have you told the constable?'

'No.' He hadn't decided yet whether he would. As soon as Porter appeared with the man from the watch, the man would run off.

'Don't kill him, Simon. Not until he tells us what happened to the clothes seller.'

'I'm not going to kill anyone,' he answered. 'Not unless he gives me no choice.'

He was skilled with a knife; a thief-taker needed to know how to handle himself. He'd been taught well and he carried three blades, all honed sharper than razors. Simon had only killed a man once. If he hadn't done it, the man would have gladly run him through. Tomorrow, though . . . in spite of what he'd just told his wife, he had the feeling that someone was going to die. He took her arm and tried to smile.

'Let's see what Jane's found.'

It wasn't much, but they were never going to find anything better or closer to the meeting tree. Jane had gone to two other wooded areas before choosing this one. Slightly better cover and the bushes gave protection from a piercing west wind.

She'd fight if Simon needed her and give him everything she had. But her mind was on her own battle. That would come later tomorrow, after dusk had fallen and the streets were beginning to quieten. Once she left here she'd go to her own meeting place and run through things in her mind.

It wouldn't end up the way she planned; she already knew that. She couldn't move pieces around however she desired, not like the old men who sat and played their chess games. Wild could be better and faster than she thought.

She could lose. With a grimace, Jane forced the idea from her head. She was going to win. She was going to have her revenge.

'What should I do?' Sally asked as they strolled back to town.

'Sharpen your knife tonight. Be ready to use it.'

Why was he doing this? Simon wasn't sure. To give some justice to Sophie Jackson, Tommy Deacon, and Jordan's friend? Janet Bristol, too? If he didn't, who else would? Or maybe it was to discover the truth hidden for years in the magistrate's papers.

Perhaps he wanted it simply because the captain had refused to tell the whole story, then threatened and publicly humiliated him. Maybe pieces from all those ideas, stirred up together in his soul.

There was no money in it. He'd walked away from Holcomb. Snubbed him.

'What are you thinking?' Rosie leaned close and whispered in his ear.

'Nothing important,' he told her. By this time tomorrow it would all be over.

'It worries you, doesn't it?'

'Of course it does,' he admitted.

'We don't have to go tomorrow. We can forget about it.'

He gave her hand a tender squeeze. She'd always been able to read his doubts so well.

'We'll be there,' he said. He'd come all this way. Now he needed to see how it ended.

Just past the Parish Church and its burial ground, Jane turned. Not for Steander this time but crossing the narrow causeway over the goit to Fearne's Island, just beyond the shore. Nether Mills were running, a few people moving between the buildings. Everything exactly as she remembered.

She retraced her steps, crossing Leeds Bridge then following Bowman Lane out to Leeds Lock, where the canal began. Jane kept to the shadows. Even with the hood of her cloak raised, she wanted no risk of anyone noticing and remembering a young woman here. A few yards away, the weir on the River Aire rushed and shouted, fast enough to carry a body away.

Jane felt someone watching. The sense had been there from the time she walked down Kirkgate. Faint, off in the distance at first.

Closer now. No threat, though; she'd felt none of that. Jane turned away. She'd seen all she needed, anyway.

She knew who it was: Sally. The girl was as good at following people as she was. Living on the streets was good training.

She was standing by the old sloop builder's yard, where workmen were tearing down what remained of the charred building. The homeless were losing one of their nighttime sanctuaries.

'Is this where you're going to do it?' Sally asked.

'Yes.' No point in lying; she'd already worked it out.

The girl stood and looked towards the water. 'How will you get him to come here?'

'I put a note under his door. An offer of work. Good money. That will tempt him.'

'You wrote it?' she asked in astonishment.

'Yes.'

'I'll be here,' Sally told her.

'I don't want you.' The words came out hard. 'I've told you often enough: this one is for me.'

'I'm going to be here, just in case. Paul Wild isn't worth dying for.'

The girl strode off. Jane stood and breathed. For moment she felt a twinge of pain from her missing finger, as if it still existed, remained part of her.

Simon played with the boys in their room, trying to wear them out before bed. All the rough and tumble was good for him, too; it stopped him thinking about tomorrow. All he had to do was grapple with a pair of squirming, growing bodies.

A few minutes and they were all laughing, out of breath by the time Rosie called them down to supper. Five of them around the table. Sally had a hearty appetite, almost gulping down the food on her plate.

They still knew nothing about her. Talented at the work, and she didn't seem to have an ounce of fear in her. He watched as she scraped up the last of the juice and gravy with a small hunk of bread and savoured it.

Who was she? After tomorrow, when this was done, maybe he'd ask. She seemed more open than Jane. Ready to smile. He'd seen her laugh with his sons.

Sally seemed to sense his eyes on her and turned towards him.

'When Richard and Amos go to bed, would you mind if I told them a story?'

'What story?' Rosie asked. No dark tales from the girl's time on the streets.

'My ma used to tell me some when I was tiny. The one with the red riding hood, and the hare and the tortoise. I think she knew them all.' For a moment, her voice was wistful. 'Would something like that be all right for them?'

'Of course,' Rosie agreed with a warm smile.

For the first time he could recall, their sons were eager to go to their bed.

Who was this girl?

Jane was caught up in *Ivanhoe*, with the Black Knight about to fight in combat for Rebecca after she'd been accused of witchcraft. The book had lifted her up and carried her back to the reign of King Richard, the Crusades and men in armour. Plenty of treachery, but chivalry and mercy, too.

None of that ahead, she thought as she marked her place with a scrap of wool and closed the book.

'You look as if you're enjoying it, child,' Mrs Shields said, glancing up from her own novel.

'I don't understand how the writer can know all these things. He makes me feel as if I'm there. I can hear every sound of the swords and the hooves on the ground.'

That calm, gentle smile. 'Think about the other books you've read. Don't you feel you're part of them, too?'

'Yes, but . . .' She struggled to find the words. 'Those all take place *now*. This one doesn't.'

'That's the beauty of a story. Do you see why I like them?'

'I do.'

A small, merry laugh. 'I'd say you were happy you learned to read.'

More than anyone would know. 'I'm glad you taught me.'

For the next quarter of an hour, as Catherine Shields prepared for bed, Jane ran her knife over the whetstone. Again and again, long, even strokes. She'd doused the lantern and worked by the light from the fire. Every so often she'd pause to test the edge against the ball of her thumb. A little more, then again, until finally she knew it was as sharp as it would ever be. She was going to need it.

Below the sleeve of her dress, Jane could make out the faded scars on her forearm. She ran her fingers over them, then pushed the fabric higher to show the whole ladder of memories. She'd done each one as punishment for a failure. Pain in her body to try and ease the ache in her heart. The sight of blood to remind her to do better.

All part of the past. She recalled the reason for every single one of them, but they belonged to a time when the future held nothing more than the next day.

After tomorrow she would do even less work for Simon than she had over the summer. Her anger at him had softened. Deep inside she knew he'd meant well when he took away her revenge, that he wanted her safe. He simply didn't understand her; he never had.

She'd still be there for anything important. But he'd have Sally. She'd fit in better than Jane ever had. She'd enjoy living with Simon and Rosie and the boys. She was the type who craved a family around her.

Jane had her own home, and soon she'd have the time to enjoy it fully once again.

THIRTY-FOUR

They gathered early in Simon's kitchen. Jane and Sally were quiet, lost in their thoughts. Rosie tried to hurry the twins through their breakfast. The tutor was due soon and she wanted them to be ready.

Simon had dozed during the night, thinking the rest of the time and wrestling with a decision. Finally, he slipped out of bed long before first light, scribbled a note and went out to deliver it. A sharp frost had turned the town white, and the factory smoke hung low and still and cold as he walked.

'We need to go,' he said. Sally and Jane pulled shawls over their hair and settled their cloaks around their shoulders, raising the hoods and fastening them at the neck. Rosie was left shaking her head.

'I can't do anything until the tutor arrives.'

'Catch up to us,' he said, and led the small procession on to Swinegate.

He was wearing an old greatcoat. It had been second-hand ten years before, tight across the shoulders now, the wool nibbled here and there by moths, but still with plenty of wear left in the fabric. That and a battered low-crown hat should make him look like Robert Jordan, at least from a distance. He picked up the small hessian sack. The evening before he'd cut up old copies of the *Mercury* to the size of banknotes. If nobody looked inside, they might pass for money.

By habit he checked the knives: in his belt, his boot, and the third up his sleeve. A loaded pistol in his pocket. He was ready. As he walked, he stooped his shoulders, becoming a smaller man like Jordan.

Well before they reached the moor, Jane and Sally moved away from him. Simon glanced back, hoping for some sign of Rosie. Nothing. Where was that damned tutor? The young man was usually reliable. The one day they needed him to begin early . . . no matter.

There was traffic on the Otley Road. A coach sped by on its way to Skipton and Carlisle. Waggoners with their heavy loads trudged into town. Boys pushed handcarts.

Simon snapped open his watch. Plenty of time before the meeting.

He ambled, trying to look like a man out for a morning walk, but his eyes took in every feature of the landscape. Jane and Sally had hidden themselves well: only once did he catch a shimmer of movement from the copse.

A few birds were singing, but out under the cold grey skies, their songs sounded lonely and mournful. Waiting was always hard. A good time for the mind to play tricks, to second-guess and imagine the worst.

Another glance at his pocket watch. Five minutes before the hour. He made his way to the tree where he'd be meeting the man. Still no sign of Rosie and he felt a nag of worry in the pit of his stomach. She'd come as soon as she could. She was probably hurrying up from town right now.

He paced around, wanting this to be over. The hour came and went, and no man appeared. Simon jumped at the tiniest sound, but he was there on his own as the seconds crawled by.

Was this a test? Or had the man realized he'd been tricked? He stood, feeling his heart lurching in his chest. Wondering if he'd given himself away somehow.

He'd wait five more minutes then give up and go home. Simon's mouth was dry; it was difficult to swallow. He kept turning his head, hoping to spot someone approaching.

Finally, a man and a woman together. Small figures in the distance at first, but there was something familiar about them. A little closer and he realized it was Rosie. An angry, quick stride. She was carrying a package.

Who was the man with a tight grip on her arm? Nobody he recognized. A little closer and Simon could see more. He was wearing a sword, walking with the erect back of a soldier. He lifted his free hand, just long enough to show the glint of light on a knife blade.

Each pace brought them nearer. Simon drew out the small sack from the inside of his coat, holding it up. The man barked a few words in Rosie's ear. With a defeated nod, she raised the package she was carrying.

Holcomb's documents. The root of all this. Coloured with death, and there would be more before another hour had passed.

From the corner of his eye, he caught sight of two girls drifting idly across the ground, paying no attention to the world. They had their heads close together, as if their conversation absorbed them. Very quietly coming closer.

The man pulled Rosie to a halt five yards from Simon.

'I'm sorry—' she began before he raised the knife to her throat. 'You can stay quiet.'

He knew that voice. The lieutenant, Holcomb's army friend from the barracks.

'I was expecting to see that little man, Jordan. Take his money, maybe leave him for dead.' He shook his head. 'So many unfortunate incidents can happen out here. Good men robbed and killed for a few pennies. You can imagine my surprise when I spotted your wife hurrying along, Westow. I wondered what brought her this way. I decided to ask.'

'We'll make our exchange and go our own ways.'

The soldier shook his head and gave a sorrowful smile. 'You make it sound so simple. But a man who'll cheat me on one thing will cheat me on others.' He raised his eyebrows. 'How do I know you really have money in there?'

'Why should I believe you have the documents in there?' he replied.

Jane and Sally were drawing closer, but still too far. At least the man hadn't noticed them yet.

The man smiled. 'I'm the one who has your wife. I think that means I don't have to prove a thing to you, Westow.'

'What do you want me to do?'

'Show it. Open it up and show me the money inside.'

He took a breath. What choice did he have? One nick from that knife, a quick slice across her throat, and Rosie would be dead. Simon had played his hand and the man had called his bluff.

He saw her body tense, the fire in her eyes, the smallest shake of her head.

He made to shake the sack open, seeing the man's eyes widen in anticipation and greed.

'Here,' he said, and tossed it to the soldier.

The man reached for it. Pure instinct. Rosie was ready for the moment, squirming out of his grasp and pulling her own weapon. Sally and Jane were running, blades drawn.

'Throw down your knife,' Simon ordered. He held the pistol in one hand, cocked and aimed at the soldier's heart.

The man looked around, bemused. 'An army of women, Westow? Is that the best you can muster?'

'Every one of them would kill you without hesitation.' His heart was racing as he stared into the man's eyes. No fear there. Nothing at all. Only an empty soul. 'Drop the knife. Sword, too.'

Still no movement. He was pushing them, seeing if they dare hurt him. Simon's gaze flickered to his wife. She was watching the lieutenant, eyes filled with a fury he'd only seen a few times before.

Jane stood silent, not moving an inch, ready in case the man tried to attack. Sally was shifting from foot to foot, anxious, eager.

'I'll give you to the count of three.'

The man smirked. With very deliberate slowness, he extended his arm and let his dagger drop to the ground. His fingertips held the sword by the hilt, drawing it from the scabbard. A heavy cavalry blade that looked as if it had seen some blood over the years.

'Let it go.'

The man opened his hand and it fell. He was poised, ready to launch himself forward. Before he could move, Rosie was there, slicing open his cheek. He reached up, then stared in horror at the blood on his hand.

'Think yourself lucky,' she told him. 'This way you can remember me. You'd have killed me if you'd had the chance.'

He was pressing a handkerchief against the cut, all the arrogance vanished.

'You'll have a good scar to show your mess mates,' Simon said. 'Tell them it came from a duel.'

'You can say you lost to a woman,' Rosie said. 'Where did you get the papers?'

He tried to stare her down, but he lost that contest. 'From a woman in Holbeck. She wasn't quite as clever as she believed. I was one of Wellington's intelligence officers in Spain. I learned how to find people.'

'What did you do with her body?' Her tone brooked no argument: the truth or her knife.

'I didn't kill her.' His voice was subdued. 'I gave her a choice. Not like those others. She could go, or fight and die. She took to her heels.' A hint of arrogance returned to his smile.

Simon could hear hooves in the distance. Narrowing his eyes, he picked out a figure on the far side of the moor, putting his animal to the gallop over the flat surface. The lieutenant hadn't noticed yet.

Sally caught the sound, worried as she glanced back at Simon. He shook his head.

Captain Holcomb drew up his horse sharply and slid down to the ground.

'I found your note, Westow.' He stared at the officer, still pressing a sodden handkerchief to his cheek. 'What's going on here, Lieutenant Jardine?'

'Your friend thought I was from the radical press,' Simon began before the soldier could plant any smooth lies. 'He wanted to sell me the papers stolen from your house.'

The captain stayed silent for a long moment, thinking.

'Is that true, Jardine?'

'No, sir. I kept an eye on him after you had me warn him off and I learned he had the papers. I was trying to recover them for you.'

'Well, Westow? What do you say to that? This man is an officer and a gentleman.'

'I trust you remember our last conversation, Captain.' Before Holcomb could reply, Simon continued, 'Maybe you should ask what happened to Mason, the soldier who was working with him. He tried to sell me the papers, the same as this—' he spat out the word '—gentleman.'

'Corporal Mason has been dealt with,' the lieutenant said.

Holcomb widened his eyes. 'How?'

But Jardine was moving. Before anyone could react, he'd stooped to pick up his sword from the ground. A turn of his arm and the point was deep in the captain's side.

As Holcomb fell, Rosie rushed to him. The lieutenant grabbed the horse's reins and pulled himself into the saddle.

'Mr Jardine,' Simon called. Without thinking, the soldier turned. He pulled the trigger.

It caught the man in his back, sending him sprawling to the ground, one boot still dangling from its stirrup as the horse dragged him along. The beast look like it might bolt, but Sally dashed forward, taking hold of the bridle and whispering to calm the animal.

'Holcomb's in a bad way, Simon.' Rosie had torn his coat open, clothes pulled up to show the deep wound in his side. 'There's a lot of blood. He needs to go to the infirmary.'

He released Jardine's foot, feeling a weak pulse in the man's neck. 'I'll go for a doctor.' He stared at Jane. 'You don't like Constable Porter, but I need you to find him and bring him here. He knows you; he'll come.'

A second's hesitation, then she turned and began to run.

'What about me?' Sally asked. She was stroking the horse's mane. It nuzzled her shoulder.

'Take that packet of documents to the house. There's a cupboard in the wall under the stairs. Put it in there.'

If anyone searched, they'd find it soon enough, but it would serve for now. He watched her leave.

'Will Holcomb live?' Simon asked his wife.

'He has a good chance, I think, as long as he's treated soon.' Her eyes moved to the lieutenant, still unmoving. 'What about him?'

'I don't know.' The man's eyes were open, but staring at nothing, although he was still breathing.

The infirmary attendants were moving off with the wounded men in the back of the wagon. Porter and the inspector had examined the scene, questioned Simon and Rosie. Jane had vanished; Sally had never returned from the house.

'The whole thing's a mess,' the constable said. 'That officer means the barracks will need to be involved. Their commanding officer isn't going to be happy.'

'Then he ought to keep a firmer hold over his men,' Rosie snapped. She pulled the cloak tighter around her body and strode off as the wind started to blow from the north.

'Maybe so,' Porter agreed mildly. 'Maybe so.' He turned to Simon. 'This man, Jardine, Holcomb had him warn you off after you walked away from the . . . business?'

'Yes.' He decided not to mention Mason. That would only make the waters murkier.

'You think the lieutenant sniffed an opportunity to make a little money for himself?'

'It looks that way. Sophie Jackson had trusted the papers to a clothes seller, a friend of her sister. She's gone, too. Not dead, Jardine said; I'm not sure I believe him.'

Porter drew in a breath. 'Christ, Westow, you make my life difficult.'

'I don't know how Jardine discovered she had them, but if he'd taken them back to Holcomb, he'd have received a reward. Nothing like what he could make by selling them, though.'

'That's how we ended up here?'

'Yes.'

'Where are these papers?' the inspector asked as he kicked at the ground.

'Safe.'

The constable gave a short nod. 'Take the horse back to Holcomb's house,' he ordered the inspector. He turned, took a few steps, heading back to Leeds. 'Coming, Westow? There's nothing more to see.'

'How much haven't you told me?' he asked once they were alone.

Simon chose his words with particular care. 'You know everything that happened here.'

'I daresay I do. You had this arranged. You should have told me. I'd have been waiting to take this bloody officer. What happened to his face, by the way? Looks like he was knifed.'

'It must have been when he fell,' Simon replied, keeping his voice level.

'Of course. You know, I've seen men with that kind of look in their eyes before. He's alive but somehow his mind isn't connected to the body any longer.'

'His own greed caused it.'

Porter snorted. 'There's probably a tale in there for the vicar's sermon on Sunday, but I doubt he'd ever use it.' They walked in silence until they reached the Head Row.

The constable stopped, rubbing a finger over his chin. 'Do you think it's over?'

'Let's hope so.' But he suspected it wasn't.

'We still don't have anything more on Wise. If your reading should turn up a name or two . . .'

'I'll make sure you know.'

'By the way, did you hear that someone burned Wise's house down last night?'

'No.' Simon hadn't been to the coffee cart that morning. He'd missed out on the gossip. But tongues would be wagging for days.

'Nothing left. Apparently the locals didn't raise a hand to put it out. What do you make of that?'

'Everything to do with him is best destroyed.'

'Indeed.' He tipped his hat. 'I'll wish you good day.'

As Simon walked home, hands deep in his pocket, it all still felt incomplete, threads dangling and twisting in the air, needing to be tied together.

THIRTY-FIVE

J ane sat, not even pretending to read. Her eyes kept moving to the clock on the mantel shelf. She hadn't wanted to be anywhere near the constable or his men. They'd arrested her once, put her in a cell, humiliated her. It had only been a handful of hours until she was out again, but simply having to speak to him brought it roaring back into her head.

She'd passed on the information and hurried away before he could begin with this questions. He could talk to Simon. She'd done what he asked. That was enough.

Now she was counting off the hours until Wild and the ending of that tale.

Mrs Shields was dozing in her chair, a book spread across her lap. Her mouth curled into a smile, as if she was dreaming of something happy. Resting, all the lines seemed to lift from her face, and Jane could see the girl she'd been all those years ago. Sweet, pretty, but with a thoughtful, compassionate intelligence. How long ago? The woman refused to say. Maybe it didn't matter, as long as they had much more time together.

Outside, in the sharp cold, she ran the knife over the whetstone again, letting the rhythm lull her. Just enough to keep an edge that would slice through flesh without hesitation.

It was still half an hour before dusk when Jane placed a shawl over her head and tucked the ends around her shoulders. The old green cloak on top, heavy and reassuring. The day dress with its thick petticoats for warmth, boot laces double knotted.

'Will this be it, child? The end?'

She hadn't been aware the old woman was watching her, worry crowding her face so she looked her age again.

'Yes.' She looked down as a thin, bony hand rested on her arm.

'Will you be careful?'

'I will,' she agreed, although this was going to be a time to be reckless, to remember all the pain. Jane knew Mrs Shields could see the truth in her eyes; the woman could read her all too well.

'Just come back to me safe. Please.'

A brief hug and she went out, hearing the latch click behind her.

Plenty of people on the streets, lights bright in the shops on Briggate. Nobody noticed her as she slipped through the crowds. Men loaded and unloaded barges by the river, breath clouding the cold air as they shouted and swore while they worked.

Jane turned on to Bowman Lane. A few of the homeless had gathered in an old wooden building by Leeds Bridge; someone had built a fire where they could warm themselves. She felt a few eyes on her as she passed, but no one followed. They were concerned with staying alive, not with her.

Closer to Leeds Lock Jane slowed, and slipped into the deep shadows. She listened, twisting the gold ring and holding her breath to catch the slightest sound, then sniffing the air for a trace of Paul Wild.

A moment of panic: what if he didn't come?

No. He wouldn't be able to resist the chance of a little easy money. She'd made the offer sound particularly tempting.

Could he read? He'd know someone who did.

One by one she batted away all the doubts.

Suddenly, she was aware of something. Someone coming closer, moving very quietly. She gripped her knife, then eased as she picked out a dark shape against the gloom.

'I told you I'd be here,' Sally whispered. 'In case you need me. Nothing more.'

Hesitation, then a nod of acceptance. She lifted her head. 'Footsteps.'

Two people. The heavy tread of men. It had to be Wild; there was no good reason for anyone else to be here with night coming. He'd brought someone.

Jane waited until they passed, then slid out and followed. They could look, but they'd never spot her. Not until she was ready.

Her eyes were fixed on the men, fingers aching from gripping the hilt of her knife. She kept ten paces behind as they walked to the towpath that ran by the canal.

'No one around.'

The voice stopped her for a moment. It took her back to that room. The questions, the man hitting her, the finger gone and the blood on her dress.

'You've been set up,' the other man said. 'I warned you—'

'Shut up.'

Good, she thought. Wild wanted to be believe.

'There's damn all here. Stay until midnight if you want. Nobody's going to come.'

Time. She took a breath and came out into the middle of the road. The hobnails on her boots kicked up a sharp sound. The men turned.

'A girl?' the man asked in disbelief. 'A girl's tricked you into coming to this damned place?'

'He knows exactly who I am. Don't you, Paul Wild?' She held up her left hand to show the missing finger. 'Don't you? You wanted to take the rest of them, too. You must remember. Here's your chance.'

Jane took a pace forward. Wild's companion turned to him.

'Come on, we can have a little fun and then kill her. It's just a girl.'

'Why don't you tell him what I did, Mr Wild?'

'She's the one who killed my brother and Gilly Harrison, then burned down the house where they were living.'

'It wasn't just her.' Sally seemed to appear from nowhere to stand beside her. 'We both did it.'

The man started to laugh. 'Look at them. They're not going to give us any trouble.'

Wild was silent, staring at Jane. The man beside him began to move. Sally raised her knife and took a step towards him.

'Paul.' There was real anger in the man's voice now. 'Come on, let's just go.'

'He's not going anywhere,' Jane said. She stared back at Wild. 'Are you?'

A misting rain began, soft and fine against her face.

The other man started to run. Three steps and he tried to barge past Sally, to shoulder her out of the way as if as if she was too small to bother him.

'You're staying, too,' she told him as her arm snaked out. He stopped, eyes wide in shock, clutching at his belly. His legs gave way and he fell to the ground.

'She's stabbed me. Jesus Christ Almighty, the damned little bitch has stabbed me.'

'No witnesses.' Sally stood over him. 'No tales floating around in the morning.'

Jane took another pace towards Wild. He was waving his knife.

'Two of you against me?' he asked. 'Is that it?' He made a poor attempt at a smile.

She shook her head. 'Just me. I've been promising myself this since you took my finger.' She lifted her blade. 'Well?'

He feinted to the right, but she remained still. Her eyes were on his face, his feet. She could smell his fear. His moved nervously, jerkily. Nothing flowed.

Jane took one more step forward. He lunged at her. She slid aside and brought her knife down on his arm. It sliced through his coat, his shirt, into his flesh. Wild cried out and pulled back. He was looking around, desperate, simply wanting to survive. Knowing it was hopeless.

Blood was dripping down the back of his hand. Soon his fingers would be slick with it, hard to grip the knife hilt. As he moved his fist around it, she darted close, aiming low, into his thigh. Away again before he could react.

He grunted and staggered. His face tightened with pain and anger. She'd hurt him.

Wild launched himself at her, trying to knock her over, to over-whelm her with his size. She ducked, shuddering as he hit her, then stabbed him in the belly. He yelled with pain and doubled over, clutching at his stomach.

He swayed as he tried to stay upright. Blood was spreading rapidly across his clothes. Whatever she'd struck inside, it was going to kill him. The light mist of rain kept falling all around them. Jane prodded at him. Wild shuffled back, dazed, fading, as he tried to avoid the knife point. She did it again, keeping him going. Out beyond the lock gates, where the navigation ran free.

It was time.

She could see he was trying to gather the final tatters of his strength, to make one last attempt to run at her. But he didn't have the strength left in his body.

Jane slipped forward. Wild raised his arm, the knife shaking in his hand. Too late. She caught him in the shoulder, cutting deep then pulling out again before he could strike his blow.

The last ounce of fight slid from him. It was easy to be hard when you had someone tied and helpless. Very different as soon as you had to face them like this.

For a moment Jane felt a flicker of pity. She took a breath and it passed. At least he didn't try to beg. Not like his brother. Billy

Wild had cried and snivelled as they questioned him. Willing to promise the world to stay alive. He didn't believe he deserved to die for snatching two girls.

Two girls. Even tonight, everything came back to them. If Emma had never come up to her and asked Jane to find her sister, Jane would still have her finger. Billy Wild and his friend would still be alive. Wise would be safe in his house.

And Harriet might be in another of the shallow graves behind it. Suddenly a finger seemed like a small price to pay.

She was sick of Wild. Sick of his face, of the slow, deliberate way he'd tried to hurt her. Jane moved closer, ready to strike if he tried to resist.

But he was past all that. No light of defiance. He was standing on the very edge of the towpath. The smallest step back and he'd be in the canal.

Wild raised his head. 'I can't swim,' he said quietly.

Then he moved away from her. He didn't cry out, barely made a splash as he vanished into the water. Very soon there would only be water where Paul Wild had once been. She turned and walked away.

Sally was still standing over the other man. His eyes were closed, his chest had stopped rising and falling. She looked down at the body.

'We can't leave him here.'

'No,' Jane agreed. She closed her eyes for a moment. Drained, everything seeping away. All her anger, her desire for revenge. It had gone now, drifting away downstream. She bent down and grabbed the corpse's wrist. 'Come on, then.'

Over soon enough. She looked out over the water. No sign of Wild. He'd disappeared. The drizzle hardened into rain.

She was hollow.

THIRTY-SIX

S imon hung up his greatcoat and hat and walked through to the kitchen. The table was covered in papers, carefully sorted into different piles. Rosie had more in her hand, glancing at one before placing it carefully.

'Where are the boys?' he asked.

'Mrs Farmer asked if they wanted to play with her brood. She's going to feed them, too. More fool her, with the appetites those two have.' She nodded at everything in front of her. 'I'm trying to make sense of all this. That one is letters, ones he received and copies of things he wrote. That one seems to be court judgements. That's the thickest one, but old Holcomb was a magistrate. Then we have the journal or diary or whatever it is, and the last seems to be notes he made on different cases.' She looked at him. 'Didn't the captain say he'd been through it all?'

'I'm not sure exactly what he did. He said he intended to make a bonfire of the papers but never got around to it. Is there anything much in there?'

'I haven't started to read properly yet. I thought it would make sense to know what we were looking at.'

'True enough.' He smiled. The woman could fashion the chaos of hell into some sort of order.

'Have you been to see him?'

Captain Holcomb had a room to himself at the infirmary. Dr Hey had bustled over to examine him as soon as he was admitted.

The man was in pain, but the physician had told him he was likely to mend unless there was an infection.

'Not as good as new,' the captain said, grimacing as a twinge ran through him. 'But in time I should be able to ride again.'

A strange priority, Simon thought. 'Someone took your horse home.'

'Good, good.' A long hesitation, then the question he expected. A long silence, then Holcomb said, 'Thank you, Mr Westow. I owe you a debt.'

'Do you? I'm a man without honour, remember? Not a gentleman.'

'I misjudged you, it seems.' Still no apology, of course. 'Do you have the papers?'

'I do.'

'What do you intend to do with them? Your gift to the Radical press?' He didn't try to hide the bitterness in his voice.

'You can have them back,' Simon told him, seeing the man's head snap up in astonishment.

'Really?'

'If there's anything in there that the constable should know, I'll pass that on to him.'

A slow, sad nod of acceptance. The captain knew he held no cards in this. 'Of course.'

'I'll deliver the rest to you once you're home again.'

'That depends on how quickly I begin to heal, according to the doctor.' He took a breath, forcing down his pain. 'Why are you doing this?'

'The politics, the injustices, they're all in the past. Too late to change anyone's life now.'

Another nod; gratitude this time. 'My offer to you still stands, Westow. You've retrieved them, I'll pay for their return.'

He hadn't expected that, hadn't intended to make money from the misery.

'There are people dead. That lieutenant is responsible for some of them. Maybe all.'

'I'll pay for their funerals. Nothing beyond that. After all, none of this would have happened if the maid's young man hadn't thought he could make some money from me.'

That would satisfy Holcomb's sense of justice.

'Very good,' Simon told him. 'I wish you a speedy recovery.' At the door he turned back. 'What did the doctor say about Lieutenant Jardine?'

'He's never going to speak or walk again. He won't be able to do anything at all. They'll arrange for his family to take him home. It might be a blessing if he dies on the way. A shame; he was a good young officer once.'

'Is Sally upstairs?' he asked.

'She went out again,' Rosie told him. 'Said she had something to do.' She sighed. 'That girl is an odd one. Did you see her with the horse? Calming it, not afraid at all. She's spent time around them, Simon. Not like someone who's been living on the streets at all.'

'Maybe she'll tell us.' He wasn't going to press her on it. 'I think she'll do well.'

'So do I.'

Plenty of chatter at the coffee cart. Talk steamed in the bitter morning air. Men kept looking at Simon as he listened to some of the wild tales. Few came anywhere close to the truth about the lieutenant and the magistrate's papers. All they knew for certain was the fighting and even most of that was fashioned from thin air.

Let them guess, he thought as he strode off. Sally stayed a few paces behind him, hidden in her cloak with the hood raised. He hadn't asked her to come; she'd slipped out of the house after him.

Maybe having her with him was a good idea, given the information in the papers he had folded in his pocket. He and Rosie had been up beyond midnight reading through everything the magistrate left. They hadn't finished yet, but there was enough to damn the man, and a few others besides.

'I feel like I've been wallowing in dirt,' Rosie said.

'We have.' He sighed and reached for her hand. 'Come on, maybe we'll both feel better in the morning.'

But he didn't. Still that ache of disgust. The magistrate hadn't hidden his sins; he wasn't even ashamed of them.

'You look like someone with plenty on his mind.' Porter was sitting in his office, smoking a pipe as he gazed out of the window. 'Spent your evening reading?'

'Magistrate Holcomb probably committed as many crimes as anyone appearing before him,' Simon said. He took out the pages from the papers. 'Details about it all. Turns out he was friends with the late Mr Wise.'

'No surprise, is it? I told you they knew each other.'

'Not like this. A serving girl accused Wise of rape. The magistrate advised him to say she'd been stealing from him. As soon as Wise did that, Holcomb issued a writ and had her dragged into the dock. Transported for seven years.'

'We're never going to be able to prove that.'

'Wise was so grateful he gave Holcomb twenty guineas.'

'Very generous of him.'

'The machine breakers he sent off to Van Diemen's land never even had chance to break the law. The factory owner had given him names and he sent soldiers to arrest them as they were walking. Not even breaking the law. He was proud of his actions. Called it nipping trouble in the bud. Kittridge, the factory owner, gave him fifty pounds. To help defray the expenses, he said.'

Porter snorted. 'He had a good little racket going.'

'There's more,' Simon told him. 'Quite a bit. Covering up rapes was common. He seemed to receive twenty guineas each time. A standard fee. In gratitude, of course.'

'Naturally. Nothing about Wise and young girls?'

'No, but there's another incident involving Kittridge. Holcomb wrote that a man came to see him. Not someone with any money or influence, by the sound of it. He accused Kittridge of snatching his daughter and using her.'

'What did the magistrate do?'

'Demanded to know what evidence he had besides a girl's hysteria. When he couldn't produce any, he warned him not to slander good men, and if he ever came back, he'd throw him and his daughter in prison.' Simon paused and sighed. 'That earned him twenty more guineas from Kittridge.'

Porter shook his head. 'What do you want me to say, Westow? Let's just be glad this one's gone.' He ran a hand through his hair. 'Kittridge is still alive. Must be ten years since he sold that mill of his.' The man narrowed his eyes. 'How young was the girl?'

'The father told the magistrate she was ten.'

The constable stayed silent for a long time. 'That's enough for me. Not as young as the ones we found. Still . . . he's had that same house, out towards Potternewton, as far back as I can recall. Might be worth a visit.'

'He'll never let you search.'

The constable's eyes shone. 'After those bodies at Wise's house, and with all that in writing, there's isn't a magistrate who'd dare refuse me a warrant. I'll let you know once I have it if you want to come along.'

'Yes.' The offer caught him by surprise. 'I would. Thank you.'

Porter shrugged. 'You've earned it. If it hadn't been for you, we'd never have known anything at all.'

'Where are we going now?' Sally asked when he emerged, looking disappointed when he told her it was home.

'We'll be out again later,' he told her. 'This isn't finished. Not yet.'

*   *   *

Jane had slept for hours. No bad dreams clawed at her heart, no feelings of guilt crept around her mind. It was long past full light when she woke. Her body felt loose and easy, all the strains of the last week vanished overnight.

Mrs Shields was bustling around the kitchen and the air was perfumed with the scent of herbs. Jane washed and dressed, brushed her hair as she studied her face in the mirror.

'You look different, child.' The old woman smiled as she studied Jane's face. 'Calmer. Maybe happier.'

Perhaps it showed. 'I think I am.'

'Is it done?'

'Yes. All of it.' Paul Wild and his friend would be far downstream. If anyone ever found them, the creatures of the river would have left them unrecognizable. One or two might wonder what had happened to them, but only she and Sally would ever know the truth.

Two hours later, she was settled comfortably by the fire, only a few chapters before the end of *Ivanhoe*, knowing that everything would end well. Nothing like life, where affairs stayed tangled and complicated.

Tomorrow she'd go to the circulating library and select another book. Nothing more than that to consider. No battles to fight, no anger to nurse. She held up her left hand. No more bandage. Just the stump of a little finger. It surprised her each time she saw it.

Her thoughts were drifting when the knock on the door, then Simon's voice.

'Porter has a warrant,' he said, explaining about Kittridge. 'He invited me. Do you want to come? Since it began when you told me to listen to Emma, I thought you might want to see how it ends.'

'Will this really be all?'

He looked into her eyes. 'I hope so. God help us if it's not.'

She thought she was already finished with it. She wanted to be. But part of her refused. It weighed on her like duty. She turned to Mrs Shields, seeing the concern on the old woman's face.

'I'll be back soon. This will be the very last time. I promise.'

A nod and a mouth turned down in sorrow.

'It'll be perfectly safe,' Simon said. 'No danger.'

Jane felt a shudder up her spine at the words. Tempting fate.

THIRTY-SEVEN

A long walk on a cold afternoon. They kept a good pace to stay warm, Simon grim-faced, ready for this to be done. Once again he'd taken the pistol from the secret drawer under the stair, primed and loaded it. His hand rested against the polished wooden grip in his greatcoat pocket. No danger, he'd said, and believed it. But a little preparation always made things safer.

God only knew what they'd find. Quite possibly nothing at all. There was no evidence against Kittridge. But Simon felt a cloud moving over his soul. He glanced over his shoulder. The two girls were silent, Sally hurrying, small legs moving rapidly.

Porter had brought eight men from the watch, carrying shovels and picks. They milled around the entrance to Kittridge's property, smoking and chattering.

The house was in poor shape, ill-kept, the woodwork in need of a coat of paint. Weeds had taken over the flower beds.

'Neglected,' Simon said.

'I asked a few questions while I was waiting for the magistrate to sign the warrant,' the constable replied. He looked wary, uneasy, eyes looking all around. There was something unsettling about the place. 'Kittridge made some bad investments. He's lost almost all his money.'

'Any servants?'

'A woman who comes down from Chapel Allerton three times a week to cook and do his laundry.'

'He could sell this place.'

'Maybe he daren't, Westow. Depends what's hidden here, doesn't it?'

He gave the order and the men spread out to start searching the grounds. Two stayed back, ready to go through the house.

Porter brought his fist down on the door. Once, twice, three times. Simon heard the sound echo inside. He took the knife from his sleeve and slipped it into his pocket, nestling beside the gun. Turning for a moment, he saw Jane and Sally holding their blades. Whatever was in the air, they felt it, too.

Elias Kittridge looked like a harmless old man. He was dressed in layers of clothes, none of them too clean. Wispy grey hair that flew all over the place, spectacles perched on his nose. A mild soul, perhaps, someone not quite of this world. Definitely not like a man who'd relish the terror of young girls.

'You can't come in and search,' he told Porter. 'This is my home. You have no right.'

The constable waved the warrant. 'We have this, Mr Kittridge. It gives us the right.'

'I want my attorney.' The meekness had gone from his voice and in its place a demand. Something very much like fear on his face, Simon decided as he watched.

'Then send someone for him.'

'There isn't anyone. What about one of your men?'

'They're here to do their jobs.' He nodded to them. 'Go on.'

A member of the watch hurried in from outside, a young, lanky fellow named Smith. He leaned down and whispered in the constable's ear.

'One of your outbuildings is locked. Do you have the key?'

'Are you allowed to search it?' Kittridge asked.

'House and everything throughout the property.' Porter stared the man down. 'Now, are you going to give us the key?'

'No.'

He turned to Smith. 'You know what to do.'

They stood in the hall, front door open to the bitter air. Simon saw cobwebs clinging to the ceiling. The floor had been swept, but there was dirt tracked over the tiles.

The minutes passed with just the ticking of the longclock. The men who'd been going through the house returned, shaking their heads. Nothing to incriminate him. Kittridge smirked in triumph.

Then Smith was back.

'You'd better come and look at this, sir,' he told the constable. The colour had vanished from his face, like a man who'd seen the dead.

'Keep an eye on him, Westow. Make sure he doesn't try to escape.'

'Westow?' The man cocked his head. 'You don't look like a member of the watch. What are you, a pimp?' He turned his head to stare at Jane and Sally. 'Take your whores everywhere, do you?'

Words. Kittridge was terrified. All his secrets and darkness were about to be dragged into the light. He looked ready to bolt if he could find half a chance.

'You knew Mr Wise, didn't you?'

The question took him by surprise. 'Thomas? Yes, why?'

'I'm a thief-taker.' Simon inclined his head towards Jane and Sally. 'We're the ones who freed the young girl he snatched.'

Kittridge twitched, blinked. His fear was growing. 'What about it?'

'Did Wise come here after he ran off?'

'I used to know him, but that was years ago.'

A lie. 'I know you didn't kill him and his servant and take the bodies back to his house by yourself. You're not strong enough. Who else is involved? It might save your neck.'

No reply, just a stare of glowering defiance. He heard the footsteps approaching, the constable stamping his feet as he entered the hall.

'It stinks of death out there. Shackles bolted to the walls. Rusted, but they've been used.' He came close enough to Kittridge to make the man back away. 'The men are digging. How many bodies are buried in there?'

'I don't know anything about bodies.' But there was no heart to his denial.

'We've found one so far,' Porter continued as if he hadn't heard him. His hands were curled into fists by his side. It would only take one wrong word. 'Small, just a child. No flesh left, just bones. It's been there a while.'

'I told you. I don't know. It could have been here when I bought the place.'

'Who else is involved?' Simon asked again. His voice was even, warm. 'You know what happened to Wise. Were you one of those friends who turned away from him?'

'I haven't seen him in years. I said.'

'Take a look. These women you called whores . . .' Simon watched as Kittridge turned to glance at Jane and Sally. 'They made two hard men tell them the truth about where they'd taken a girl they snatched. It's what led us to your friend Wise.' He paused, just long enough to let the idea fill the man's mind. 'They'd enjoy hearing what you have to say, too. I don't think it would take long.'

'You can't let them do that,' Kittridge shouted at the constable. He was shaking.

'I'll be outside. We need to see what else is in that building. See if you can talk some sense into him, Westow.'

Another moment and he'd gone.

'Well?' Simon asked. 'It's your choice.'

From the corner of his eye he saw Sally beginning to edge around behind Kittridge. The man's time was running out. Jane moved to stand next to Simon.

'You want Cornelius Ellis and John Faulkner.' He bowed his head, defeated. 'They were part of it. Wise and his man ran here. I told them to go. I hadn't had anything to do with that in a long time.'

'You can't shrug off your sins that easily,' Simon told him.

'I sent word to Ellis and Faulkner. They killed Wise and his servant here and took the bodies back to his house when it was dark. I didn't have anything to do with any of that, I swear.'

Kittridge was a broken man. Fear and imagination. They held plenty of power, especially with the guilty. But they could be dangerous; they had nothing left to lose.

'Watch him. I'll go and tell Porter.'

As he turned away, Kittridge leaped forward. He dragged a hand from his pocket, clutching a knife.

Jane shouted and threw herself at him. He turned his blade, slashing at her arm, drawing his hand back for more with a madman's fury.

Sally jumped on him. One hand dragged his head back while her knife sliced through his neck. The blood spurted. Simon watched Kittridge's face as he died. He had something like satisfaction in his eyes as his light faded.

'How bad is it?' he asked Jane, taking out his handkerchief and pressing it to the wound.

She was pale, breathing fast, but she shook her head. 'A cut. He didn't have much of a knife.'

She showed him the wound. A little blood, but not deep. There wouldn't be a scar. He wadded the handkerchief over it and hacked a strip from the bottom of his shirt to tie around her arm.

'Thank you,' he said. He raised his eyes to include Sally. 'Both of you.'

Porter was talking to his men. He raised his eyebrows when he saw Simon and Jane cradling her wounded arm.

'Dead?'

'After he gave us a pair of names.'

'Of his own free will?'

'Cornelius Ellis and John Faulkner.'

He saw the constable's face harden. 'I know where they live. I'll pay them a visit as soon as we're done here. Bones, Westow. We'll never know who she was.'

Some small justice for the dead. Perhaps it hadn't all been in vain.

THIRTY-EIGHT

Late November, 1824

'I'll go,' Simon called as he heard the knock at the door.

He opened it to see a large-boned woman with a ruddy face. Not someone he knew at all.

'I'm looking for Mrs Westow.' Her voice sounded almost apologetic. 'My name's Janet Bristol.'

'I'm her husband. The thief-taker.' He smiled. 'Come in.'

'I'm sorry for arriving out of the blue. You probably heard I had to run from Leeds . . .'

'I did.' He moved aside. 'My wife will be very glad to see you again.'

THIRTY-NINE

December, 1824

T he house was scrubbed, shining and neat. Simon was wearing his good clothes, Rosie in a dress she rarely had chance to wear. The boys were clean. Sally had a proper gown, her hair clean and brushed until it shone.

Jane hung up her cloak. Her arm had healed. Most of the time she was scarcely aware of the missing finger these days. She hadn't been sure she wanted to come here for this visit by the Caldwell family; she'd been wary of the bad memories it might evoke. But Mrs Shields had persuaded her, even coaxed her into unwrapping her good dress. Deep chocolate brown, modestly cut, with a pattern the shade of raspberries.

She'd been content to do very little. Cooking and cleaning at the little house behind Green Dragon Yard. Tending Mrs Shields. Visits to the market and the subscription library, lost in *The Children of the Abbey* and *Clermont*. Escapes into other worlds.

Sally was sitting with the boys. Simon and Rosie were talking quietly, waiting for the knock on the door.

Emma ran straight to her, hugging her close. She looked so different. Poised, carefully dressed, as if nothing had ever happened to her. A young lady. But when Jane gazed into her eyes, she could see the history. It would always be there, surviving, holding on and hoping.

'Your finger . . .' She stared at it, horrified, then at Jane's face. 'What happened to it?'

'Nothing important.' The girl didn't need to know.

A moment, then Emma took Jane by the hand and led her over to her father.

'Papa, I've told you all about her. This is the one who listened. She believed me.'

'Ma'am.' He bowed to her. 'My wife and I can't thank you enough. If it hadn't been for you—'

'Not just me. Sally, too.' She beckoned the girl over. 'And Simon and Rosie.'

'We're more grateful to you all than we can ever express in a lifetime.'

Harriet stayed close to her mother, shy and silent as she looked up at them. Maybe that was the only place she felt safe now.

The gathering became a welter of conversation. Too much for her, too many people in a small space. Jane slipped out into the hall. Sally followed.

'Are you leaving already?'

'Nobody will notice.'

'I did.'

She nodded. 'Do you like it? Working with Simon? Living here? Are you happy?'

'Yes.' The girl smiled. 'I am.'

Jane had reached the front door before another voice called her name and Emma ran down the hall.

'You didn't even say goodbye.'

'No.'

'You . . .' She couldn't find the words. A final tight hug. 'I pray for you every night.'

Emma dashed off again. Jane closed the door behind her. She set off along Swinegate, reaching into the pocket of her dress to cradle the hilt of her knife. Faint, in the distance, she heard the notes of Davy Cassidy's fiddle.

AFTERWORD

This was the darkest book I've ever written. Earlier versions were darker and more violent than this; in the end, I toned it down. Even now, though, it goes into some desperate, uncomfortable places. But all industrial towns, not just Leeds, had plenty of homeless people. Not just families, but groups of children. The casualties of profit. Before 1834 and the Poor Law Act, there was no real safety net to help them. We'll never know how many wandered the streets and how many died.

I'm the one with my name on the cover, but many more than me have helped make this book a reality. Sara Porter, my editor, and all the team at Severn House, who believe in what I do, and keep letting me do it. All of them are wonderful, and I'm glad to have been associated with them for so long. Lynne Patrick, who's gone over almost every book I've written, and made each one of them so much better. All the booksellers and the reviewers who help spread the word. The librarians, who do such sterling work in the face of funding cuts. I'm so grateful to every one of you.

Finally, of course, to Penny, who reads these things first and offers a good, honest critique, and much more.